D0929683

SOUTH CENTRAL NOIR

EDITED BY GARY PHILLIPS

BROOKLYN, NEW YORK

Published by Akashic Books
©2022 Akashic Books
Copyright to the individual stories is retained by the authors.

Series concept by Tim McLoughlin and Johnny Temple
Map of South Central Los Angeles by Sohrab Habibion

Paperback ISBN: 978-1-63614-054-4
Hardcover ISBN: 978-1-63614-055-1
Library of Congress Control Number: 2022933226

All rights reserved
First printing

Akashic Books
Brooklyn, New York
Instagram: AkashicBooks
Twitter: AkashicBooks
Facebook: AkashicBooks
E-mail: info@akashicbooks.com
Website: www.akashicbooks.com

ALSO IN THE AKASHIC NOIR SERIES

LOS ANGELES

SOUTH
CENTRAL

NORTH
PACIFIC
OCEAN

UNIVERSITY OF
CALIFORNIA,
LOS ANGELES

CHEVIOT
HILLS
RECREATION
CENTER

405

MEMORIAL PARK

BALLONA
WETLANDS
ECOLOGICAL
RESERVE

LOS ANGELES
INTERNATIONAL
AIRPORT

NORTH
PACIFIC
OCEAN

MIDTOWN
SHOPPING
CENTER

SOUTH CENTRAL

KOKUSAI
THEATRE

EXPOSITION
PARK

CENTRAL
AVENUE

SNOOTY FOX
MOTOR INN

DUNBAR
HOTEL

LEIMERT PARK
VILLAGE

MARTIN LUTHER
KING JR. BLVD.

SLAUSON
PARK

CRENSHAW
BOULEVARD

SLAUSON
AVENUE

SOUTH
FIGUEROA
STREET

INGLEWOOD
PARK
CEMETERY

SOUTH PARK

WATTS
TOWERS

IMPERIAL
HIGHWAY

10

110

105

TABLE OF CONTENTS

PART III: THE WORLD IS A GHETTO

INTRODUCTION
INNER-CITY CONFIDENTIAL

L ike "Hollywood," the term "South Central" conjures up not a geographic location so much as specific imagery and impressions derived from the news and pop culture. Examples include Ice-T's "6 in the Mornin'," "*Looked in the mirror, what did we see? Fuckin' blue lights, LAPD*"; Ralph Fiennes as volatile gang boss Harry Waters snarkily decrying the need for an assault weapon in the film *In Bruges*, "An Uzi? I'm not from South Central Los fucking Angeles"; the movie *South Central* based on Donald Bakeer's novel *Crips*, with Glenn Plummer as Bobby Johnson, an ex-con on parole trying to steer his son away from the gang life that's consuming him; and *Moesha*, a slightly edgy network sitcom starring singer Brandy Norwood, about coming of age in Leimert Park.

In 2003, the Los Angeles City Council rechristened the whole of it "South LA" to blunt its infamous reputation—though they maintained a 2.25-square-mile area within its boundaries as "Historic South Central," whatever that's supposed to mean. Nonetheless, the South Central where I grew up remains a locale where the majority of the residents work hard and share many of the same concerns as those who reside in Westside neighborhoods. It's a place where the demographics and physical characteristics have changed since my youth, where even gentrification has crept in.

This, then, is the backdrop to *South Central Noir*. Within these pages you'll find stories of those walking the straight and narrow—until something untoward happens. Maybe it's someone taking a step out of line, getting caught up in circumstances spiraling out of their control. Maybe they're planning the grift, the grab . . . whatever it is to finally put them over. Other times the steps they take are to get themselves or people they care about out from under. You'll find the offerings in these pages are a rich mix of tone—tales told of hope, survival, revenge, and triumph. Excursions beyond the headlines and the hype.

The settings herein reflect South Central today or chronicle its colorful past, such as the days of the jazz joints along Central Avenue, venues like Jack's Basket and the Club Alabam. The LAPD's intelligence squad infiltrating left organizations is threaded in here, as well as what jumped off at Florence and Normandie that fateful day in April 1992, the flashpoint of the civil unrest that garnered world attention. Key landmarks also figure in these stories, such as the Watts Towers, the old Holiday Bowl on Crenshaw where people of various races used to congregate, and the Dunbar Hotel, built by Black folks to cater to people of color in a segregated city.

For the purposes of this collection, South Central is defined as roughly thirty-three square miles: Washington Boulevard to the north, Imperial Highway to the south, Alameda Boulevard to the east, and Crenshaw Boulevard to the west (bearing in mind that those boundaries are somewhat fluid). From South Park to East Martin Luther King Jr. Boulevard, from the borderlands of Watts to the one-time Southern Pacific railroad tracks paralleling Slauson Avenue, take a tour of a section of Los Angeles that may be unfamiliar to you but you will get to know, at least a little, by the time you finish reading this entertaining and engaging anthology.

Gary Phillips
Los Angeles

PART I

ALWAYS AND FOREVER

ALL LUCK
BY STEPH CHA

South Park

T he whole city was on fire—good, fuck them all—and Sang-woo sat in his car and smoked. He'd promised Hana he'd quit, but she was eleven, she didn't make the rules. If her teacher told her to say no to cigarettes, that was fine—great, even—of course kids shouldn't be smoking. But he was an adult, and he wasn't about to rearrange his life just because his daughter asked.

The sky crackled, thick and burning. Night was here, the sun gone down, but Sang-woo didn't see stars; he couldn't even find the moon. Only the bright colors of arson wrapped in the gray pall of smoke and ash. It was really something. Sang-woo was born after the Korean War, and just late enough to avoid the Vietnam War too, where his older cousins fought with the South Korean military, committing war crimes and fathering war babies, for all anyone knew. People said South Central was a war zone. The men at church who avoided war, like him; them and their fearful wives. It was true, he got scared once in a while, but his customers knew him, his days were spent selling liquor and groceries, taking cash, counting out change. He kept a gun behind the register because it was stupid not to, but war? No, this place was something, but it wasn't a war zone. At least not until now.

Two blocks down Avalon, he could see Mary Yoo's hamburger stand on fire. That was a shame. Mary was a nice woman—ugly and quiet, but nice. Maybe Black people saw an ugly, quiet Korean woman and thought she was rude and racist. Or maybe they just lit the place up because they were mad and it was there. Sang-woo didn't know what his own wife was thinking half the time, how was he supposed to know what went on in the minds of Black people?

For example: why did they torch Happy Hamburger—Happy Hamburger! poor, flat-faced, unsmiling Mary—and leave South Park Liquor alone?

South Park Liquor. It had felt like destiny, in its way—he was from South Korea, his last name was Park, it seemed like a solid business, and it came up for sale right when he had enough money to get something going. Opportunity! The whole reason he left Korea, to find opportunity, to grab it with both hands the moment it appeared.

Eun-ji had told him to stay home, said it was too dangerous to go back. She wasn't wrong, he knew that, and if she'd begged him instead of scolding him in that huffy way she had, like he was an insufferable idiot, like it wasn't about this thing, today, but every decision he'd ever made—why did he lease a Camaro, why did he throw money away at the casino, why did he move her across the ocean, away from her family and friends, so she could live like a pauper?—maybe he would've listened. He'd closed the store early yesterday, after the verdict came down, and stayed away for over twenty-four hours, watching the riot unfold on TV. He wanted to give it some time, and besides, there was no reason to open up. All his paying customers would be waiting out the chaos at home.

That's what he thought, anyway, but there was Anthony, right in front of the closed doors, facing the street like a palace guard. He was a fat man, the kind of fat where his pants fell down, not on purpose like the young guys, just drooped low every five minutes so he was always pulling them back up and tightening his belt in frustration. Maybe he was young too—Sang-woo could never tell how old Black people were, and he hadn't bothered to ask. Anthony had kids, Sang-woo knew that much. Two of them, their picture in his wallet. Sang-woo saw their chubby faces whenever Anthony turned the wallet inside out, looking for hidden dollars.

Sang-woo got out of the car, threw his cigarette on the street, and put a new one between his lips.

Anthony nodded, like he'd been expecting him. "Crazy, huh?" Sang-woo walked over to Anthony and lit the cigarette. He took a drag, filling his lungs with smoke, with bitter, sooty air. He shook another cigarette loose from the pack and offered it to Anthony. "What are you doing here?" he asked.

Anthony took it with a grin. "Came to check on your place," he said. "Can't have my luck burn down."

Sang-woo shook his head. He was moved, he couldn't help it, even if he knew Anthony meant exactly what he said. Anthony was a gambler, like Sang-woo—the most superstitious kind of man. They weren't friends—Sang-woo wasn't friends with his customers, it wasn't like that and he didn't pretend—but they did scratchers together every time Anthony came in, sometimes four, five times a week, ever since Anthony hit it big last July. He'd won five thousand dollars, the biggest score in the history of South Park Liquor, and neither man could believe there wasn't more coming.

It was the same mistake, he realized now, the same one that defined Sang-woo's entire American existence. The notion that *this*—South Park Shibal-Sekki Liquor—was some kind of golden goose, a place of good fortune, and not a shithole money pit where all his dreams came to die.

He looked at it now: his store, his life's work, its shabby pink walls inappropriately cheerful, surrounded by so much destruction. He thought of a pretty Vietnamese blackjack dealer at Commerce, her nails long and shell-pink as she tapped the felt, shaking her head, then raked in another stack of Sang-woo's chips.

He hated this place. He hated that it was supposed to make him proud, all his toil and sacrifice so his kids could have good lives, so they could go to school in America and tell him to stop smoking. If he worked hard, and they worked hard, he could pay for them to go to college. It was a good bet, American college. Positive expected value. But the return wouldn't come to Sang-woo. That was for Hana, for Eric. He and Eun-ji would take care of themselves with what they had left. But the work was hard, and after eight years running the store, he had worse than nothing to show for it.

Somewhere nearby, he heard sirens. He wondered if they were going to Happy Hamburger or another fire—Sang-woo saw one raging on his way here, and at least a dozen buildings that had burned overnight. He asked: "You think you're lucky, Anthony?"

The big man shrugged. "Don't know about that. But this is my lucky spot."

"What happened to the money? The five thousand?"

"That exact money? I don't know. Gone, I guess."

Sang-woo had done the math. In the last year, Anthony had bled over three thousand dollars on scratchers, and Sang-woo had bled right with him. But every time they hit—fifty dollars on a ten-dollar ticket, twenty dollars on a five-dollar one—they felt the euphoria of possibility, the big score waiting, hidden in the next card. Sang-woo understood—had probably always understood, somewhere in his broken, idiot brain—that the chase wasn't worth it. Between the scratchers, the cards, the horses, the sports—all the bets he made to sprinkle his long, dreary days and nights with brilliant little crystals of chance—he was in the hole for almost $100,000. For weeks now, he had been gathering the courage to tell Eun-ji. She'd put some money away in a savings account that wouldn't mature for a few years. She said it was for Hana and Eric, but he knew what it was really for: an emergency fund she could shield from him.

He would tell her, he'd decided, on Hana's twelfth birthday, the first week of May, when Eun-ji would have to keep her composure. Then, with less than a week to D-Day, everything changed.

"How long you stand here?" he asked Anthony. "You here yesterday?"

"Yeah, came last night with Wallace."

"Wallace?" Wallace was another customer, but he had no special reason to care about Sang-woo or the store. "Why?"

"He borrowed a hundred dollars from me when I hit that jackpot. I know I ain't never seeing it again, so I figure he owes me. It's a good thing too. We chased some kids away."

Sang-woo crushed his cigarette with his shoe and gave a hard kick to the metal frame of the doorway. The glass rattled.

Anthony stared at him, his eyes wide and alert, like he was ready now to face down a looter who'd come for his store. "What'd you do that for, Sang?"

"It's no good, Anthony," said Sang-woo, kicking again. "You say it's good luck? No. It's bad luck—for me, for you. You know what my wife say?"

"What?"

"She say when you gamble, all luck bad luck, even good luck." He'd shouted at her to mind her own business, even broke a plate—but it stuck with him, the way things did when they came spitting out of her mouth. "Forget luck. *Fuck* luck. I got something better."

Anthony laughed. "Yeah, what's that?"

Sang-woo lit another cigarette and watched the flames rising from Happy Hamburger, not a fire engine in sight. "A sure winner," he said.

$280,000. It was more money than he'd ever had in his life. With $280,000, he could pay back his creditors, open another business—in the Valley this time, somewhere safe—and who knows, maybe even have some left over. Enough to put aside for the kids or play the stock market—no use letting it sit in a low-yield bank account when it could grow with some careful investing, maybe double or triple by the time Hana went to college.

Sang-woo never felt better than he did after the fire, South Park Liquor turned to a crumpled skeleton of metal and rubble and ash. It was all he could do to hide his glee, his winning ticket stashed away in his home desk drawer.

Eun-ji was livid, of course she was, but what could Sang-woo have done? She'd warned him against going to the store at all—now did she think he should've been there, armed and standing guard, night after night after night? She cried and wailed, lamenting the loss of their livelihood, and Sang-woo let her. Then he mentioned, as if he'd just remembered, the insurance policy he'd bought from Mike Koh. She'd stared at him, agape: "Mike Koh? That useless bastard?"

But even Eun-ji came around when he showed her the policy from Pacific Marine and Fire. Signed, dated, everything in English, and the bottom line: in case of total loss caused by fire, $280,000 of coverage. It didn't stop her from pouting, or worrying ceaselessly about the future, but she went back to washing his clothes and cooking and serving his meals without complaint. He knew that for once he had done something right.

Except a month had passed with no word from Mike Koh, a man Sang-woo usually saw two or three times a week. He wasn't at church, he wasn't at his usual tables—Sang-woo looked every time he dipped into Commerce, hoping to double some of his future payout money. Sang-woo called and called, left multiple voice mails on Mike's phone. He started getting that roil in his gut, the gambler's vertigo, the hope and nausea he felt watching the torturous turn of a make-or-break card. It pissed him off: this was not a gamble; Sang-woo had signed the papers, he'd even made the payments on time, he had the policy in his pocket; he'd already won.

So why was he standing on the corner in front of his burned-out liquor store, watching the street with Anthony and Wallace like a trio of low-level drug dealers?

Wallace looked at his watch. "You think he'll show?"

Sang-woo put out his cigarette, lit another, and wondered idly if Mike would be scared of Wallace. Anthony, he didn't bother wondering about; he would never count on anyone being scared of Anthony, only figured that both of these jokers would be better than just the one. But Wallace? He looked young, not like a kid but like he could be twenty, twenty-five, prime gangbanger age. He was thin, maybe even skinny, but Mike was no Schwarzenegger. Mike was an insurance salesman. He sold policies to Korean merchants in South Central, but he found them at church, at birthday parties, not in the actual neighborhood. When Sang-woo named South Park Liquor as their meeting place, Mike asked if there were still National Guardsmen around, then said he'd only drive down in the middle of the day. Sang-woo guessed that Mike rarely saw Black people. Yeah, he'd be scared of Wallace. Maybe even of Anthony, if he thought the big man might have a gun.

"He'll come," said Sang-woo. "He has a girlfriend. I met her at the casino. If he don't come, I told him next voice mail I leave for his wife."

Anthony laughed into his fist. "Sang! You savage!"

A minute later, Mike's 4Runner drove cautiously down Avalon. Sang-woo made eye contact with Mike through the windshield and motioned him toward the carcass of the liquor store.

Mike stopped the car at the intersection and rolled down his window, leaving a lane between the car and the corner. Sang-woo suppressed a smile—Mike was scared, all right, the greasy little weasel.

"Park the car!" Sang-woo shouted at him in Korean. "I just want to talk, but you better talk to me."

"I'll park across the street," said Mike. "We'll sit on that bench. Only us."

"What's he saying?" asked Anthony.

"He wants to talk alone. Over there." Sang-woo gestured toward the bus stop on the other side of Avalon. "You guys stay here. Watch us—do the mad dog. Then five minutes, you walk over."

Mike parked his car and got out while Sang-woo crossed the street. There were a few other people at the bus stop, but they watched for the bus and paid the two Korean men no mind. In every direction, Sang-woo could see broken windows and burned-out buildings, but in some ways, it felt like things were going back to normal. The fires had stopped. The soldiers were gone. People left home. They walked the streets. They took the bus.

Sang-woo sat on the bench next to Mike and pulled the policy out of his pocket. "Remember this?"

Mike nodded. He looked tired and sheepish. Sang-woo could see his sunken eyes, his armpit sweat, the shape of a wifebeater under his thin, rumpled shirt.

Sang-woo unfolded the paper. It was creased and limp, but the print was clear. "It's worth $280,000."

Mike leaned over to glance at the numbers. "That much? Are you sure?"

"You should know what it says. You sold it to me. 'South Central is so dangerous. Who knows what could happen? Protect your business. Think of your kids.'"

"Let me see it."

Sang-woo set the paper down on his lap and jabbed the number with his middle finger. "Total loss, $280,000. Are you telling me that isn't what this says? Are you telling me you lied?"

"I didn't lie!"

The sweat stains on Mike's shirt had spread. It felt good to see him squirm after weeks of talking to his answering machine, but Sang-woo knew what that meant: Sang-woo's sure winner, his insurance and most responsible bet, had been a gamble after all.

"Look around, brother," said Mike. "You think you're the only one trying to get paid?"

Sang-woo hadn't spoken to Mary Yoo—he'd felt lucky and

didn't want to catch bad luck from a sad-sack virtuous immigrant sucker like her. But maybe *he* was the sucker. Happy Hamburger was gone, but maybe Mary had insurance. And if she did, surely she'd had better sense than to buy it from Mike Shibal-Sekki Koh. "What do you think your job is? Selling pieces of paper? I *paid*. What did I pay for?"

Mike said nothing. Sang-woo grabbed him by the collar.

"I want to talk to your boss. Where's your office? We can go now."

"The office? It's not—" Mike pushed Sang-woo's hand away. "My boss doesn't work in LA."

"What do you mean? Where does he work, then?"

"The company is in Antigua, okay?"

"Antigua? Where the fuck is that, the East Coast?"

"It's in the Caribbean."

The Caribbean—Pacific Marine and Fire wasn't even in America. It hit Sang-woo like a punch in the gut. "You sold me a cruise-ship island insurance policy, you son of a fucking dog?"

He could hear Eun-ji now, telling him he should've listened to her, should've gotten insurance from a reputable place, like the companies that advertised on TV. But no, this one wasn't on him. Sang-woo had called those places, had been told, more or less, that they didn't do business in South Central. The one quote he managed to get was so laughably high, it wasn't worth considering—they couldn't pay the premiums and keep enough profit for the business to make any sense. Mary Yoo could have done no better.

"I swear, I thought they were legit. You have to believe me." Mike cowered, and it made Sang-woo want to throw him down, stomp him into the pavement.

He did believe him. Mike Koh was a loser, the kind of guy who spewed cash on lucky numbers, who put more chips on the table—without fail—whenever the dealer was a woman with big breasts. He was a smiling optimist, the stupidest type of gambler, who went along with whatever felt good without stopping to think for a single second in his shibal-sekki life. So yeah, Sang-woo believed him, but he didn't care if Mike had conned him on accident instead of on purpose.

Mike wouldn't look at Sang-woo, though he couldn't stop himself from taking nervous peeks across the street, where Anthony and Wallace had been glaring, just as instructed. Sang-woo knew from Mike's expression when they left the corner and started making their way across the street. He had to tamp down a grin—Anthony was putting some real menace in his step. Sang-woo owed him whether or not the policy paid, but Anthony knew as well as anyone that you couldn't wring money from a broke Korean with a burned-out store.

"You're gonna get me that money," said Sang-woo, gesturing at the two Black men coming in their direction. "Or I won't just talk to your wife. I'll send these guys to talk to her."

Mike stood up like something had bitten him in the ass. "Come on," he said, almost shouting. "You might get paid still, you know? Why threaten me, huh? I'm nobody. That's why I wasn't ready to talk to you—because they don't tell me anything. I promise, none of this is my fault."

He pleaded, and Sang-woo said nothing, just tuned him out while Anthony and Wallace closed the distance.

"I'll do my best, okay? I promise you, I'll do my best, it'll just take time."

Sang-woo stood up and faced Mike, so close he could see the sweat pooling in the creases of his forehead. He stared at this idiot's idiot forehead and before he knew what he was doing, he raised his hand and flicked it, right in the middle, as hard as he could.

Sang-woo hadn't done that since his school days in Korea, and he was pleased to see he still had the bully's touch—it looked like he'd almost broken skin. Mike let out an indignant sound, a choked little whimper, and cupped a hand over the fresh injury.

"Your best isn't worth shit, Mike. Get me the money." He threw his eyes at Anthony and Wallace, now just fifteen, maybe ten feet away. "Go."

Mike did as he was told, all but running to his car, and Sang-woo sat back down.

Anthony sat next to him with a heavy sigh. "I don't know, Sang. I don't like your chances."

Sang-woo laughed.

Maybe the moron would come through, like morons sometimes do, or maybe Sang-woo should just accept that he'd lost this one: thousands of dollars in premiums and the payoff he was owed, all burned up with his store, his only stable means of making a living. It felt bad—like getting stacked in Hold'em when he'd gotten his chips in good.

He crushed his cigarette under his shoe and put a fresh one between his lips. He took a deep, steadying breath, letting the cigarette dangle. Weeks had passed since the last of the fires went out, but he could still smell smoke in the air. It clung to the neighborhood like a grimy film, the way it stayed in Sang-woo's clothes and hair, hot and sooty and shameful, so that Hana always knew when he'd had a smoke, when he'd let another day go by without even trying to keep his promise.

"Shibal," he said. He snatched the unlit cigarette from his lips.

A jolt of optimism ran through him as he returned it to the pack, aligning it with the others—a small white circle, so neat, so clean. He had gambled and he had lost, yet life was long, he could make it up. He'd brought them here, hadn't he? His wife, the kids, their lives—they were American now, wasn't that something? He'd staked a claim on this place once, and he could do it again, why not? Eun-ji would be furious, but she was always furious, and the kids—well, he was their father.

He would quit smoking today. He could do that much. He closed his eyes and made a silent promise, a prayer, a wager: if he could make it a week without smoking, he, Sang-woo Park, could do anything.

HOW HOPE FOUND CHAUNCEY

BY Jervey Tervalon

Snooty Fox Motor Inn

Hope found Chauncey in the oven where she thought he'd be. Maria ran by searching everywhere in that filthy house, but Hope saw that the oven door in the kitchen was open. She walked to it slowly, knowing if she saw the wrong thing she'd be broken. But there he was inside of that cavernous old oven in his baby blanket curled up sleeping, clutching emptiness. She gently lifted him up, determined not to wake him, but her infant brother woke with a scream. She cooed and sang to him until he rested his head on her shoulder and wearily returned to sleep.

She figured he'd exhausted himself and had no energy left to cry; that he had been crying for a long time in the dark, filthy house that her mother somehow still owned. It wasn't the first time Hope had found him there, though Rika said she'd never put him in the oven again for safekeeping, but Hope knew she was lying, and she returned daily to check on him. It was about dark outside, and almost black inside the house; Hope didn't want them to be there a minute longer than they had to be. She skipped over trash, avoiding all the madness and filth that had accumulated in what used to be her home.

"I found him," Hope said, just loud enough for Maria to hear.

"He's okay?"

"She put him in the oven again, but he's okay."

"We gotta go," Maria said, her voice edging on panic.

Hope nodded. Chauncey might wake screaming his head off

and Rika could appear like she would do, straight out of nowhere, like a horror movie monster, and snatch him from her arms. Not this time, she'd never give him up.

"You think she has any formula?" Maria asked.

"Under the bed. She hides it there."

They burst into the bedroom, holding their breath because Rika never would take the time to throw away soiled diapers; instead, she just tossed them into what had become a mountain of shitty diapers; but the bedroom reeked of something worse than that.

"I don't want to put my hand under the bed," Maria said, shaking her head.

Hope understood. Anything could be under there, but when Rika had some extra money and sense enough to pay a basehead to gank formula for her, that's where she'd hide it from that same basehead who might steal it back. She'd get enough cans of formula for a month so the baby wouldn't go hungry even if she spent all the rest of her cash on rock. All she needed was water; she could find that from a neighbor's hose even if the water was off in her house like it was now.

"Hold him," Hope said, gently handing Chauncey over to Maria. Because Chauncey was blond with blue-green eyes and pale skin that contrasted against her dark skin and even Maria's light-brown skin, Hope knew that some people said she stole herself a white baby because there was no way that baby could be her brother.

She squatted down, gripped the bedframe, and lifted the bed high off the floor. "I see it. And I see all kinds of shit."

"Can you get it? I don't want to put him down," Maria said.

Hope could tell Maria was even more scared of what kind of nastiness she might touch than she was. Hope pulled up, flipping the bed over. The cans were there like they were supposed to be, but she couldn't bring herself to reach for them. They saw Booty, the pit bull that Rika was supposed to love, lying there dead and so close to the formula that his rear paw rested on a can. She had no idea of why it had gone under the bed to die, but it made as much sense as anything else that had happened to them.

"Can we go? Just leave the cans. It's no good now."

Hope nodded; she needed to breathe, seemed as though the entire time they were inside of the house she hadn't taken a breath. Outside, the sun was just setting at the western end of the palm-lined, nearly deserted avenue, and Hope began to feel Maria's panic run through her, making it hard to think clearly.

Hope wanted to catch the bus to the Snooty Fox, but Maria never went along with that idea. It was a waste of time, but she still had to try to get Maria to go along.

"Come on. It's a short bus ride."

"No, it's too crazy."

Maria would hardly take the bus in the day, but night, hell no, she just wouldn't consider it. She'd developed a way of walking so fast that nobody could catch her unless they sprinted, and then she'd just run. If she ran, no one could stay with her. She ran the 400 and the 800 at Locke for that pervert track coach—before things really fell apart. Hope hated trying to hang with Maria, and carrying heavy-bottomed Chauncey made it twice as hard.

"Do you want me to hold him?" Maria asked, but Hope shook her head. She'd keep up while holding Chauncey; she had no choice.

Hope glanced at the house she was raised in, praying that it would be the last time she'd ever see it; words couldn't explain how much she hated it. Maria had gapped her; doing that run/walk thing. Hope wrapped Chauncey a little tighter in his favorite Dora baby blanket and worked hard to catch Maria. Maria did have a point about it being safer to run everywhere you go; by the time the Kitchen Crips kicking it by the liquor store noticed them, they had already blown past. If they tried to catch them, they'd realize it was hopeless, and even if the knuckleheads burned out in a car, Hope and Maria would just cross against traffic and go in the opposite direction. It worked, but it was so hard; Hope was already winded. The relief she felt when she saw the motel in the distance made the burning in her lungs go away.

The Snooty Fox Motor Inn wasn't really the kind of motel you'd stay in with a baby; it wasn't the kind of place you'd stay in with a family or by yourself. Purple—everything was shades of purple except for the shag carpet which was thick and white. The ceilings were mirrored and so was the bathroom. Neither one of them could figure out why anyone would want to see themselves on the toilet. First time Hope saw the mirrored ceiling above the toilet, she shrugged and said, "Freaks got to be freaky."

She had the key so Maria waited by the door warily looking about, ready to bolt. Soon as they entered the room and locked the door, Maria put a chair against the handle and they both collapsed on the bed with the baby between them. He was wide awake, bright eyes casting about, taking in all the purple and then, to Hope and Maria's delight, his own image above them on the ceiling. When he waved at himself they both laughed, then Hope's stomach churned when she realized that the night hadn't ended.

"We've got to go back out."

"Why?"

"We need formula."

Maria shrugged and slipped on her sandals. It never seemed to be over because it was never over until you were dead. Neither wanted to go anywhere, not when they could kick it in the motel room, watching cable TV, eating cold pizza, and not having to dodge fools or answer to anybody; but there was no way to consider doing that when Chauncey needed a bottle and they had nothing for him, except sugar water. They wrapped him up again in the Dora blanket, and again they were off at Maria's break-ass pace. In front of the yellowish glow of the Food 4 Less they parted ways; Hope headed for the interior of the store, picking up a bunch of bananas and diapers, all the time feeling eyes on her. Security there, an even-at-night-sunglass-wearing, grim-faced Latino with tattooed, bulging arms watched her with an ugly smile that was more a leer or a smirk. Once, awhile ago, he'd said something in Spanish that she wasn't supposed to know. She knew it and it might have been worth six months in juvenile if she had let herself go and smashed him in the face with a jar of pickles, but she'd just shined him on. Those days of acting a fool were gone; everything she did now had to be cold-blooded serious. It was about Chauncey and it was about Maria and then herself. It was about getting the hell out of Dodge before things got worse, and though that was hard to imagine, she was sure that things *would* get worse.

She glanced at the checkout line and saw Maria conversating with Hector, the used-to-be gangster who now had a job and a wife and kid, but still wanted some of Maria. Hope returned the smile of the security guard scoping on her, and he grunted an acknowledgment. She approached him and stopped close enough to make him take a step backward.

"I need a ride home. You know someone who'd hook me up?" She could see herself reflected in his sunglasses, her long braids hanging about her face, her pretty full lips, and the tightness of her button-up shirt.

"Where do you need to go?" he asked, looking down with a puzzled expression at Chauncey's bright-blue eyes.

"Somewhere with you," she said, stepping even closer to him.

The alarm went off at the front of the store and the guard took off to see what was going on. Hope followed.

Maria stood in the path of the electric eye of the sliding doors. She held two cans of formula, the stuff they keep in locked cabinets, waiting for him to arrive.

"Puta!" the security guard shouted, and charged to catch her as she ran. Hope trailed, still clutching the diapers and fruit in one hand and in the other Chauncey, who seemed to sense that something was about to happen and was wary and quiet.

"Fuck you!" Maria shouted as the big-armed guard chased her into the parking lot. Hope set off the alarm too, but the bagger, a big Black footballer she knew from Locke, shrugged and didn't try to stop her.

Hope waited for the guard, waving his gun above his head, to get closer to Maria, and then she stepped quickly in the opposite direction. As she retreated, she heard the security guard lustily cursing Maria with a surprisingly high-pitched voice, daring her to return. Hope laughed as she hurried away, delighting Chauncey, who laughed along with her.

They arrived at the motel pretty much at the same time. Hope suspected Maria must have run backward the entire way as she sometimes did. She unlocked the door and they exploded inside.

"We can't go there for a while," Hope said.

Maria laughed. "That's what you said last month."

The baby had finally had enough excitement and began whining for a bottle. Hope walked to the bathroom and carefully rinsed the Donald Duck bottle. She should have gotten another bottle and nipples too, now that Chauncey had started gnawing through the nipples. She'd save the banana for morning; now at sixteen months, Chauncey wanted much more than formula. She looked at herself in the mirror as she mixed formula, two scoops and slightly warm water, and he was good. Chauncey didn't look like her; he had their mother's face, her straight hair and white skin. Hope had met her own dad a few times, a Black firefighter who used to like to kick it with her mother, but he got off drugs and left town and Hope's mom could never find him to make him pay child support, or so she said.

Chauncey's dad was white, she knew that, but Rika would never admit to who he was, like it was some kind of secret. Hope had some ideas; sometimes Rika would visit her old school, so she thought it might be a teacher. You couldn't put anything past a teacher, but maybe the father wasn't a total loser. Chauncey was handsome and playful and with the sweetest disposition; he hardly cried and was so smart. When he was really little, when he was hungry, he'd point to his mouth, and when he was tired, he'd cradle his head. When Rika brought him home from the hospital, she seemed to want to live a different life. She even went to church for a little bit, but that didn't last. Hope had seen her decline over time, going from trying to be a good mother to just not giving a fuck.

Rika would say, "I'm going out, watch Chauncey."

That would be it; she'd bail and leave Hope with a baby. So, there she was, sixteen and trying to take care of a two-month-old. It was the most overwhelming thing that Hope had every experienced, and it changed her. She realized she could *do*. She could be the mother for her little brother, at least she would try, and that was more than Rika ever did. She was sure she could do a better job than anybody else.

"Hurry up with that bottle!" Maria shouted.

Hope returned. At the sight of her, Chauncey squirmed out of Maria's arms to reach for the bottle and couldn't get the nipple into his mouth fast enough.

"He's hungry, this one," Maria said with satisfaction.

"Yeah, he is."

"Think we should take him to school tomorrow?"

Hope sat on the edge of the bed, surprised to hear the word "school" slip from Maria's mouth. "Maybe we should go, see what's happening."

"Yeah, maybe . . ."

Hope didn't think much of the idea and thought that Maria must be tripping. They both knew the score, what it meant to go to school with Chauncey.

"You go, Maria. I'll stay here."

Maria paused before she said another word. She put her hand on Hope's arm.

"I don't care if you go. But you know I can't go up there. You know Rika will be looking."

"I know," said Maria. "You're doing your best for him. I just wanted to see what's going on."

Hope nodded. Seeing what was going on didn't just mean seeing how much classwork she had missed. Hardest thing about doing what they were doing was giving up on the life they had before, no matter that that life was shit for the both of them.

"I'm not going to go to Locke without you."

"You need to do what you need to do. I ain't stopping you."

Maria started to cry then, softly like it wasn't really happening. Hope knew that Maria had a sister, but something had happened between the two of them and they hadn't talked in a long time.

"Do you want to catch the bus to the beach?" Maria asked.

Maria always wanted to go to the beach, especially when things were going bad. Things weren't there yet, but one more night and they had to be out of the Snooty Fox Motor Inn. Hope knew they had to plan. They had options but not good ones. If Chauncey got sick, or if they just couldn't stand another night at Aunt Thelma's, they'd do what they had to do.

"Manny comes back Saturday. We need to be out of here before that."

Maria shrugged, though it was her that Manny fiended over. Hope knew that if it was *her* the asshole wanted, she sure as hell would be trying to make sure they were long gone before he got back.

"We'll see Aunt Thelma. She'll help us out, but we can do that Saturday. We'll go to the beach tomorrow."

Maria smiled lazily, closed her eyes. The baby finished the bottle and began drifting off. Hope slid out of bed and checked to see that the lock was on and that the chair was secure under the knob. She made sure the half-sized bat was where it was supposed to be, near the bed, and the raggedy cell phone, the last gift her mother had given her before she went crazy, was where it was supposed to be, in the diaper bag, alongside the rusty .38. The .38 was Maria's, but Hope doubted that it worked or even that it was loaded. She hated guns and didn't want anything to do with them, yet Maria insisted they keep it.

Hope reached into the ridiculously small pocket of her jeans where she had five twenties rolled tight inside of a straw. That money would never be spent unless things blew up and they had to get out of town fast. Getting out of town seemed more and more likely, since they had already used up most of the favors they had coming from the girls they were down with; they were left with Aunt Thelma and Manny the Perv. She wouldn't consider help from people she didn't know well ever since that social worker tried to take Chauncey away. Hope had called her because she thought she had no choice; Rika and her boyfriend at the time were squabbling in front of the house and it got to the point that Rika had pulled her duce-duce on him.

That's when Hope figured that she had to do something, so she unfolded that barely legible number for Child Protective Services she had saved to do the right thing, but the right thing turned out to be so wrong. The social worker arrived the next day, a small, dark-skinned Asian woman who listened quietly and took a lot of notes. Soon, it became clear that she knew all about Rika and that she already had a thick folder on her. Hope realized that the social worker wasn't going to take Rika away, just Chauncey. Hope changed course and threw out the incontestable fact that Rika was the best fucking mother in the world and that she'd made up the thing about Rika chasing her fool boyfriend in the street, trying to shoot him in the ass.

Rika had realized that Hope was on her side and came on

strong with lies knowing that she was a fly's finger from losing Chauncey.

"Oh yeah, the house is messy because I been working long hours—I don't own a gun and I've never shot at anybody—I've been off drugs and living a healthy life." Rika continued lying her ass off with the best butter-couldn't-melt-in-her-mouth routine. Hope nodded with fake enthusiasm at all the right places. The social worker shrugged, realizing that she didn't have a case and left with a bitter look on her face. After the social worker cleared out, Rika charged Hope and brutally slapped her. Rika was a re-lentlessly neglectful parent, not a physically cruel one, and rarely hit Hope, but this time she looked murderous. "If I had time, I'd beat your ass good," she had said, and disappeared into the street. That was just the start of the times when it went from really bad to unbelievably fucked up.

Hope wanted to fall asleep; it just wasn't going to happen. What she needed more than anything was a chance to catch her breath; she didn't see how she could. She had to calm down, to rest, maybe even sleep, though she didn't like her dreams.

First headlight beams flooded the room, then steps, a key in the lock. The chair stopped the door from opening.

"Open up! Don't keep me out here!"

"Oh shit, he's here," Hope said, still whispering as though Chauncey could possibly sleep through all the shouting. He wailed and Maria put her hands on top of her head as though she were trying to keep it from flying off.

"Hey, I hear you. Open the door!"

Hope knew the voice though she didn't want to. Not him, not now.

"It's Manny, he's early," Hope said, fear and anger in her voice.

Maria turned on the light and reached for the diaper bag and held it close to her chest. Hope held Chauncey in one arm and with her free hand pushed the chair away and opened the door. Manny stood there in the doorway, silhouetted by the ample off-street lighting radiating from the parking lot—lighted parking lots supposedly kept gangsters away like sunlight did vampires, though vampires didn't shoot the lights out.

Hope ignored him as she cooed to the baby, doing her best to calm him. For whatever reason he didn't close the door behind him. Hope couldn't bring herself to do it either. Somehow it closed itself.

With liquor stink all over him, Manny stumbled over to the bed, sat on the edge of it, and unlaced his boots. Suddenly this room with all the mirrors and purple everywhere looked like what it was: a place that pervs like Manny could get their freak on. He was a little man who walked with a cowboy swagger when he wasn't staggering, and who drove a SUV so big it had a ladder. Brown-skinned and weathered like he earned a living outdoors, he was a building inspector for the city of Los Angeles. The owners of the motels around the bedraggled central city, all Patels and Kupuys—South Asians trying to make a living on some of the worst streets of Los Angeles—knew Manny's kind, and comped him rooms to keep him smiling and happy as he had his way with underage girls.

"Where'd you find the boy?"

"He's my brother."

"Good, good. Didn't know you had a white mama."

"My mother's not white."

Manny grimaced like talking to Hope was too much work. He looked away from her and focused on Maria. "I finished my vacation early, just so I could get back here and spend time loving on you."

Maria looked stricken, and it didn't help when Manny reached into the bag and came out with a brown leather jacket with fringes like you see on girls who dance to ranchero music.

"I got this for you. Come over here and try it on."

Maria took one step and, like a dog snapping at a fly, he grabbed her wrist and pulled her down onto his lap.

"I . . . wait," Maria said, still clutching the diaper bag.

Manny didn't wait; he clamped one of his hands onto Maria's leg and squeezed it. He tried kissing her on the mouth, but she turned her head, and he caught her ear. It didn't seem to bother Manny that Maria cringed every time he touched her. Actually, he seemed more than comfortable with her discomfort. Hope, though, was losing her mind. Maria put up with Manny because she felt she had to—of all the bad shit she had to deal with he wasn't the worst—but she really didn't have to live like that anymore. They both swore that they'd never let that kind of shit happen to them again.

Maria held out the diaper bag for Hope to take.

"You could party with us, but the baby would probably yell his ass off."

"No, I don't party."

"You don't?" Manny said with a frown while massaging Maria's leg.

"No, I'm watching my brother. I don't have time to party."

"Oh well. Maybe you need to give us privacy. Take the kid into the bathroom or something."

Maria pleaded with her eyes for some kind of help as Hope walked away into the sanctuary of the bathroom. What was wrong with them? They should have seen this coming. Manny had done it before to Maria, but times had changed, or at least that's what they wanted to believe.

Hope sat on the toilet and rocked Chauncey asleep, glancing up at herself in the mirror and feeling disgusted as she listened to what was happening on the other side of the door, whispers that weren't whispers; the grunts of a drunken-ass old fool and the sounds of Maria protesting.

Soon as Chauncey was sleeping, she put him into the tub on top of a nest of bath towels, and then took the .38 out of the bag and looked it over. Would it work if she pulled the trigger? Unsure, but determined to make things different, she swung the door open and stepped into the other room.

Manny was on top of Maria, grinding his tattooed body into her, grunting mightily. Maria had her arms across her face to keep his nasty mouth from kissing her, and Manny was too into it to notice Hope kneeling down and rolling the bat from beneath the bed.

Hope thought about what she would do next. Should she shoot him or hit him? She had promised Maria that she'd get her back, just like Maria said she'd get hers. Hope stepped forward, lowered the gun, and lifted the bat high, then came down on the back of Manny's head; the sound was sick like a coconut cracking, but at least Manny stopped with the grunting.

Maria kicked him off of the bed and scrambled to her feet and stood there shaking. She still had on those tight-ass Levi's cutoffs that would take industrial scissors to remove.

"He was too drunk to get them off," Maria said.

"How is he?" Hope asked, unable to look at Manny twisted up in purple sheets.

Maria bent down next to him for a long moment, then straightened up. "He's breathing."

Hope sighed, "I guess that's good."

"Yeah, I think so."

Now that she knew he was alive, she squatted next to him and fished keys out of his pants that were crumpled around his ankles.

"What now?" Maria asked.

Hope stood up with Manny's wallet in hand and shrugged. "Visit my aunt. Figure it out."

Maria nodded.

Chauncey started to cry.

Hope hurried into the bathroom and lifted him from the tub into her arms. "We'll figure it out," she said, as they ran for the hulking SUV outside of the motel room.

THE GOLDEN COFFIN

BY EMORY HOLMES II

Dunbar Hotel

1

September 24, 1935. Riverfront Substation, LAPD

I heard crowds outside the window. Every now and again, a shout would break out far off, down the way—and closer, in the hall outside. The colored folks that got rounded up with me was getting pushed around. Sound like they was pushing back, fighting, banging the walls.

The cop that arrested me would sometimes stare out the window. Like he was expectin' to see another colored girl pulled out the river, dead. Wasn't but one light turned on in the room and the room was dusk dark except for where I was sitting. His boots was so heavy, even when he was behind me I could follow him. And every time he came into view, clomping past, light came in the window, and I could make out the scars and wrinkles in his face.

There was a knock at the door. The cop went over. Laid his ear against it. Like he could tell who was knocking just from the sound. He cracked the door, "Whatd'ya want, officer?" he said.

A lady cop answered, "Detective Hanniday, the chief wants to know when you'll be finished with the colored boy. The niggers are rioting. He needs to see you, pronto."

"Tell the boss I'm 'bout done," Detective Hanniday said.

He closed the door and, before I could track him, snuck up beside me. Bent close. "You kill that girl?" he said.

My throat clinched. "Naw, naw," I finally told him.

"I ain't got devilment enough to torment a fly. I was hiding near the river with some Oklahoma white boys and some Mexicans we fell in with when we jumped off the train. We was looking for something to eat. Some fellers from the camp tore past us shouting that a white girl been kilt. Colored boys did it, they said, and the cops was coming to kill us all. I took off. Tripped. On a stump I thought. In a slippery place, up from the water. I looked 'round. Seen that poor girl tangled in the weeds. She was a goner. Dent in her head. Blood 'round her neck. Dress pulled up. Her bloomers was gone. I like to died, seeing that."

"And?" Detective Hanniday said.

"Cops drove up. One stepped out a long black Packard. His lights shined right on me. He was big as a mansion. Two guns on his hips."

"Chief Hopalong," Detective Hanniday said, talking to hisself. He walked to a picture on the wall. Pointed to a fat man—the one in the Packard.

"That him?" Detective Hanniday said.

I nodded.

"You've met our remarkable chief of police," Detective Hanniday said. "Shirley 'Buster' Hemingway." He looked back at me. "Then what?"

"The cop doors flew open. Dogs jumped out. The chief blew a whistle. Sicced 'em on us. They tore acrost the riverbank. Two ran up on me. They was biting the little girl too. Some cops pulled 'em off."

The memory of the dead girl raised the hurt and scaredness I was trying to forget. Detective Hanniday had took off my handcuffs. I was grateful for that. My wrists was still stinging. I tried to mash the hurt down. Didn't work. I touched my legs where the dead girl touched them. The blood was drying quick and hard.

"Go on," Detective Hanniday said.

"'Round up them niggers,' Chief Hopalong said. And they

did too, but not just colored. They beat on anybody they fount. That's when Chief Hopalong came over and started to whup me. Accusing me of killing the white girl. He was whupping me good and proper, till a colored cop came over and stared at the dead girl. 'This ain't no white girl, Chief,' the colored cop said. 'She just a yella gal.'

"'A yella gal?' Chief Hopalong said. 'We wasting all this time tending to a nigger?'

"He stomped back to his car, getting madder and madder just from saying that. That's when he called you over. Remember?"

The detective didn't say nothing. Staring out the window, smoking his cigarette, studying nothin' but his own thoughts. Then he said, "Yeah, I remember, kid. I'm the resident nigger-lover 'round here. Pride of the LAPD."

He kept quiet a spell, then looked at my naked feets. "Damn, boy, you got the biggest feet I ever saw on a child. How tall are you?"

"Five something," I said.

"Five something? What was your name again?" the cop said.

"Theus," I told him, like before.

"How old are you?"

"'Bout fourteen or fifteen, I 'spect."

"And you say you came in last night with that gang of Okies camped on the river?"

"Nawsuh, I came in with some new Okies. And I didn't meet up with them till I left out from home . . ."

"Home? Where's home?"

"Jardin," I told him. "Jardin, Mississippi."

"Where are your folks?"

"My pa got kilt sassing a white lady back in '29. Then ma got the nervous sickness. My big sister Paradise caught it too."

"So, why here? This is a white man's town. Why not run to Chicago or Detroit? Your people seem to be getting on there."

"I'm huntin' my Uncle Balthazar. 'Fore Ma quit talking right, she showed me his picture and said he a big pooh-bah in one of the colored hotels downtown. Figure if I throws in with him, I might can make it."

"What hotel?"

"Can't remember. It start with a D or a G."

"You mean the Dunbar?"

"Yeah, that's it. Dunbar. Ma said everybody that stays there's rich. Pullman porters, movie stars. If I throws in with my Uncle Balthazar, I figure I can get somethin' to eat. Get rich too, by and by. That's why I had to come here."

Detective Hanniday thought on that a minute then pressed a buzzer on his desk. A colored cop, Officer Kimbrow, came in. "Unlock the charity bin and find this boy some clothes. Forget shoes, he'll have to get those clodhoppers shod elsewhere. Once he's decent, drop him off at the Dunbar."

2

We drove up from the river through some mean-looking streets. Officer Kimbrow didn't say nothing. Then he looked at my feets. "Damn, son, those is some gigantic feets!"

Seem like he couldn't decide when to look at the road and when to stare at my feets. It tickled him and he told me when he was 'round my age he had big feets too. "Nature evens it all out quite nicely as you grow."

He started talking. Told me colored folks ain't got a chance in hell to make a life in this mean ol' town. Said he believed white folk, not colored boys, was killing all them Black girls—it was a warning. *Keep out*, the warning said.

We drove past ragged shacks, me thinking about the warning. Directly, we turnt onto a pretty street named Central. Seem like the whole town cheered up. Stores and buildings everywheres, brand new. Fancy cars and jalopies pushed in around us. Like we was joining a parade. Loud music played a ways down. Horns honked, folks jumped on the running boards, cheering.

I asked Officer Kimbrow, "What's the matter? They all happy. Ain't they heard 'bout the poor girl?"

"Naw, they ain't heard," Officer Kimbrow said. "They happy about the fight."

"What fight?" I said.

"Goodness, boy, don't you know? Joe Louis just knocked out Baer in four. He's the number one contender now. A colored man is gonna be champion of the world. And there ain't nothing these crackers can do to stop it."

3

Officer Kimbrow fount a parking space and pulled me through the crowd. When we reached the hotel, seem like the whole block reared up right in front of me. Balconies and windows jumped into the clouds.

Officer Kimbrow said, "Hurry up, son," and walked in.

I couldn't move. That Dunbar Hotel looked like a secret golden palace for white folks, tucked smack in the middle of Negro town. The white folks I knew about didn't truck no colored boy walking, bold as a prince, in through the front doors of they personal palaces. I wanted to hunt for the colored entrance.

"Come on, boy," Officer Kimbrow said again. I followed him, on the lookout for a whuppin'.

There was fountains, paintings, and flowers everywheres. Some ceilings was glass, staring at the cloudy sky. Walls was done up with sand-colored tiles. Flowers and gold curlicues twisted 'round them. The front rooms and all the shops was filled with peoples.

Nobody talked about the murdered girl. Everybody was trying to say something important about the big fight. We went to the front desk. A man, around seventeen, asked if we was booking a room. He was dressed in a fantastic brown suit covered with buttons. A little red hat sat on his head neat as a cherry. On his pocket was the words *Tiger Smalls, Bell Captain*.

Officer Kimbrow told Mr. Smalls we was looking for my uncle, Mr. Pin. When Mr. Smalls smiled at me I could tell my uncle was sho-nuff a poo-bah of some quality there.

"Captain Pin is in the barbershop," Mr. Smalls said. "Follow me."

The shop had four brass chairs. The barbers moved like dancers. They conks slick as race cars. Pearl buttons ran acrost they white shirts. A sign above the mirrors said, *House of Style*.

A giant radio sat beside the front window. Folks was watching it like a picture show. The colored station KGFJ was replaying the fight.

The head barber seen us come in. Before we could talk, he pointed to a tall, prosperous-looking gentleman getting his conk did back of the shop. The gentleman peeked his head out from the hair dryer as we approached. His conk sparkled like glass. He stepped to the mirror. Patted his doo, studying hisself. He looked back at us in the mirror. "Something the matter, officer?" my Uncle Balthazar said.

4

His office was big enough to fit a desk and a visitor's chair. A sign on his desk said, *Balthazar Pin, Plant Captain*. The walls was decorated with photographs of my uncle in his brown tuxedo, posing with rich colored folks. I didn't recognize but one of them, the famous runner Jesse Owens.

Uncle Balthazar sat at his desk; I sat in the visitor's chair. The cop talked about murdered girls—four since June. They'd died awful ways. Cut, beat, strangled, raped—then kilt and throwed away.

Just before he left out, Officer Kimbrow said, "Mr. Pin, I am honor bound to tell you, you can't rely on any of the sworn officers of the LAPD, colored nor white, to protect you. I suggest you look to your own menfolk. To stand up as men must; and, if it comes to it, to trust in the authority of Mr. Smith and Mr. Wesson to deliver due justice on our behalf."

5

Uncle Balthazar stared at me a long time after Officer Kimbrow left out. Then he came 'round the desk and studied me some more. "Mercy, you got some big feets, boy," he said at last. "How tall is you?"

"About five seven," I said.

"Well, that won't last long."

He took a step back. Studying me. "Your daddy was a runt as a kid. Grew tall and big as a bear. Mean too, quiet as it's kept. I loved your ma, though. She was God-fearing and sweet-hearted. Prettiest in the bunch."

"She ain't pretty no more. Nor God-fearing neither," I said. "She stopped loving the Lord when Pa got kilt. She stopped being pretty when the nervous sickness got her. It ruint her. Ruint Dise too."

"Well, boy, the Good Lord done sent you to me. If you works hard, I'm your man. But if you come up shiftless and short, you out the door—understand?"

"Yes suh."

He pressed a button on his desk. Directly, a lady, 'bout eighteen, stepped in. Pretty as a movie star. The writing on her pocket said, *Cleopatra Chimes, Chief Housekeeper.*

"Miss Chimes, take his young man down to the infirmary. Dress his wounds, give him some proper vines, and feed him."

"But there ain't no room, Captain Pin," Miss Chimes said. "We full up with help: janitorial, bellboys, waitstaff. We don't need no more staff."

"Then we'll just have to make a place outta no place," my

Uncle Balthazar snapped. He thought on it. "He'll serve as my personal factotum until we can find him suitable employment."

They was using words I'd never heard of. "Fact . . . fact . . . tote . . ." I tried.

"Factotum," my uncle corrected me. "That mean, every damn thing I say is a fact. And if I point to a heap of satchels yonder by the elevator, I expects you to hop up and tote 'em where they needs to go. Fact-tote-um—get me?" He turnt to Miss Chimes, said, "Now, he can't bunk here. F'now, get one of the bellhops to make him a pallet back of the pantry. He can stay there till we find lodging downtown."

"Yes sir, Captain Pin," Miss Chimes said.

She cleared a space behind the pantry. A bellboy named Chipper came with the bedding. He didn't say nothin' to me, nor hardly look at me all the while he made the pallet. He knew there wasn't no jobs, and here I was, the captain's pet, getting one.

Chipper left out soon. In the infirmary Miss Chimes brought in supper, some cornbread and a bowl of gumbo. I swallowed it all before it stopped steaming. Then Miss Chimes pulled out a first aid kit. "Be strong, shorty. This is gonna hurt," she said.

'Cepting my ma, I ain't never had a growed-up woman touch me like Miss Chimes did that night. Now, she wasn't trying to touch me in no sinning way (I don't think), but all while she was rubbing me and dabbing me with Vaseline and stinging cream, and sticking bandages and cotton balls all up and down my legs, seem like my privates (which she never touched) was getting healed and scrubbed and rubbed and pampered some too. I thanked the Lord when she quit.

6

The smell of biscuits got me up 'round four a.m. 'Round five, Flip

Cromwell, one of the busboys working mornings, brought me a pressed white shirt and pants and a white-and-black cap a milkman would wear.

My first uniform!

Flip Cromwell said, "We ain't got no ski shoes to fit your big feets, so you gotta wear socks till we can find some. So, get cleaned up, scrub. Breakfast's waiting in the break room. Chow down and report to Captain Pin in the lobby. Six sharp."

The break room was all white, with a long counter, stools, and booths. Photos of celebrities was on every wall. Most of the talk was about the big fight, where the great Joe Louis knocked out Baer in four. When Miss Chimes came in with the maid staff and heard what all them folks was talking about, she banged a fork on her water glass and yelled, "Stop!"

Everybody stopped.

"The fight? The fight!" Miss Chimes said. "What about the colored girl dead by the river? What about her? What about *her* fight? Why ain't none a you talking about her?"

Nobody said nothing after that. The only sound was the clinking of forks on plates. Miss Chimes glared at us the whole time. We was happy to run out of there at about a quarter to six.

Uncle Balthazar stood in the middle of the lobby. Wearing glasses, like a professor, and a chocolate tux with a bright-red bow tie. We sat around him on the big leather couches. He called for reports from the top peoples: head chef, bartender, waiter. Then said, "Friends, there is a killer among us. Killing our babies. Discarding them like garbage. The damn cops won't help us. The damn mayor won't help us. We alone and must be vigilant. Ever vigilant and ever ready to ensure our homes are safe for our chirrens, our grandmothers, and for our own selves. It's up to us. So, be careful and be aware."

A discussion of the murders followed. Once the speakers had their say, Uncle Balthazar turnt to me and said, "On a final note, comrades, I'd like to introduce you to the newest member of the Dunbar family. Master Prometheus Drummond. He my nephew and go by the nickname Theus. I have seen fit to establish the post of factotum for him. That mean he a lackey, lowest rail on the stool. Please spy on him. Torment him. If he slip up and sass back, I'm gonna kick him back to the river where he come from."

He said these shocking words then looked around at all the faces. All but mine.

"Understand?"

They nodded, yes suh, Captain Pin.

"Okay. Now, get to it," he said.

They hustled to they posts.

7

Uncle Balthazar sat at his desk signing papers. Cold as an icicle. Ack like he didn't know me. "So, I took a chance and hired you last night, nephew," he started off, "but you ain't legit and on the books, official like, till daybreak Monday. That give you six days to familiarize yourself with your responsibilities as a steward and representative of the greatest colored hotel west of the Mississippi. Or six days to mess up. Got me?"

He pushed the button on his desk and directly Miss Chimes walked in. "Miss Chimes will give you a comprehensive tour of the facilities," he said. He winked at her and began his rounds.

My uncle wasn't gone good before Miss Chimes grabbed me by my factotum shirt and jerked me outside, back to the trash bins in the alley on 42nd. She shoved me against a bin. Smiled. Her bottomless brown eyes was especially frightening.

"Now listen, squirt," she said. "I know Captain Pin said I got to work with you. But I ain't got to like you. Understand? If you don't pull your weight, I'll kick your Black ass myself." She jerked her hand inside her pocket and took out a pack of smokes. Pulled one out. Perched it between her lips. Stopped fussing long enough to stare at me. "Got a light?" she said finally.

Said it like a girl who don't want no light but just want to shame you and show you that you ain't got nothing she can use. So don't try to ack like you do. *You ain't got nothing I want, Negro,* she was saying without saying it.

I searched my pockets and shook my head no. Shamed.

"Thought so," she said, real mean.

I liked to died when she pulled a lighter out her own pocket and lit the smoke. "You mens is always buttin' in where you ain't needed," she said. "And as for protecting me, I don't need no damn man, 'specially no half-squirt half-a-worm like you running behind me. If that killer or any-damn-body run up on me, he gonna take his johnson home in a thimble. We clear?"

"Yes, Miss Chimes," I said.

I was shaking inside, looking for somewheres to run. She blew out a cloud of smoke and said, all serious, "Now, here are the rules, Wormboy. More important, these are my personal laws for getting along with me anytime you walk past me in this fabulous hotel. First, ain't no cussing on the premises. Got that, mutherfucker? And two, ain't no smoking, at no time, and that mean from right now till Doomsday, y'understand?" Another toke. She added: "No drinking, no dawdling, no overt familiarity with the guests— they're our patrons, not your buddies—no offensive or boisterous behavior, no spitting, in the street or nowheres, no stealing. And no sassing your betters, that mean me. Understand?" She flicked the butt into the street.

8

There are a hundred bedroom suites in the Dunbar. Sixty of them luxury, with private bath, sitting room, and gardens. Radio in every suite. Phonographs when requested. Miss Chimes pointed out the quirks in every room. Each flaw and flourish now my personal responsibility. She showed me what she called "hidden nooks" where dust and the occasional spider hid. How the beds must be made, pillows fluffed, linens folded; the daily flowers set out, watered, and arranged.

She showed me lockers lined with mops and brooms; shelves of brushes and rags. Disinfectants, bleaches, candles, soap, scents. I managed to pocket a small box of matches.

When I was 'bout wore out, I followed Miss Chimes into the cool darkness of the ballroom. Seats for a hundred. She summoned the head chef and all the waitstaff. Made me tell my name and shake hands. Our tour took four hours to complete. When we was done, Miss Chimes took me to the entrance on 41st.

"Look down, little Negro," she said.

My big socks was standing on the threshold of the hotel. The flagstone was imprinted with the words *Hotel Somerville*.

"They calls it Dunbar now," Miss Chimes said. "After the poet Paul Laurence Dunbar, and that's all well and good. But every time I say 'Dunbar' with my mouth, I say 'Mrs. Somerville' in my head. This is her hotel, not his'n. Sure, Mrs. Somerville had a good man—Dr. Somerville—to help her, with love and support and cash like a good man should, but she was a doctor too, and rich as hell, and all this pomp and majesty you see around us is her doing; the work of a single colored woman—Mrs. Vada Somerville. Her husband didn't do shit but get married to a lady genius. Understand?"

I did.

9

A sharecropper's boy ain't no stranger to hard work, and I decided I was gonna make my Uncle Balthazar, Miss Chimes, and all them California Negroes confess I was the hardest-workinest feller, colored or white, any of them ever seen. I shot up at four a.m., threw on my factotum uniform and cap, swallowed a biscuit, and had the bannisters, tables, and main room floors sparkling before the six a.m. meeting. I kept up a hot sweat till well after quitting time. Made sure every wandering eye seen me. I didn't take no break, nor dawdle, nor cuss, nor sass back at my betters, nor slacken my pace till moonlight rose over the avenue.

To help with my chores, I'd been given a bike, with *Dunbar Flyer* painted on the frame. My Cadillac. Uncle Balthazar fount me a place downtown, walled in with some Okie tents and run-down shacks for families on the dole. My neighbors was poor and grief-worn. From sunrise to long after sunset, when they wasn't walkin' around looking pitiful and stunned, they filled the air with curious sounds and voices; singing and playing mandolins, guitars, fiddles, and accordions, all mixed in.

10

The Dunbar paid for Rosalinda and Delroy Teal—the parents of the murdered girl—and all seven of they surviving children to come to LA as guests of the hotel and the legal fund of the NAACP. Saturday, after the murder, the Central Avenue Colored Women's Brigade held a rally and a march from the steps of the Dunbar down Central to the river. Where Magnolia Teal was fount.

Fount by me, folks was saying.

'Bout five hundred protesters showed up for the march. The speechifying was led by Mrs. Charlotta Bass, editor of the colored paper, the *California Eagle*. That tiny lady was as loud and convincing as a Holiness preacher. The real target of the murders, she said, was Negro life and culture itself.

"I want to address the Negro women, here and across our great city," she said. "Ladies, it is up to us to do something about the violence being done to our bodies, our hopes, our families, and especially our children. Many are the stories of heartrending courage that Negro women of the slave period have handed down to us. They endured as our sisters, our daughters, our mothers, and the mothers of a hundred rebellions—all of which our standard history texts have conveniently forgotten. Well, *we* have not forgotten. And we will not fail to root out this cancer festering in our midst."

The crowd got quiet when Mrs. Bass stepped aside and introduced the parents of the murdered girl.

The Teals put me in the mind of my own ma and pa. Unschooled, dirt-poor laborers. They words was sorrowful and heartbreaking. They sobbed the whole time they was talking. So did they children. All the speakers expressed outrage at the murder of one more colored girl—four since June.

Cops, white and colored, was out in force. Marchers called them buzzards. *Eagle* reporters passed out posters with pictures of the girls—Etna Pettipeace, Marietta James, Paulina Crabtree, and Magnolia—all who, Mrs. Bass said, was defiled and left like garbage on the street.

Uncle Balthazar made me meet the Teals. It all but wrecked me. They was kissing and hugging and thanking me for finding Magnolia, when all I did was trip on her. Their mistake kept me embarrassed the whole time I was meeting them. Uncle Balthazar seen I was too emotional to hang with the Teals. Told me I could take off.

On the way downtown, I fixed posters on every post and tree I passed. Following the rally, all the colored hotels—the Dunbar, the Monarch, the Clark, etcetera—pledged escort services 24/7 for any colored womens and children requesting them. I volunteered.

11

My job as factotum gave me the perfect perch to learn my new hometown. My duties took me into every corner of the Dunbar and acrost the far-flung districts of the city. Uncle Balthazar told me places a Negro could go, and which ones they couldn't. My uniform was my ticket in, he said. White folks welcome coloreds long as they think theys working for them. My coworkers and several of the old customers took pride in schooling me.

12

Sister Chimes was my standout teacher even in that bunch. One of her most thought-stirring ideas was the "golden coffin." She explained it one day when we was delivering gumbo and sweet potato pies to some rich white folks in the Hollywood Hills. They was hosting a fundraiser for LA's mayor, Fineas A. Stankey, who lived in a segregated neighborhood just above the *Hollywoodland* sign on Mount Lee. Mayor Stankey was a Canadian boy. Had a fondness for hamhocks and greens, but not for the peoples that cooked 'em.

The delivery shoulda been done by bellhops or waitstaff, but Miss Chimes, boss of housekeeping, insisted on delivering it. We met at the Dunbar garage off 39th, and picked out the longest limo in the fleet to tote the grub. She wanted to show them crackers that Black folk could arrive in a limo too, if they felt like it.

We delivered the order and Miss Chimes fount a wide-open space overlooking the city. Dusk was coming. We parked, got out, walked a minute, under the trees. Directly, Miss Chimes pulled out a cigarette. "Gotta match?" she said. She smoked it down to a twinkle. Mashed it out and said, "Let's ride."

We took the limo west, down Sunset. Past the Strip. The expensive hotels. The mansions in Beverly Hills. Miss Chimes pointed out places where movie stars lived and the famous restaurants for white folks where exciting things was happening. Next, the Pacific Ocean rose behind the hills, wide and black as the sky. Snow-white waves curled along the bottom of the blackness, marking the waterline. The boulevard curved back and forth under the headlights.

We reached Malibu and rolled south. Past Santa Monica, Venice, past the scrap of beach set aside for colored folks. "White folks calls it the Inkwell," Miss Chimes said. We took Washington east, back acrost the city. It was a thrilling and breathtaking trip.

I was still tingling when we dropped the limo off at the garage. I asked Miss Chimes if I could escort her back to her quarters at the Dunbar. The killer was still loose, after all, and although I was pretty sure Miss Chimes was capable of kicking the ass of any street hoodlum she met, having a friend at your back in a fight with a monster has advantages.

I said it and Miss Chimes looked surprised, like she was amazed I even knew her name.

Neon lit the avenue. We could see the Dunbar just ahead, growing brighter as we approached. The King Cole Trio was headlining next door at the Club Alabam. Fans was milling in the street waiting for the doors to open for the eleven o'clock show.

Miss Chimes paused. I lit her cigarette, and we stepped into the street to admire the scene. After a while, she said, "So what did you think about your tour of our beautiful city?"

"My tour?"

"The hotels, the mansions, the ocean."

I took a good while expressin' amazement for all I had seen.

Then, bluntly, Miss Chimes said, "Well, my wide-eyed worm, ain't none of that for you—the hotels, the mansions, the ocean— you ain't welcome in none of that. None." She turnt to face the avenue, waved her hand acrost it. "Look at all this joy and prosperity. Cadillacs and jalopies scrubbed and waxed like they heading to a wedding. Eager customers, flashin' and frontin' everywhere you look, broke as a joke but dressed to the nines. What you think of that?"

"Beautiful," I said, confused a little, trying to figure where her speech was heading.

"Well, this is your coffin," Miss Chimes said. "A golden coffin stuck in the mud beside a deadly river. There ain't no signs on the streets showing the walls of the coffin, but if some lost Negro step a foot beyond First to the north, Alvarado to the west, Slauson south, or cross the river, east, they begging for a beatdown. Our liberty is an illusion. Look around you, boy! Watch! Listen! The neon, the moonlight, the music, the dancing, the glow of prosperity, the hundreds of colored homeowners nestled safe, hopeful, and happy all around us—that is an illusion too."

"Illusion?" was all I could say.

"Tell me, Wormboy, what do you call a trough—a gorgeous, golden trough, filled with pretty flowers, that every day gets dumped on with fresh flowers and soil? Well, soon the trough fills up. But there ain't no way for the flowers that's already inside to crawl out. Nowheres to get sunlight nor nourishment. No air. And the gardeners tending the box just keep dumping on more dirt and flowers, covering the pretty flowers already inside. Soon, them at the bottom—once sweet-smelling and exotic—grows withered and stale. Start to suffocate. Rot. Dying inside the trough. That's what's happening on Central now, but we can't see it for the golden walls, dazzling us, seducing us to keep inside. It's a coffin, a golden coffin. Life and beauty overhead, all untouchable. And in the beautiful coffin, no air, no sunlight, no escape."

Miss Chimes was attracting a crowd.

"Mind what I say: one day soon, this coffin gonna explode," she told the crowd, "its golden prettiness flying and burning across the sky. Scalding and smoldering and rotting and stinking up the streets. And folks will be asking themselves—what happened?"

She mashed her cigarette in the street.

"Just wait," she said.

13

Seem like the escort services was working. Wasn't no murders from September to November. Once more mens signed up, I allowed myself a day off. Took a part-time job Sunday afternoons working the stockroom at Komix & Kandi. My favorite spot on the whole damn street.

Komix & Kandi not only had chocolate bars and red hots, they carried the spookiest comics in the city: *Dr. Fate, Hourman, Captain Zog*. Candy was sold in front, comics out back—in a room hid behind a curtain, so the scary scenes on the covers was out of view of lady customers.

Mr. Zimmerman, the owner, hired me, he said, to show solidarity with his Negro customers facing not only a killer but the LAPD. Mr. Zimmerman was a shutterbug. A two-dollar Brownie, each with a neck strap, sat ready on every shelf. He used them to snap photos of the kids that came in.

The shop was closed Sundays, while I swept the back room. Out front Mr. Zimmerman sat at the register, balancing his books. My chores took twenty minutes to finish. The rest of my three-hour shift I relaxed with a 3 Musketeers, reading *Krazy Kat*.

Last Sunday I heard pounding at the door. Mr. Zimmerman told the customer we was closed. Didn't stop the banging. When I peeked out the curtain I seen Mr. Zimmerman, mad as hell, grabbing his keys to let the guy in.

It was a colored cop. Big ugly high-yeller bald man with muscles like a boxer. Looked like a Fisk gym coach. Didn't look like no cop. Wore sneakers. Uniform didn't fit. It wasn't no friendly meeting neither. He cussed Mr. Zimmerman. Dragged him to the register. Pinned his neck against the wall with one hand, banged the register open with the other.

Something made me snatch up a Brownie. Poked it through the curtain. Snapped some shots. It was over in a minute. After he stolt Mr. Zimmerman's money, he stolt a fist of candy too. Then left out laughing.

I ain't no kind of hero, but soon as that mean ol' cop went away, I pulled the Brownie 'round my neck and ran out back where I'd parked the Flyer. Raced 'round the block in time to see the cop's brand-new Plymouth chugging down Central. Most of the shops was closed till after church, but the cop seemed to know which ones had somebody inside working inventory. He went in nine shops. Robbed them all. I was able to sneak up to the window at three of them. Snapped the crook red-handed.

Mr. Zimmerman got the pictures developed two days later. I showed them to my Uncle Balthazar. Officer Kimbrow came down soon as my uncle called him. He flipped through the photos, amazed at each one he studied.

14

From late September when I first arrived in the city, until the beginning of November when I got promoted from factotum to bellhop, finally making some money, I'd growed like a weed. An impossible weed. Once five feet seven on its tippy-toes, now a towering palm tree, six feet five on naked feet. I was growing so quick, I ran through four factotum uniforms before I graduated to bellhop. Puzzling as it sounds, I didn't notice the changes in my body till Miss Chimes started looking at me different. She started calling me Prometheus 'stead of Wormboy.

15

It got to be a hot December.

Tripple digits since the third. Leftovers from Thanksgiving supper was barely out the icebox when Christmas decorations went up all over Central. Coal-black Santas and chocolate elves and angels was seen on every street from 1st to Slauson.

In the main lobby of the Dunbar, a steady stream of tourists lined up to see the baby Jesus, brown as a nut, lying in a manger, with his colored family and admirers kneeling nearby. A big ol' tree got shipped down from Sonoma. Miss Chimes and her girls dressed it with blinking lights and sugarcanes.

16

Off 8th and Central was a curious house painted curious colors. Yellow and pink. At first I thought it was a settlement house for orphan girls, 'cause the chairs and davenports on the porch was always filled with poorly dressed young womens, looking lonely, with nothing to do. Then I thought it was a pet store run by ladies and specializing in expensive cats, until Tiger Smalls told me that ain't what a 'cat house' mean. It was a shop all right, Tiger said, where pretty girls was rented out for dates. If they sold anything, he said, it was love.

The girls came onto the porch at sunset.

Didn't pay no mind to the weather. Fanning theyselves when it was boiling hot; playing cards and reading magazines when it was cool. The broke sign over the porch claimed it was a hotel called the Come On Inn. But that was a sign from the old days, Tiger said. Pink House is what folks calls it now.

Don't need no sign.

Madam Carmelita Sweet was the lady that ran it. Miss Sweet was old like a grandma, but she wore big hats and high heels, like she was a pretty young girl fixing to go to church. Her lips and cheeks was painted bright red.

I started to notice that mens that shopped there would drive past the inn real slow first, picking out the girl they wanted to date, then hunt for a parking spot out back. Or they'd park way down Central, pretending they was shopping somewheres else. Then sneak back.

The entrance was somewheres in the rear.

Both Miss Chimes and Tiger Smalls warned me to steer clear

of Madam Sweet and her girls. And I did too, till one night when I was heading home. Just past 26th I rode over some glass. Blew both tires. Had to walk the Flyer thirty blocks home. Past Pink House.

One of the ladies on the porch called out to me. I'd have stopped for that voice even if it wasn't calling me. Was like singing. Like Ma calling me, when I was a boy. I looked around. There musta been five girls on the porch. I could only really see one of them, the girl in the middle. She was dressed in yellow, her face ink-black in the shadows of the awning.

She got up. Kept her eyes on me and descended the steps. Thirty-nine paces in all from the porch to the street. I counted every step.

She came close.

I could smell her body.

Her perfumes and her sweat.

Lord, she was fine.

Eyes bigger than spotlights at the Club Alabam. Her face round like a walnut.

She pulled out a cigarette. "Got a match?" she said.

'Course, I seen that California trick before. Was ready. I pulled out a match, smooth, like Humphrey Bogart. Lit her cigarette.

She smiled. Could have studied that smile all night. "Lordy, you tall. How big is you, cutie?"

"Six foot five," I said.

"My goodness, tall as sugarcane. Sweet inside too, I bet," she said, studying, making sure it was so. "Mmm, you a whole lotta man to drink in. So, where you headed, handsome?"

"Home," I said.

"Oh yeah? Where's home?"

"Couple blocks up Broadway."

She thought about that a moment, smoking her cigarette, looking me up and down, not saying nothing. Her eyes was fingers, searching me.

"I seen you gliding by," she said finally. "On your pretty bike. In your pretty uniform. Watching me. You been watching me, sweetie?"

"No ma'am," I said. "I just be going home. I don't look at nobody."

"Don't look at nobody, huh?" she said laughing. "Well, you ain't having no trouble looking at me now. Is you, cutie?"

"No ma'am," I said.

"What's your name?"

"Theus. Theus Drummond."

"Work at the Dunbar?"

"Yes'um," I said.

"Man, I'd love to go there. I hear it's like a palace. A palace run by colored folks. I just love thinking about that."

She got serious a minute, smoking her cigarette, then she said, "Say, Theus, you think maybe one night when you ain't got nothing to do, and I ain't got nothing to do, you can maybe show up and take me out to see what's going on at the Dunbar? Mix in with all those rich folks and celebrities? I'd like that fine if you could."

She said that, then turnt away real quick, then back, like she was 'fraid I was fixin' to say no. Instead, I said, "Yes'um. We can do that."

"Oh Theus," she said, like a little girl, amazed at what I said, and before I could say nothing else she'd threw her arms 'round me and kissed me full on the mouth.

I ain't never been kissed like that.

I suspect nobody has.

She fixed her dress where us mashed together had mussed it, then looked at my busted tires. "I see you got work to do. I won't keep you. Just wanted to make your acquaintance—Mr. Theus Drummond. I been wishing for a strong handsome man to squire me 'round this fabulous city. Back home they say Central Avenue is glamorous and fun. But it ain't been no fun for me so far. Anyways, a girl without a companion is looking for trouble. Can't be too careful, y'know? With that killer on the loose. Raping and killing women who's unprotected and all alone. Alone like me."

"Yes'um," I said.

I don't remember walking the Flyer home. Only that when I got there, and fixed the busted tires, I was too happy to sleep. All I could think about was the lady in yellow. I popped open a Coke-Cola, pulled up the window, and listened to my neighbors fussin',' playin' music, and laughin' outside. Listened till the sun came up. Then I realized, *Damnit, Theus, you ain't got her name.*

17

Whenever I rode past Pink House, I was on the lookout for the lady in yellow. Didn't see her nowheres. I started to fret she left town. Finally I got up the gumption to knock on her door at Pink House. I tapped real polite-like, at first. Could hear folks stirring. Nobody came to the door. I gave it a bang. Could hear Madam Sweet howling inside, like she'd been shot. "Bust that door, boy, and you done bought it," she said through the closed door.

"Sorry, ma'am, I was huntin' for one of the ladies that stays here."

"What lady?"

"The pretty girl in yellow," I said.

Madam Sweet was quiet a minute, pretending she was looking for something. Then said, "Ain't nobody here matching that description."

"Y'mind if I come in? Look around?"

"Fuck yeah, chile. 'Fore you can step up in here you gots ta show me the dough-ray-me."

"I got money," I said.

She cracked the door open. "Show me."

I pulled out my wallet, fat with greenbacks.

Madam Sweet pulled the door wide open. Inspected me head to toe. "Why, you just a baby. How old is you, son?"

"Almost twenty-two."

"And youse a lyin' sack a shit," she said. "Come back when yo' dick grows big as yo' feets."

She slammed the door.

18

Uncle Balthazar allowed me to work the graveyard shift Thursday night, December 12. I could spend all my time Friday shopping for Christmas gifts. Mostly, I was trying to figure what the glamorous lady at Pink House would like—something shiny and expensive, I was thinking.

I decided to take a break from all that thinking and hunting, and rode the Flyer over to Komix & Kandi. I happened to glance in my mirror: I was being followed.

A Model A, long as a boat, had eased up behind me. It was still light out, and plenty of folks was on the street. The driver paid 'em no mind. Like there wasn't nobody on the street but me—and him. I hollered at the creep. He ack like I was talkin' French. 'Round 55th, that raggedy boat jumped right onto the sidewalk. Penned me against the fence. The driver left the motor running. Jumped out. Ran around. Jerked me off the Flyer.

It was the phony cop from Zimmerman's. I felt the cold edge of a straight razor layin' against my throat. He took his time. Made the blade flash and flare under my chin.

"Now listen, you pissant beanpole," the phony cop said. "I know you been following me."

"Following you?"

"Yeah, following me!" he shouted. "Like you don't know. I gots eyes every-fuckin'-where. Don't you think I seen you? And you tryin' to ack like you ain't doggin' me? Snapping nasty pictures. Niggah, please."

I was tryin' to tell him I ain't never followed nobody, and even if I did, I . . . The pig-ass punk hauled off and punched me in my eye. I fell hard. My beatdown commenced from there.

Folks yelled. Honking they horns. Telling the man to let me go. But nobody got out to help me.

When the phony cop was done whuppin' me, he kicked me in my eye. Got in the car.

"If you know what's good for you, ya little roach, you'll keep my activities out yo' mutherfuckin' brain. You dig?"

I did.

He drove off.

That was December 13—the night of the Louis fight. A right uppercut to the body stopped Paulino Uzcudun at the Garden in four rounds. From the main stem, all the way downtown, the streets was swarming with fans. Cheering the champ. Dancing wild. Crazy drunk. Acting a fool. Like nothing serious was going on, 'cept the fight.

They fount another murdered girl that night, off Avalon, behind the dugouts at Wrigley Field.

I learnt about the murder Saturday morning after I got to work. Uncle Balthazar made me wear an eye patch all day. Just before my shift ended he called me into his office. Officer Kimbrow was there. Wasn't in uniform. Was dressed like a colored banker: briefcase, Borsalino, pin-striped blue suit, beat-up brogans.

He couldn't stop staring at my busted eye.

"Lord amighty, Theus, is you missing a headlight?"

"I rather not talk about it," I said.

"Well then, let Officer Kimbrow talk," my uncle said. "Tell him."

"I've been fired," Officer Kimbrow said.

"Cops get fired?" I responded.

He explained all the troubles he'd been having as a colored cop, serving a force openly hostile to colored folks. Following the noninvestigation of the Magnolia Teal murder, Officer Kimbrow launched his own investigation. Snuck 'round, copied files, surveilled suspects, took photos. All firing offenses.

"I started to notice a pattern," Officer Kimbrow explained. "All the killings was at nighttime. On some festive occasion that brought large crowds of Negroes together. All the killings was perpetrated on pubescent girls, helpless and alone.

"Those is the facts. Any event that inspires happiness and civic unity is a target. Etna Pettipeace was kilt on June 19, Juneteenth; Marietta James was kilt on the Fourth of July; Magnolia Teal was kilt on September 24, the day Joe Louis stopped Baer in four. Last night, again after a Joe Louis fight, LaDora Ragland got kilt.

"The ringer in the bunch is Paulina Crabtree. She was kilt on August 22, a curious choice for your run-of-the-mill murdering simpleton. August 22 is obscure, neither a local nor a national holiday. But those historically in tune, like I is, knows August 22 marks the arrival of the last slave ship on American shores—Mobile, Alabama, August 22, 1859. Now how many folks knows that?

"That's how I knew the killer was a Black man; a Black man with deep knowledge of Black history; a Black man with a deep hatred for Black life, for himself, and for Black womens in particular.

"I developed detailed profiles of likely suspects—all noted Central Avenue intellectuals. My list topped twenty souls. Only two suspects stayed uppermost on my list, both graduates of Black colleges. Two brothers. Theotis Palsey, notorious con man, wife killer, and rapist. That's the cat you photographed at Zimmerman's. Ten years ago, he ran a bullshit church west of the Furlong Tract named the Holy Temple of the Living God the Redeemer of Zion. Meaning himself.

"He began his killing there. First his teenage bride. Then

two girls in the choir. Theotis is supposed to be rotting in county prison, but he ain't. He escaped from a maximum-security cell back in March. While he was on the lam, he put out a statement blaming Black womens for his incarceration. The colored girl killings started three months later, in June.

"His younger brother, Cleotis, is a disgraced former vice cop. He was a proud henchman for Chief Hemingway before he was indicted for raping a colored girl in custody two summers ago. Once Cleotis got canned, his connections landed him a plush job as a tax assessor for the city. The extortion con works like this: Using city records, Cleotis identifies a mark, some mom-and-pop struggling to make the rent. Theotis sneaks out of hiding, shows up at the business. Flashes a tin badge and phony documentation alleging the victims are tax cheats. Those that don't pay get beat up or worse.

"I realized these colored crooks couldn't operate without protection. And the protection racket points to the top. To our trigger-happy chief, all the way to our sleaze bag mayor, Fineas Stankey."

Officer Kimbrow laid his briefcase on the table, snapped it open, and pulled out two large envelopes. On top was one addressed to the mayor. The next one to Chief Hemingway. Each envelope contained photographs I took of Theotis Palsey, dressed in fake cop clothes with his dime-store badge, shaking down shopkeepers. But the killer snaps was took by Officer Kimbrow hisself.

Cleotis and the chief, on a quiet street 'cross town in the white neighborhood of Leimert Park. They was took the night of the La-Dora Ragland murder. The men was photographed in the back of the chief's Packard, laughing like school kids. There was a note in each package that read.

Enclosed are photos of brothers Cleotis and Theotis Palsey, the criminals bringing blackmail and murder into our community.

These violent felons are well-known to you and their crime spree has been executed under cover of your authority.

If these extortions and killings don't cease—and immediately—our agents will be compelled to publish copies of this damning evidence of your complicity in robbery and murder, in communities you are sworn to protect and serve. Beware.

We are following you, we are watching you. Should you fail to heed this warning, copies of these files will be sent to every media outlet in the southland—both white and colored— and the consequences for you and your cronies are certain to be dire. Fatal to your careers and, most likely, your lives.

The note was signed, *The Universal West Coast Protection Committee.*

I'd never heard of any Protection Committee. Officer Kimbrow shrugged and said, "I'm it." He musta seen I was confused. He picked his next words careful.

"I've started a small detective agency on Vernon. I calls it Central Security and Detection. I've rented office space and applied for my license. My agency has initiated its first civil action today. Charging the city with corruption, extortion, and complicity in murder. If my suit goes through, you'll certainly be called to testify, Theus. Can you stand up in court and tell the truth of all you have photographed and seen?"

When I didn't say nothin' Officer Kimbrow got nervous. "Come on, son," he said. "You can do it. Steadfastness and courage are all we have."

Testify? Court? Didn't know what the hell he meant by that crazy talk. I nodded anyway.

"So, if called, will you testify?" he said.

I thought a minute. "Mmm. No suh," I decided.

19

That meeting with Officer Kimbrow got me upset. Scared too. I promised myself I wouldn't never talk to him again. That night, I was lyin' in my crib tending to the shiner that punk-ass thug put on me. I heard a knock at the door. I hustled out of bed and fount a butcher knife in the kitchen.

When my front door banged again, I jerked it open. Ready. Standing on my doorstep was the lady in yellow, now a beauty in pink.

I liked to keeled over.

She smelled like roses.

"I followed you home a couple of times, cutie. Hope you don't mind," she said, strolling in. "I was too shy to knock."

She seen my beat-up face. My eye shining like a coal. Said, "Oh my, Theus. Your gorgeous face! Who did this to you? Come here, darling." She kissed my wounded eye. "There, that should fix it."

We chatted a bit—the murdered girls, the heat—then she said, "Say, Theus, I heard the Dunbar is hosting concerts Christmas week to New Year's. Bessie Smith, Chick Webb—top stars. The Will Mastin Trio is headlining Christmas Eve. If you ain't busy, I was wonderin' . . . you think we could go out on a real date? Mix in with that glamorous crowd? I'll pay."

I couldn't say yes'um quick enough. She told me I couldn't pick her up at Pink House no more 'cause Madam Sweet put her out. She'd hired a room somewheres west of Figueroa. On the night of our date she'd just walk to 9th, down the street from Pink House. We could take a taxi to the Dunbar from there.

She got halfway down the walk before I ran to stop her. "Excuse me. Miss?"

She turnt. Smiled. "Something I can do for you, prettyman?"

"I don't know your name."

"My name? It's embarrassing to say out loud, but . . . my name is . . . Angel. Angel LaBrie."

20

Officer Kimbrow's evidence must have arrived on Chief Hopalong's desk early Monday morning. On Mayor Stankey's desk too. Like Kimbrow figured, they thought the photos and all was from somebody white. In the chief's afternoon press conference, he mentioned, for the first time, the murders of Negro girls taking place along the Central Avenue corridor. Dogged police work, he said, had brought the monsters who did the killings to light.

A dragnet was set to snare the wrongdoers—two brothers, Cleotis and Theotis Palsey. One a corrupt county official, the other, a bloodthirsty homicidal fugitive. No Angelino was safe. Updates on the investigation would be forthcoming. Neither the mayor nor the chief mentioned their involvement in the crimes.

21

Next morning at daybreak, LA Vice tracked the Palsey brothers to an abandoned horse farm in Compton. Surrounded it. The brothers was ready. Started shooting, battled more than an hour. Two officers kilt. The LAPD set the farm afire. Cleotis got burnt to a crisp but his murdering brother got away. There was a citywide alert: Theotis is crazy, armed, and deadly. Vowing vengeance. Womens and girls in extreme jeopardy.

22

Them relaxed, rich hotel guests went buck wild. Poured out the doors like cattle. Hunting for taxis: to Union Station, the Valley. Anywheres but here. Uncle Balthazar gathered the staff in the break room, tolt us to keep calm, stay professional. Assure the guests they was safe long as they stays inside the Dunbar.

Didn't work.

The customers that was left hurried over to the House of Style.

Crowded 'round the radio. The mayor was making an announce-
ment. The fugitive, Theotis Palsey, sent a warning to all the radio
stations and newspapers in town. Promised murder and destruction to a long list of folks: the mayor, the chief, everybody in the
phone book. The radio guy read the outlaw's message:

> "*To Mayor Stankey and my former friends at City Hall:*
> *I have been thy steadfast ally and defender.*
> *Have done labors for thee lesser men could not stomach.*
> *I counted thee as my brothers,*
> *Brothers in the fight against the encroachments*
> *of a repugnant race.*
> *But ye hath betrayed me*
> *And killed my dear brother.*
> *Ye hath sown the wind*
> *And ye shall reap the whirlwind.*
> *Mark me: the shadow of death*
> *Is upon thee.*
> *Ye shall not escape.*
>
> *Yours in Eternity*
> *The Living God the Redeemer of Zion.*"

23

Streets was deserted from the river to the ocean. Cop cars, bumper
to bumper. Beat cops prowling alleys. Dragnets laid acrost the city.
The thin blue line swelling everywheres.

Theotis was a ghost. Seeping through the holes in the net.
By the start of my morning shift Tuesday, two more murders was
alleged in his tally. White folks. A old white lady, home alone,
raped, beat, and stabbed to death on Miracle Mile. A few hours
later, a banker, shot to death, ten blocks south of there. Changing
a tire.

The Redeemer of Zion wasn't just killing colored folks no more.

24

Uncle Balthazar canceled the Will Mastin show around noon. The Memo, the Last Word, Club Congo, Murrays, and the Basket Room canceled they Christmas shows too.

Soon as my shift ended, I flew down to Pink House. I had to find Angel. I banged on the door, begged Madam Sweet to let me know where my Angel was staying.

"You tell that thieving bitch if she step her ugly feets 'round here, I got a .22 slug with her name writ all over it!" Madam Sweet yelled through the door.

25

I raced home. Maybe Angel had stopped by. I got crazy wondering when I would see her again. A couple blocks from my crib, I seen a gathering. Gave me a sick feeling. I got closer and seen cops stringing tape acrost the alley. I squeezed in close enough to see a body wedged between two dirty row house walls. The sheet thrown over it failed to cover the victim's blood-streaked hair. The bloody fringes of her dress.

I pushed in under the police tape. Ran to the body, pulled back the sheet.

There was my Angel. Her teeth broke out, scattered acrost her chest like glass busted out a window. Her forehead was bashed. She had been stabbed. Her red dress was pulled up. She was naked from her tits to her feets, with a red line curved acrost her neck, where she had been slashed.

The sight of her burned my eyes. Seem like the garbage and the weeds and the peoples in the alley was hot coals rather than folks and things. The nosy crowd flicked flashlight beams acrost the body.

* * *

I couldn't sleep that night. I paced through every corner of the crib. Like I could walk away a million miles of pain just by turning 'round and 'round.

26

Only staff without families was allowed to work the next day, Christmas Eve. Uncle Balthazar tried to make me go home, but I insisted on staying. I wanted to be out. Hunting the killer.

27

Around eleven a.m., our skeleton crew met in the break room. Miss Chimes was determined to deliver a load of food and toys to the needy. Especially to the mission off Santa Barbara, and the Salvation Army on 5th. Uncle Balthazar was against it. "We've exposed our family to too much risk already," he said.

Miss Chimes allowed it was true. Wasn't having it anyway. She dropped a quarter in the cuss jar and said, "I'm not letting this evil fuck steal my Christmas."

I dropped a quarter in behind her. "Fuckin' right," I said.

Uncle Balthazar finally agreed to it, but only after Miss Chimes told Officer Kimbrow he could escort her.

28

Officer Kimbrow showed up at two. The plan was to get done before sundown. I loaded the gifts. Couldn't shake the notion the killer was watching us.

Officer Kimbrow taped a mug shot of the suspect, Theotis Palsey, on the dash. 'Fore we left out, the officer had second thoughts. Tried to get Miss Chimes to let him go alone. She reached into the pocket of her smock and pulled out a tiny .22. "Look what Santa brought me," she said.

"Cute," Kinbrow said. "You know how to work that popgun?"

"Watch and learn," Miss Chimes said.

I asked Officer Kimbrow if he had another firearm lyin' around. Case of a gunfight. Miss Chimes laughed out loud. Said I was too young to get turnt loose on the street, crazy, armed, love-sick, and inexperienced. She searched among the gifts, pulled out a Louisville Slugger.

Ash wood.

Jet black.

Hard as iron.

I gave it a couple of test swings and climbed in the cab.

Our route took us down Central, from 51st to 5th.

29

Streets was deserted, but I wasn't scared no more. Was ready to fight or die. If Officer Kimbrow and Miss Chimes was willing to risk they lives in a Christian act of love, why not me? I was doing an act of love too. Avenging Angel, my murdered girlfriend.

30

We'd made fifteen stops by the time we turnt the corner on 5th Street—heart of Skid Row. We was passing an alley when Officer Kimbrow noticed a rusting Buick twenty yards in. The hood was raised and a burly Black cop was leaning over it doing something with the engine.

The wreck was on blocks. No other cops, colored nor white, was in the area.

"What the hell?" Officer Kimbrow backed up. Nosed the truck into the alley. Rolled to a stop, unholstered his Magnum. Opened his door and eased one foot into the alley. Half in, half out the cab, he leveled his pistol. Said, "Turn around slowly, offi-cer. Let me see your hands."

The cop spun.

Shot Officer Kimbrow right through the windshield. Splatter washed acrost the cab. Kimbrow grabbed his throat, gasping. Blood spurting through his fingers. Slipped behind the open door, shielding hisself. Miss Chimes fumbled for her gun. Fell out the door, on top of Officer Kimbrow, firing as she landed. The Black cop ran toward us, Miss Chimes's bullets thumping acrost his chest.

He kept coming.

I grabbed the Slugger. Raced 'round to where Miss Chimes and Kimbrow fell. Got there in time to whack Palsey acrost the jaw. He turnt, gave me a scolding look. Quick as Joe Louis, I swung the Slugger down acrost his neck. Then the rib cage. A combination.

His pistol dipped. Dropped. Bounced into the weeds.

"Devil!" Palsey cried, snatching at me. His reach was short. I stepped back and whacked him again. He caught the barrel of the bat and pulled me forward like a fish. Seized me. Swung me 'round. Throwed me in the weeds.

He hunched down. Pulled a knife out his waistband. Miss Chimes rolled clear of him, emptied her pistol. Palsey looked confused. Had blackened his skin with greasepaint. Like an actor in a minstrel show. He swung the knife, stabbing nothing. Frantic. Huntin' 'round for his pistol.

I seen it first.

Scrambled to it.

Felt the iron settle in my grip.

I turnt.

Palsey raised the knife.

I fired. His eyes bucked. A bright-red dot, the size of a nickel, appeared on his forehead. A little stream of blood, edged in black, spurted out the wound.

He fell acrost Miss Chimes.

Dead.

31

I didn't celebrate no Christmas that December, 1935. Not no New

Year's neither. When Uncle Balthazar took me down to Angelus Funeral Home to pick out a casket for my Angel, the undertaker met us in the showroom and said, "We have several elegantly crafted vessels where your loved one can abide in comfort and peace till Jesus comes, Mr. Drummond. Models in mahogany, teak, copper, platinum, silver, brass, and gold. Which would you prefer?"

I had to think on that a minute.

"Anything but the gold one," I told the guy.

THE LAST TIME I DIED

BY JERI WESTERSON

Crenshaw Boulevard

1

I watched the police officers take away the weeping Negro janitor from the St. Vincent's Academy on Crenshaw and Slauson. They arrested him for murder. The headlines screamed it, hinting of other things that might have happened to the girl, things I didn't quite understand. Story after story in the *Los Angeles Times* made much of her whiteness and his Blackness. In the end, his trial seemed like a foregone conclusion despite his pleading innocent. The jury wore hard faces throughout the trial, and those who read about it were ready for the verdict they expected.

Except . . . none of it was true.

2

All Jesus had to do was be crucified. He never had to go to an all-girl's Catholic high school.

I hadn't wanted to go. I wasn't even Catholic. But my mother had said I was "out of control" and needed "guidance" and since there were no military schools for girls in 1961, this was it.

I borrowed some smokes from the janitor, a nice Negro man who didn't mind sharing. I tried smoking in the bathroom between classes and sometimes during, but too many goody-goody girls reported me. Damn nuns smacked you good with those rulers. Later I discovered going behind the gym. *No one* went there. I could lean back against the fake-stone building and feel the bounce of the volleyballs inside me, like a drumbeat in my chest.

My friends were just as wild as I was, straining to break out of the box the nuns tried to crush us into. Conformity. Sameness. It was in the uniforms, the skirts at just the right length from knee to hemline. Moral training with prayer and sacrifice. Reading, writing, arithmetic. Certainly no boys. And smoking was strictly forbidden, even though the nuns couldn't tell me exactly why.

I knew why.

Even though I'd seen *them* smoke in the walled gardens of their convent.

Later that evening in the dormitory, we all lay on my bed. "I am honestly sanguine about this whole thing," said Josie, chewing on a straw she had stolen from the cafeteria. Her new favorite word for the week seemed to be "sanguine" and she used it all the time in almost every sentence, trying it out even when it didn't quite work.

Maggie glanced at her over her horn-rimmed glasses. "I don't think you know what that word means. It means the opposite from what you're saying."

"No, it doesn't," Josie said defensively, before she flipped over on her stomach. "Anyway, this dance is going to be extraordinarily lame."

"A dance with no boys," I sighed.

"What's the point?" said Josie, twirling her dark ponytail in her fingers.

"*Comportment, ladies!*" crowed Maggie, suddenly sitting up and imitating the deep voice of Sister Conception.

The others laughed, even as they glanced at the clock. It was lights out soon. Lights out was the time we liked to go exploring.

3

I lay on the cold floor. Am I dead? Must be, I decided, as hands clasped my ankles and dragged me along the concrete. Of course, I didn't feel it. But I was curious as to what would happen next. It should have scared me that "next" didn't seem to involve clouds, angels, and the face of God, but instead the dark of a basement in this damned Catholic academy. Poor old St. Vincent's. I wondered if there were many murders at the school . . . or if mine was the only one. Because I could only remember so much. And I didn't like the thought of it.

I could hear crying, but I wasn't sure where that was coming from.

I zoomed up to the top of the ceiling, in a corner. Didn't even have to make it happen. I was simply . . . there. And looked down.

The figures dragged me. They were the ones weeping. Did they think they were rescuing me? Were they frightened about what could happen to them? They were surely in danger. Was there a way to help?

4

Ben Washington, the Negro caretaker, mopped the floors at night when all the students were supposed to be asleep. It worried him, sometimes, as the wet strands of the mop, like a dead woman's hair, swished over the linoleum floor. These high school girls had no respect. This was supposed to be a religious high school. But not one of these girls had the respect they should have had for it.

The nuns had their hands full with these girls.

Sister Conception seemed to be the mildest about it. She was a stern-faced woman, as they all seemed to be, with starched white wimples cradling their faces, and their severe black veils and black habits that made them look more like shadows than women. Were they women anymore? If you gave up God's gift of procreation, could you be considered a woman? A woman who gave it all up to live cloistered in this place?

Ben shook his head. There was one nun who scared him the most. He wasn't Catholic, so it didn't matter to him how he felt about her, even though his own fiery minister would tell him to love his neighbor. It was hard to love your white neighbor, to turn the other cheek, when they called you "boy" when you were a man.

Sister Sixtus didn't treat him bad because he was colored. She treated him bad because . . . well, she treated *everyone* bad. He supposed she thought it would help their soul. "Crazy white woman," he muttered, sweeping the mop from side to side in ever-growing arcs. He once saw her twist the arm of one of the students so bad the girl had to go to the doctor. They thought she'd broken it, but it was only a sprain.

He was glad he wasn't married with children. How would he handle it if some white woman teacher sprained his own child's arm?

He mopped more vigorously, until the floor shined in the dark.

5

Sister Sixtus had a face like a middle-aged man, even though she was supposed to be this side of thirty. That's what all the girls said. And when she was angry, she never changed expression. She only got red in the face.

I tried to look contrite, with my eyes lowered. But the truth of it was, if I looked at her, I'd crack up. And then she would be even madder.

She caught me smoking and was yelling at me about it. "You need to pray about this, young lady! At your flouting the rules at every turn!"

"The nuns smoke."

"What's that you said to me?"

I raised my face then. I didn't feel like laughing anymore. "I said, *the nuns smoke*."

A sting and then my head rang. She'd slapped me . . . oh good and hard. I was like a doll with a spring for a neck because my head just knocked back.

I stared at her. My hand went to my cheek and it was hot.

"You bitch." It came out of my mouth before I could stop it. The hand came again and slapped me a second time.

"You will pray ten Hail Marys for that outrage, young lady."

"I'm *not* Catholic!" I shouted back at her. "I'm not gonna say your witchy spells!"

Another slap.

"Sister Sixtus!"

My face burned. I turned toward the doorway where Sister Conception and two other nuns stood in horror. Like they never slapped anyone.

Sister Sixtus brought herself up, adjusted her habit and the rosary hanging from her belt, and walked away from me.

The nuns in the doorway parted for her, but all they did was stare at me. I sneered at them for just standing there, for doing nothing, for not even stopping her, for not defending me.

I stomped out of the room, pushing them aside because they weren't moving for me like they'd done for Sister Sixtus.

6

Tonight's expedition meant spying on Mr. Washington. He didn't live on the premises, but he often stayed late. There were always spicy rumors about him, and we wanted to be front and center to see it.

I was not an instigator, but I liked to participate. We mostly got along with each other, though we also found pleasure at being cruel to one another. I seldom understood their cruelty, vaguely owing it to their indifference to the images of saints being tortured with arrows, being cooked on hot grills like a barbecue, or getting chopped up . . . all with those vacant expressions on their faces. The sisters liked to have those images around as teaching tools. As if this was the sort of thing the students could expect in the modern world. I often wondered if the nuns thought this was a real possibility. Or were they trying to be subtle? No, not possible from those stern faces that seldom cracked smiles. I was sure they fully expected that I would turn on a spit if I got out of line, dating the wrong boy or doing a little petting. I wasn't sure if I believed in Hell, just the Hell of sitting in class and listening to the nuns babble on. That was surely Hell on earth. Say ten Hail Marys and get it over with.

We waited ten minutes as usual after lights out before we slipped on our regulation flannel bathrobes and set out.

The corridor outside the dorm was dark. Shadows were always moving from the roving headlights of traffic along Crenshaw. Light kept sweeping over our faces, and I caught a secret glance between Josie and Maggie with smiles meant only for the dark, and didn't attribute it to anything other than our mutual eagerness.

I liked roving the empty corridors at night, seeing the closed doors on the sleeping classrooms. The quiet. I imagined the nuns settling down in little nests, like black-and-white-feathered chickens, clucking softly to one another, plotting their evil for the day to come.

First place we headed was the basement, because that was where Mr. Washington had all his tools, his shelves filled with cans of paint beside stiff brushes, coils of wire, buckets, electrical tape, coffee cans of nuts, bolts, screws, nails.

He wasn't there so we poked about, looking into the cans of oily-smelling nails, brown with grease. We pried opened paint cans and sniffed their pungent fumes.

It was Josie who got the idea.

She took a bucket and filled it with the smelliest white paint. We got a rickety old stepping stool, and placed it on the landing so we could position the bucket over the door, pulling it ajar. We had to figure out how to get out of the room *and* set it up, and we finally did. Then we scrambled around the corner in the dark to watch what happened.

It took a long time. We were getting bored waiting, and had to keep reminding each other it would only be really good if we saw it happen. But it seemed like hours. It might have been.

Finally Mr. Washington came around the corner, the squeaky wheel of his dented metal mop bucket echoing down the corridor. He pushed it forward, leaning heavily on it, like he had the whole world on his shoulders. He looked tired. For a second, a short one, I thought of stopping him . . . but then the idea of white paint all over that black face was starting to make me laugh, and I threw my hand over my mouth, stifling the sound.

He scuffed to the basement door and stopped. His eyes traveled up and down that doorway. I guess he wondered why it was ajar, but he didn't think long about it before he pushed it open. The bucket came down on him, dumping a sheet of white on his head. It looked like a cloak, covering the roundness of his head and then his shoulders, before the bucket hit the floor with a loud clatter, and then bumped down each step. He swore some bad words that I wasn't quite sure the meaning of, and slipped down a few of the stairs, yelling some more. He fell on his back and just lay there, swearing and crying.

We jumped up from our hiding place and tore through the corridors back to our dorm, slippered feet slapping the linoleum. When we got back inside the dorm, with whispered warnings to be quiet that only made more of a ruckus, one of the girls sat up in bed and scolded us, saying that they'd *all* get in trouble because of our shenanigans.

And all night I sort of regretted doing it. Though it had been funny at first, he was crying real tears because it had hurt when he fell, and maybe it wasn't all *that* funny, and then I got mad at Josie and Maggie. And I knew we'd get in trouble bad in the morning.

But nothing was ever said about it. And when our guilt faded away, we plotted again.

7

Mr. Washington had a shed where he kept the lawn mower and other garden tools and bags of manure. He did a lot of work in

there, sharpening shears and clippers. I hung around, eating pea-
nuts in the shell that he always had.

And he'd always tell me, "You shouldn't be in here, miss.
You're gonna get dirty with all them tools and grease."

I hung out there sometimes because I wanted to get away from
my friends. One day I asked him, "Where do you live, Mr. Washington? Do you live here at the school?"

"No, little miss. I live not too far from here in a house."

"You work late. Why don't you live here?"

"It ain't right for me to live here. And I got a house."

I wanted to ask more personal questions, but I didn't know
how to.

I don't know why we played pranks on him. I liked him. But I
liked doing things with my friends. Even though . . . even though
they played them on *me* sometimes.

I have found dead frogs in my bed. I have found my tooth-
brush floating in the toilet. Once, they hid all my clothes.

I never got back at them. I don't know why.

8

The corridors were quiet and dark. I liked to glide through them.
Sometimes I'd come across the nuns in the hallways and I'd swirl
around their silent figures. I whispered something nasty in the ear
of Sister Sixtus once. Her face drained of color, then she babbled
a prayer and ran to the chapel.

I began whispering to all the nuns, but only a few of them
heard me.

Not one saw me.

9

Josie and Maggie stopped doing things together once I was dead.
They never sat near each other in class, never passed the ball to
each other in phys ed. Their voices sounded hollow and muffled

to me. It seemed . . . they *were* hollow and muffled to everyone else. They didn't seem to have any other friends.

Say ten Hail Marys and hope for the best.

10

"I don't want to do those pranks again," I said to my friends, when we nearly killed Mr. Washington with a wire strung across the corridor.

"He's fine," said Maggie.

We all sported the same ponytails on the backs of our heads, high as we could wrap the rubber band. I watched them bob on my friends' heads as we prowled the corridor. The pranks seemed to be getting worse, and I don't know why we did it to Mr. Washington when he did no one any harm.

"Why aren't we doing pranks on the nuns? They're the ones we don't like."

"Beca-a-a-a-use," said Maggie, "we can get in trouble if we pull pranks on the nuns."

So what? I was always getting blamed for things anyway. Things I didn't do. Some of them.

That night we got a bucket of dirt and sprinkled it out on a floor that Mr. Washington had just mopped.

11

I stood next to Mr. Washington in his cell at the Lincoln Heights Jail near the LA River. If I had thought the basement was pretty bad, it had nothing on this. Bars as far as the eye could see. Trash, noise, dark. I was glad I couldn't smell it.

Mr. Washington often stood in his cell at night, looking out through the bars. There were a lot of Negroes in the cells around him. Sometimes I'd drift by the others and peer within. Some cried at night. Some plotted with words muttered through gritted teeth. But no one else stood at their bars like a guard on the wrong side.

I stood with him. I didn't know what to say, to whisper. I

didn't know if he'd hear me anyway. The other men slept and made noises. Their cheap bunks squeaked as they turned over and over. I could see Mr. Washington's eyes in the dark. They looked sad . . . and scared. I peered down at his big hands, with their big fingers and flat nails. I thought briefly of holding his hand, but I'd forgotton how.

12

I stood in the corner of the courthouse as the trial went on. When I was little, we'd take the streetcar downtown past the courthouse. But recently they'd started ripping up the tracks.

The seats were filled with people and reporters. The jury sat to one side in a sort of box next to the judge on his high desk. One lawyer sat with Mr. Washington at a table covered with papers facing the judge. The other lawyer—he had two helpers—sat at the opposite table. That lawyer wore a smug look on his face. He argued against Mr. Washington and yelled a lot, and talked about me as if I were someone else. Told how innocent I was, how bright a future I had. None of that was true.

But back at the academy, I did whisper to Sister Sixtus at night. She spent a lot of time in the chapel alone, crying. I whispered to her how horrible she was and that she was going to Hell. She was ugly when she cried.

13

"Why do we always have to bother Mr. Washington?" I lamented for the umpteenth time. "Leave him alone. Let's do Sister Sixtus."

Maggie pushed her glasses up to the bridge of her nose. "It's too hard to prank the nuns."

"Go check to see if Mr. Washington is in the basement," said Josie.

I rolled my eyes and crept toward the basement door, pushed it opened. It was dark. He couldn't be down there if it was dark.

"He's not there," I whispered.

"Are you sure?" Josie had a little laughter in her voice.

"Yeah, I'm sure."

"Go look over the landing," said Maggie.

"Jesus Christ," I mumbled, then stepped onto the landing and looked over. The basement smelled like oily grease and furnace.

I took another step just to get a good look . . . and that's when the wire caught me at the neck. I tried to jump back but one side tore loose and it wrapped around my throat.

I heard their laughter behind me. Goddamnit.

I slipped off the step and suddenly the wire tightened. I couldn't get a grip to tear it away. I couldn't breathe. Panicking, forgetting it was a prank gone wrong, I twisted hard to try to free myself. It tore the wire completely loose, but by then I was leaning too far and I was disoriented by lack of air. I felt myself go headfirst over the stairs, hitting more steps as I fell.

I seemed to fall forever, tumbling, tumbling, and everything hurt, but mostly the terror took over and I couldn't breathe.

When I finally toppled to the basement floor, I didn't move. I couldn't. I still couldn't breathe because the wire was tight around my neck now and my head and shoulder hurt bad.

A scream vaguely in the background, hurriedly hushed.

Hands were on me. "Are you all right?"

"You're okay, you're okay . . ." like a prayer.

Then they tried to drag me up the stairs but that wasn't working. I heard their feet running and stomping up the stairs, and I wondered if they were coming back.

I lay that way for a long while as I got groggier, coming in and out of consciousness. A figure loomed out of the darkness looking down at me. I thought it was Mr. Washington at first. But slowly, I realized the shape was wrong. It was like a pillar. A black column. And then I could see the edge of their face in the light from the street through one of the basement windows. A nun.

She knelt. "Looks like you got yourself into real bad trouble at last, young lady. You really are such a troublemaker." I thought she was praying over me, but I kept thinking, *Why aren't you doing anything? I'm hurt!*

She prayed for a bit more . . . or *was* she praying? Maybe she was just looking at me. After a while, she glanced around the dark basement and saw something. She rose and moved away from my vision. I heard something rustle and something like a wrench clatter to the floor. She came over to me and glanced down before kneeling again. "You can just be quiet now," she said, and something rectangular came toward me. It was a smelly old towel. And she pressed it to my face. And then I *really* couldn't breathe.

I struggled, but not much. My poor body was too broken for that. It smelled like oil and dirt and I couldn't get any air. The darkness swallowed me up like a tunnel slowly closing in.

My heartbeat slowed . . . and then it was done.

14

I sat on top of Sister Sixtus's wardrobe and watched her at her prayers. They were so fervent, so full of emotion. Yet I wanted to laugh because they wouldn't do her any good.

Not that I could remember how to laugh.

15

The nuns met for their evening meal. Some would eat with the students, while the others would stay in their own dining hall. Separate. Away. This made them holier, they must have assumed.

The Mother Superior stood at the head of the table. "We must pray for poor Mr. Washington, that he understands his sins and confesses them. Pray for his soul."

I sat on an empty chair next to a quiet nun. Even in profile she looked like a man. But she wasn't praying.

Later that night, I whispered to Sister Sixtus and she finally got up from her knees and left her room. I followed her as she passed door after door of each sister's cell through the dark corridor, until she came to one at the end. She hesitated a long time, just standing in front of the door. I thought I would have to whisper some more to her. But she finally raised a shaky hand, balled it into a fist, and delicately knocked.

"Come in," said the voice from the other side of the door.

She grasped the doorknob and pushed it open.

"Sister Sixtus, what do you want? It's late."

"I . . . I . . ."

"Yes? Are you all right?"

I whispered to Sister Sixtus of Hell and the fires of damnation, and she took a step into the room. "I . . . I . . . know . . ."

"You know what?" She was irritated. She was in her starched white nightgown, with a cap on her closely cut hair. I could tell she just wanted to go to bed.

"I . . . know what you did."

She tied the strings of her cap under her chin. "This isn't getting any clearer."

Sister Sixtus took another step inside. "I know that you killed that girl."

Sister Conception seemed to freeze. She slowly lowered her hands to her lap before she turned and rose. "That's a strange thing to say."

"I saw you. I saw what you did."

Her eyes narrowed. I'd been trying to whisper to her though she never seemed to hear me. Funny thing.

"You supposedly saw what I did . . . but you never told anyone."

"I'm going to tell. But I'd rather you confess it."

She laughed. "Me? Tell what? Something you dreamed?"

"I didn't dream it. I saw it. I can give details. Confess it before they convict that poor man."

"He's a colored man."

I didn't like the way she said that. To us, grown-ups weren't one thing or another. They were just grown-ups. Mr. Washington was easy to pull a prank on because he never told. But you couldn't get away with it with the nuns. They were the worst, as far as grown-ups went. You sure wouldn't tell them your problems.

"He doesn't deserve to die!"

Sister Conception took a step toward Sister Sixtus, who backed up. "I'm not going to confess. I didn't do anything. That girl wasn't Catholic and hadn't the grace on her. It was better she was gone. Her friends did most of it to her anyway. Her own friends. They're the ones who killed her. These are the hearts of the little heathens we have in this place. It would be better to tear the whole place down than to have these girls here."

Sister Sixtus stared at her. I could see it all on her face. She was scared. If she didn't get out of there, Sister Conception would get her too. Even I could read as much in her eyes. Maybe it was already too late.

Sister Sixtus spun on her heels and ran down the corridor.

I watched Sister Conception stand there in her nightgown, glaring at the open door. She was trembling in her fury, when she had been so passive as she pressed that towel to my face in that dark basement. I was dead anyway. I wasn't going to survive that fall. She didn't have to kill me.

She pulled the door closed and stomped to her bed. No kneeling to make her prayers. I watched her douse the light and lie in her bed, her blanket clasped to her chest, her hands like claws. She was fuming. I didn't remember what anger was like. So I watched her to see if I could remember. Steps in the corridor. Lots of them. She hadn't bothered to lock her door. She was too angry. The steps got closer. What was she going to do?

16

The newspapers covered Sister Conception's trial. The *Sentinel*, the colored paper, wondered why Mr. Washington was still in jail. I didn't return to the courthouse to see Sister Conception. She couldn't hear me whisper about Hell anyway.

17

It's quiet in the academy now. Too many families took their children out. Sister Conception was going to get her wish. They were going to tear down the school. Cut down the big magnolia trees along the sidewalk out front. It was all going to go. Build something else in its place. Los Angeles was like that. Get rid of the old. Cover it up. Build something on top of it. Until that was old . . .

As the years tolled on, I lost more and more of my memory, and never remembered why I was there . . . or even who I was. Or . . . if I was anyone at all . . .

ALL THAT GLITTERS

BY GAR ANTHONY HAYWOOD

Watts Towers

I t was a strange place to work as a security guard. The fabled Watts Towers in Los Angeles. What the hell was somebody going to steal at the Watts Towers?

Before he got the job, all Eric knew about the Towers was what he'd learned in elementary school. Way back in 1921, some crazy Italian immigrant named Simon Rodia had started constructing what would eventually become, when he was done thirty-three years later, seventeen giant spires and interconnected structures on the site of his 107th Street home. He combined steel rebar, concrete, and anything else he could get his hands on—scraps of porcelain, tile, glass—to create what was now either the biggest eyesore or the greatest piece of man-made art the city of Los Angeles would ever see, depending on your taste for the bizarre.

Today, looming almost a hundred feet off the ground at their highest point, the Towers were a California State Historic Park, one that saw forty thousand visitors annually. Eric Pound was one of six people on the security staff charged with keeping the Towers safe and unmolested. Which, to Eric's mind, was like being tasked to make sure nobody made off with the doorknobs at a Motel 6.

Not that Eric didn't see his share of undesirables at the Towers. Like at any public space, the people who came here covered all kinds of emotional, psychological, and socioeconomic ground. Some were stone criminals and others were simple drunks. Words got exchanged, fights broke out, and sometimes blood was spilled. The Towers were situated in a patch of South Central turf the

Bloods and Crips had been fighting over since before Eric was born, so it was only natural that violence would break out on the grounds from time to time.

But it wasn't visitors intent on harming each other that Eric saw most often during his daily rounds at the Towers. It was certifiable crazies. Drug addicts, alcoholics, or clinically disturbed individuals on or off their meds, who showed up hallucinating, walking the lines to get into the park on unsteady feet as they held two-way conversations with themselves. They rarely bothered anybody but some were a nuisance requiring intervention.

The guy in the green jacket was one of those.

Today made the third time Eric had seen him at the Towers in the six months since being hired. As before, the guy had come in wearing a tired, oversized green overcoat he didn't need for the current weather. He was a Black man with small teeth and a head spotted with bald patches whom Eric had initially thought was homeless, because he had that sad, hunched-over set to his frame and his clothes and shoes matched the green overcoat's thrift store aesthetic. But he always had money for the park's entry fee and when he spoke—which he did only sparingly—it was with a clarity that life on the street usually denied people over time.

Still, whomever or whatever he was, today was the third time someone on the security staff had been forced to remove him from the park for attempted vandalism. Eric caught him using a common spoon he'd somehow managed to slip through the gate to try to pluck a piece of yellow glass from its concrete setting in one of the tower walls.

"That's her," the guy in the jacket said with some excitement, as Eric and his supervisor, Melvin Barnes, escorted him out to the sidewalk. It was the same thing Eric had heard him say the last two times.

"You need to let it go, Pops," Melvin said when they got the guy outside. "Next time we call the cops. Understand?"

The man in the green jacket didn't seem to understand at all, but he walked away without an argument.

"What the hell is his story?" Eric asked Melvin after they'd gone back inside the park.

Melvin smiled. "Nobody. Go back to work."

"Hold up. You act like you know the guy. Tell me."

"Forget it. Curiosity kills. You ever heard that?"

"Come on, Melvin. Who is he?"

From the pain on his face, Eric could tell it wasn't a story he wanted to tell. But Melvin sighed and told it anyway.

Seven years earlier, another guard at the Towers had his curiosity piqued by a regular visitor to the park. A young man named Darrel McNeil was the visitor, and Jimmy Dutton, the guard, found him fascinating. Darrel was somewhere in his midtwenties but had the mind of an eight-year-old. He usually came alone, but every now and then his older brother Greg would either join him or drop him off and pick him up later. Darrel was a favorite of the park's personnel, sweet and funny as hell, but nobody paid much attention to Greg. He was a nonentity, more polite and warm than a clothing store mannequin, but only by the slightest margin.

The two brothers lived with an invalid mother in Baldwin Hills, up in the heights where Black people with real money lorded over those with less. The mother was the widow of a man who'd made a fortune in insurance but had died too young to spend it, the victim of a fatal stroke at the tender age of forty-four. Darrel and Greg were Carol and Thomas McNeil's only children.

Their mother loved both her sons desperately, but she doted on Darrel. He was her baby, and a baby with special needs at that, so she gave him the lion's share of her attention and affection. But Greg did not go without; far from it. He was given everything his brother had and more. All Carol McNeil asked of him was that he be both a father and a brother to Darrel at all times. Carol Mc-

Neil had been confined to her bed since her weight had ballooned to over three hundred pounds and diabetes had taken both her legs above the knee. Greg had been twelve and Darrel only nine, and the boys' father passed away just two years later, so Greg had to pick up the parental slack his mother couldn't provide his little brother. Help dress and feed Darrel, watch him and protect him, teach him how to take care of himself in all the limited ways he was capable. It was a full-time job, and it only became more so as the boys grew into manhood.

But Greg never seemed to mind. He met all his brother's needs dutifully and efficiently; no complaints, no hesitation. A casual observer would have taken Greg for a loving, if emotionally distant, sibling. He was all things to Darrel. But the role he filled most was that of escort. Everywhere Darrel wanted to go, Greg was obliged to either lead or follow. The park. The movies. Children's theater plays and the Natural History Museum in Exposition Park.

And the Watts Towers.

Darrel developed a particular obsession with the Watts Towers. He loved stories about knights and dragons and kings and castles, and to Darrel, the Towers were the closest thing to a real-world castle he had ever seen. Darrel was also a collector, a hunter-gatherer of random objects of little value that he considered great treasure: buttons, bottle caps, board game tokens. Anything colorful and shiny captured his attention like nothing else, so the rainbow surface of the Towers and the walls that surrounded them, pebbled with thousands of pieces of glass and tile, were tailor-made to dazzle him.

In the beginning, Darrel sometimes visited the Towers twice in the same week, a fanny pack of his favorite baubles cinched to his waist and his older brother in tow. But as they'd grown older, Greg's tolerance for monotony would only allow for a schedule that had he and Darrel appearing at the park twice a month. Even that would have been too much for most people, after years of visiting the Towers enough times to draw each spire from memory, but Greg's silent resilience to Darrel's eccentricities seemed to have no bounds.

What no one knew, until the curious security guard Jimmy Dutton discovered it years later, was that Greg was simply biding his time. His greatest quality was not devotion at all, but patience. What his mother and others mistook for imperturbability was in fact cold calculation. From the age of eight, Greg understood the simple math of his moneyed existence, the wealth he stood to gain as Thomas and Carol McNeil's oldest and most self-sufficient son, if he could just wait long enough to inherit his father's fortune. So he set himself up to do exactly that, in the best way he knew how: by playing the perfect child to his parents and loving sibling to his brother.

Finally, three weeks after his twenty-first birthday, Greg's long-game gamble paid off: Carol McNeil died.

Almost overnight, Greg became the beneficiary of the family fortune, Darrel's legal guardian, and the trustee of the irrevocable trust Darrel's mother had set up for him. There was no one to contest their mother's will and no grounds to base a case against Greg even if there had been.

In short order, he was living the life of a free man of independent means he had always dreamed of. He dropped out of school, shedding any pretense of requiring employable skills anytime in the near future, and began to enjoy himself and his parents' money. He developed an appreciation for expensive cars and women who loved to gamble. Greg was no ladies' man, never had been, but he learned to date and date well, only driving the Porsche or the Corvette out to Vegas alone if that was his preference. Sometimes he came back with the same woman and sometimes he came back with a new one; in either case, he usually returned to Los Angeles a poorer man than he had been at the start.

As the months, then years, went by, two things happened that took Greg completely by surprise.

The first was the realization of how little he wanted things to change between himself and Darrel. He knew he loved his little brother on some level—what kind of monster wouldn't?—but he hadn't counted on loving him to the extent that he would still want him around even after their mother's passing. All those years of faithfully shadowing the boy around like a Siamese twin, it seemed, had left him with more affection for Darrel than resentment. In portraying his little brother's great protector, he had unwittingly *become* his great protector, so that now he had no desire to ship Darrel off to some assisted-living facility somewhere and forget about him, as he had always thought he would the moment the opportunity presented itself. Instead, by choice, he maintained much the same life with his brother they had always shared; the only difference now was the price tag of the car Greg drove to take his brother to the park, or to the movies, or—where else?—the Watts Towers.

The second surprising thing Greg discovered after his mother died, and which proved much more alarming than the first, was how fast he was able to burn through the $1.4 million he'd inherited. Within two years, he had whittled that figure down to the point that Annette Thomas—his accountant and financial advisor—was strongly recommending that he slow down, go back to school, and start thinking about working for a living. Of course, Greg just thought Thomas was being an alarmist, but she soon enough proved to be prophetic. The numbers she eventually showed him didn't lie: Greg was staring down the barrel of impending insolvency.

If he could have found a way to dip into Darrel's trust for the cash he needed to reverse his fortunes, he would have done it. But Thomas would not allow it. Greg had made the crucial error of hiring the same money manager to watch over his own financial affairs who had for years watched over his mother's, and Thomas's loyalties to Carol McNeil's sons—*both* her sons—were nearly the equal to those she'd demonstrated for the woman herself. Under Thomas's eagle eye, Darrel's trust fund was as safe from Greg as the paintings in the Louvre.

In a desperate, last-minute attempt to avoid financial ruin, Greg throttled back on his spending and began liquidating assets. But it was too little, too late. The day soon came that what he owed and what he could pay were less than equal, and some of the people his gambling activities had put him in debt to were inclined to do him harm. He was in over his head.

He went back to Thomas again. Was there anything besides his parents' home left to sell? Something he could turn into cash *fast?*

"Well, there's your mother's jewelry," Thomas said.

"Her what?"

This was the first Greg had ever heard of any jewelry. He was a small boy when his mother had last been healthy enough to go out socially, with or without his father, so jewelry was something he had no memory of seeing Carol McNeil wear. According to the fine print in Thomas's books, however, an heirloom collection of fine rings, bracelets, earrings, and necklaces that Greg's mother had inherited from her own mother was included in the McNeil estate, valued at just over seventy thousand dollars.

Greg couldn't believe his ears. His problems were solved, at least temporarily.

Except for one small thing: Thomas had no idea where this jewelry was.

It had been fourteen years since the collection was last assessed, and Thomas had never laid eyes on it. As far as she knew, it was locked up in one of Carol McNeil's safety deposit boxes, but Greg had already gone through those and found only personal documents and stock certificates, the latter of which he'd cashed out months ago. Had his mother sold the jewelry before she died without documenting the sale? That seemed unlikely. She would have had little reason to do such a thing, and even if she had, the proceeds would have surely gone toward something tangible and easily identified.

No. This jewelry had to be somewhere, Greg decided. Hidden away in the house where only Carol McNeil had known where to find it.

Annette Thomas had photographs of the nineteen pieces: seven necklaces, four rings, two bracelets, and three pair of earrings. With the photos in hand, Greg proceeded to take the house in Baldwin Hills apart, room by room, starting with the bedroom his mother had spent the last nine years of her life occupying.

He found nothing.

Until, as a last resort, he showed the photos to his brother.

"Darrel, have you seen these? This was jewelry that belonged to Momma."

Darrel looked the photos over carefully and smiled. Nodding, he said, "Our secret treasure."

Greg's breath caught in his throat. Feeling light-headed, he sat down on the end of Darrel's bed. "Say again?"

"Momma called it that. 'Our secret treasure.' She gave it to me to protect."

It made a ridiculous sort of sense. It was exactly the kind of game their mother would have played with her favorite son. Jewelry she never wore anymore, a fortune in the bank—what harm could it do to give them to Darrel, whom she thought of as a harmless child?

"Darrel, where is it now?" Greg couldn't keep the desperation out of his voice. The people he owed money to had given him one last chance to pay; he had less than forty-eight hours. "Your treasure?"

Darrel grinned, thinking his older brother wanted to play the game too, and went to the large toy chest in the corner. He got down on his knees, reached under the chest, and slid out a large, flat black-velvet box. He handed it to Greg.

Greg opened it, hands shaking. Now he did feel faint. There was nothing inside but a pair of earrings and the skeletal remains of everything else: the bracelets, rings, and necklaces had all been plucked nearly clean of the diamonds and gems they once held.

Greg couldn't remember the last time he'd been angry at his little brother. There seemed so little point. But there was a rage building up in him now he wasn't sure he could control. "Where are the stones? The diamonds, the emeralds?"

Proud of himself, Darrel said, "I hid them. Momma said protect them, so that's what I did."

"Hid them *where?* What the fuck are you talking about?"

"You said the F-word."

Greg took hold of his brother's shoulders and shook him, hard enough to rattle his bones. "Darrel, where the hell are the stones?"

"In the castle!" Darrel began to cry. He couldn't understand what his brother's anger was all about.

The castle. What Darrel called the Towers. The Watts Towers. "Oh, Jesus."

Greg released his hold on his brother, his mind retracing all those visits to the park, that funky little fanny pack attached to Darrel's hip like a colostomy bag. When had it started? Before their mother died or after? It had been years since Greg had actually walked through the park right alongside his brother, and even when he'd been that invested, the focus of this attention had almost always been elsewhere. Boredom and a watchful eye did not go hand in hand. Greg realized now that Darrel could have left a live snake at the park without his noticing.

He told Darrel to show him the fanny pack, already certain of what he would find. Inside, along with all the pieces of chipped glass and shiny detritus the man-child collected like a vacuum cleaner, was a fat tube of glue. Greg himself had probably bought the tube for Darrel on one of their regular shopping trips, never giving a second thought to what purpose his brother might have for it.

He had no more questions to ask. He finally understood what had happened, the ludicrous game of make believe his mother's favorite son had been playing with their inheritance. Without conscious thought, Greg threw one punch. A straight right hand that struck Darrel flush in the face and knocked him halfway across the room. It was the first time he had ever raised a hand to his brother and it would prove to be the last.

Darrel cracked his skull on the corner of his desk and died at Kaiser Permanente in West Los Angeles four hours later. The coroner's official cause of death was blunt-force trauma to the head.

"Whoa, hold up," Eric said when Melvin stopped talking. "That's it? That's the end of the story?"

"That's it," Melvin said.

"So you're telling me . . ." Eric glanced around the park at all the colorful, gleaming objects studding the walls and towers surrounding them. "That seventy grand worth of diamonds and shit is all here somewhere?"

Melvin just shrugged.

"The brother had been gluing pieces here and there every time he came in?"

"Not every time. Just every now and then."

"And nobody every noticed?"

Melvin laughed. "Noticed how? Man, how close do *you* look at all the glass and tile and shiny plastic in this park? You think you could find a ruby among it all, even if you were looking for it?"

"But somebody would have seen him do it. Right?"

"He was careful. He didn't want to be seen. He called himself 'protecting' his mother's 'treasure,' remember? You never knew a kid who could do something for years without his parents ever knowing about it?"

Eric fell silent. Going over it all in his mind. "I don't believe it," he said finally.

"I didn't think you would," Melvin said, "which is why I didn't want to waste my time telling you."

"It's crazy." Eric shook his head. "So this older brother. Greg. How come he's not in prison for murder?"

"Well, he was locked up for a while. But for manslaughter, not murder. His brother's death was an accident and he was halfway insane, so they only gave him a few years."

"And he's been coming here ever since, picking what he thinks are his mother's jewels off the towers with a damn spoon?"

"Oh, that's not him," Melvin said. "That's Pops. The brother died a couple years ago, from what I hear."

"Wait, what?"

"You heard me." Melvin was finding Eric's confusion extremely amusing. "The brother's dead."

"Then who—"

"Greg and Darrel used to come in here like clockwork, for years. Then they stopped. Three years later, Greg shows up twice, all by himself, and Jimmy wants to know why. So he follows Greg out of the park and asks: 'What happened to your brother?' And Greg tells him. The whole story, exactly as I just told it to you."

"Jimmy?"

"Jimmy Dutton. The guard who used to work here I mentioned. Only nobody calls him Jimmy. Everybody calls him—"

"Pops."

"Exactly. That was Pops we threw out of here today, not Greg. Greg figured out pretty quick it was hopeless, trying to find a few dozen needles in a haystack of thousands, but Pops?" Melvin shook his head. "He's lost his mind trying."

Eric couldn't think of anything to say.

"Now you know why I didn't want to tell you," Melvin said. "It's a sad damn story for everyone involved."

Eric nodded.

"But now that I have told you, there's one more thing you need to know."

Eric waited, afraid to ask.

"First time I catch you in here with a spoon, your ass is fired."

PART II

COLD SWEAT

COLLECTIONS

BY ERIC STONE

Central Avenue

There's never enough fucking hours in the day. Not if you want to get in a nap. The bedside clock said seven thirty. Vince laid down for a minute around six. He was supposed to have called in a half hour ago. You don't want to piss off the Lucca brothers. They're nice enough guys when you do what they want, exactly what they want. They aren't so nice otherwise.

His mom was out, working the night shift, hoping like hell they weren't gonna let her go to make room for all the soldiers coming back. She'd left some dinner on the table. He sniffed at it, got a Lucky out of the icebox instead, and lit a Pall Mall before sitting down to make his call.

"Where ya fuckin' been, Ears? You're supposed to call half hour 'go. The boss don' like you guys callin' in late."

Ears, shit, why'd they have to call him that? He hated it. The name's Vince, Vincent, even Vinnie, but just because he has big ears. Hell, his father's were even bigger. No one had ever called Harold P. Lasker "Ears." Not more than once anyhow.

But there sure as shit wasn't anything he could say to Earl about calling him that.

"Yeah, sorry, some trouble at home. Got anything for me tonight?"

"Sure do, Ears, lotta mooks took it on the chin in the sixth at Holly Park last Sunday. Seems some popular tipster got it wrong."

"Okay, gimme."

"Gotta pencil and paper, kid? There's a bunch of 'em."

Earl rattled off a dozen names and addresses. They were all right around Central Avenue and it was mostly guys who wouldn't give him too much trouble.

"No names? I like it when there's names, Earl. Don't you have any movie stars for me? A singer? Someone?"

"Nope, not this week. Jeez, kid, they can't all be Jimmy Stewart."

Vince hadn't ever actually gotten to work over anybody as famous as Jimmy Stewart. That'd be a story that would buy him a few drinks. He'd had his share of drinks off of pounding on a few B-grade actors, a singer or two, a pretty well-known horn player. Tonight's list was mostly small-fry, working stiffs, schmos into the Lucca brothers for a few hundred, no more than a grand or two tops. That was never much fun. They were just regular guys trying to get ahead, who'd screwed up.

Still, they were chumps and it wasn't Vince's fault they were deadbeats. Maybe he was doing 'em a favor. He'd thump 'em and collect. Maybe they'd learn their lesson and either stay away from the ponies and cards or at least not get in over their heads next time. If someone had knocked some sense into his dad back when he was starting out, maybe the family would've been better off.

He got off the phone and cracked open another Lucky. Charly'd know who was where over on the Avenue, so he called him next. Vince was hoping Eckstine was playing somewhere. The singer always brought out swarms of girls. A set or two of that voice and they'd be easy game. On a good night it wasn't all work.

"Nah, sorry, Vince, no Eckstine tonight. Billie Holiday's over at that big place on Western. I might drop by there later."

"It's all junkies and dykes, isn't it?"

"That's the one. If you're looking for company, it isn't the place. But she's got a hell of a voice."

"And a lot of depressing songs. No thanks."

No problem—if Eckstine wasn't playing it just meant less distraction for getting the job done. Vince looked over the list and numbered the names in the order he'd get to them.

The closest one, Bob Wilson, was familiar. The guy almost always had the dough. It was an easy commission. But still, "I'm not your fucking errand boy" is what he'd told Wilson the last time he'd had to hunt him down to collect. He was gonna pop him one this time. Nothing much, just something to get the point across. Vince wasn't hard to find. The guys who'd come to him were the ones he never gave any trouble.

He wasn't really in the mood. He had to get up for it. He dumped the rest of his beer in the sink and got out the can of Maxwell House. He packed it down hard into the top of the percolator and filled the tank with half the water it called for. It'd take a lot of sugar to make it drinkable, but he liked it sweet.

He lit the stove, set the pot down on the burner, and went to get ready. He splashed water on his face and combed his black hair so that some of it hung down over an eye. People said he looked menacing that way. He fished a couple of whites out of his sock drawer and swallowed them dry. Once the speed and the coffee kicked in, Vince'd be pumped.

It was too early for the serious night owls. Wilson was one, which meant he might still be at home. If he wasn't, there was a poker-and-slots parlor in the back of the drugstore over on 67th. He'd be there sometime tonight, although not for long. His credit wasn't any good until he forked over a payment.

Vince parked his Buick across Wilson's driveway in case the jerk got any bright ideas. He tramped through the flower bed on the way to the front door. Might as well give the guy some extra grief. There was gonna be the late penalty and at this point a little something more for making Vince come over here so damn often.

Things were likely to be better than the last time Vince had to drop by. Wilson's wife had left him and taken the kid since then.

Nothing he hated worse than having to pound on some dummy while the little lady was hollering at him and a brat was yowling.

It was a small Spanish-style place, one of the few single houses on a street of four- and six-unit buildings. There was a light on in the living room and Vince could hear a ball game on the radio.

He rang the bell and stood back. He didn't try to hide or anything, not wanting to tip Wilson off that he was going to get a beating.

Footsteps shuffled up to the other side of the door.

"Yeah, who is it?" The peep hatch opened and Wilson looked out from between the bars.

Vince didn't say anything, just made sure Wilson could see his face.

"Oh, hey, Vinnie." At least the slob knew better than to call him Ears. "I've got money for you. I was gonna look for you when I went out tonight."

Yeah, like hell he was.

Wilson opened the door and waved Vince in. The place was a mess, empty beer bottles, moldering food cartons, a couple of weeks' worth of newspapers and racing forms, most of it covered with dust. If the poor bastard was going to chase away his wife, the least he could do is get someone to come in and clean up from time to time.

Vince didn't really want to sit down. The whites and coffee were buzzing in his veins. He just wanted to collect the cash, put a little hurt on the fool, and get to his next customer.

But he sat anyway, took a couple of deep breaths while Wilson went to the kitchen. It was better if he remained calm. He needed to bust the guy up, but not too much. Dead or disabled doesn't make anyone a repeat customer.

Wilson came back with two open bottles of Blue Ribbon. It wasn't Vince's usual brew, but it would do. Wilson handed one to Vince then walked over to turn down the volume on the radio.

He sat on the sofa across from him and took a long swallow of his beer. He set it down on the coffee table too hard. He was trying not to let it show, but he was nervous.

"Look, Vinnie, I'm a little short right now. I been having to send money to the wife. She's staying at her mother's. I don't know what she does with it all."

Vince took a swig from his bottle, then pointed the mouth of it at Wilson. He didn't say anything. He scowled and cocked his fingers to look like the bottle was the barrel of a gun.

"No, Vin, Vinnie, it's not like that. I've got the vig and another C-note on account. I just couldn't pull it all together to-night. That's okay isn't it? So long as I've got the vig."

The Lucca brothers weren't going to mind. That was the point anyhow. Let a sucker lay down some bets, loan him some dough, carry him when he's late, and keep racking up the interest, a lot of interest. It was a chump's game. But so long as he could make a payment, and there was some hope he'd be around to make the next, bigger payment, Vince's bosses were happy. And when they were happy, they made *him* happy.

He tilted the bottle back toward himself and took another swig. He smiled when he held out his hand. "Okay, Wilson, so give."

The jerk stood up from the sofa to get into his right front pocket. He pulled out a thin wad of greenbacks and held them out to Vince. "This should cover it. I'll have the rest next week, promise."

Vince nodded. "Count it out."

He watched as Wilson laid the bills out, mostly fives, a couple of tens, some ones. In the end, it was a hundred short of what the guy had said he'd pay. Did he think Vince wouldn't notice?

"Where's the C-note on account, Wilson?"

He looked startled, like he'd expected to get away with some-thing and was surprised that he hadn't. He reached into a back pocket and came up with two old, filthy fifties. He held them back for a moment. "Hey, Vince, can you let me hang onto one of these for tonight? I was gonna go meet some pals on the Avenue. I could use the scratch."

"Shoulda thought of that before you promised me the hundred, Wilson. Hand 'em over."

Vince took the two bills, then scooped up the others, folded them all, and put them in his shirt pocket. He set his bottle down gently on the table, took a deep breath, then let it out slow as he stood up. He walked over to the radio, where the ball game was burbling low, and twisted the dial up loud. He turned, walked around the coffee table, and stopped, towering over the stupe.

Wilson had a dumb, surprised look on his face. He had to be an idiot if he wasn't expecting something like this. Vince just hoped he'd cooperate, make it easy. He'd hurt him less if he did.

"I'm going to have to beat on you a little, Bob."

Wilson'd been a standup guy. Once he figured there was no way out, he didn't beg or try to fight back or do much of anything other than protect his puss and the family jewels. Vince considered leaving him be after one quick hard shot to the gut. But what the hell kind of lesson was that? By the time he'd get halfway back to his car Wilson would be nearly over it, sitting on the sofa, opening another beer.

So he followed up the gut shot with a hard jab to the chest that must've made Wilson feel like his heart was trying to get out through his throat, then peppered his kidneys with some pokes he'd be feeling for the next couple of days. After that, Wilson was on the floor, curled up, moaning, steeling himself for one of Vince's pointy-toed Florsheims in the ribs.

But Vince cut him a break. He leaned down toward Wilson's ear.

"I appreciate you not making it too tough on yourself. I'm

gonna leave you alone now. You'll be okay, might piss a little blood next day or two, but nothing's broke. Just don't make me come to *you* from now on, got it?"

Wilson's body sagged with relief. He got it. He nodded and cleared his throat to show he did. Vince headed to the fridge, got out two Blue Ribbons, walked back to the coffee table, and popped them open. He put one down on the floor by the beaten guy.

"No hard feelings, Bob," and walked out raising his to his lips.

George Meyer was as henpecked a slob as there was. He liked playing the ponies, liked hitting the bars, but the little lady made damn sure he was home early most nights. Vince just about had time to find him on his last drink, crying in his beer in front of some couldn't-care-less bartender wiping down his glasses getting ready for the real drunks to show up.

George was on a budget. His wife counted every penny of his paycheck. It was mopes like that who always got into the most trouble. Get a hot tip on a horse from some jokester and the wife won't cut loose even twenty bucks to lay down a bet. So he borrows the twenty off some friendly-seeming shylock. Hell, it's such a good tip, why not make it fifty?

But then his horse comes up lame in the backstretch and so does George. Where's he gonna get the fifty bucks and interest he owes? So the shark carries him for a week. But a guy like George, he can't cough up the seventy-five it's gonna cost him to get square the next week. So the not-really-so-friendly lender carries him another week and the seventy-five magically becomes a hundred and that might as well be ten thousand bucks to a guy like George.

So then the shark lays off the bet to the Luccas. He pays them for his territory anyhow. Then the Luccas, they send someone around, someone like Vince, to let George know it's now a hundred twenty-five bucks and at the end of the week it's gonna be one fifty. Week after that it's up to two. Sure, they've got some convenient payment plans, convenient to themselves.

That fucking George. Should've just played the twenty. Should've gone home and taken the heat from the wife like a man when he lost it. Instead, he'd let it get out of hand and was into the Luccas for six hundred bucks. That was twice as much as he'd ever been into them before and it was a problem.

Vince guessed George would be at the 54th Street drugstore. They didn't serve booze, but they'd sell a man a setup at the soda counter and there was always somebody hanging around out front hawking half-pints of the cheap stuff.

It was only a little before eight, but George was nursing his last rum and coke at the counter before heading home. He coughed on a swallow when Vince sat down next to him.

"Don't choke yet, George. I might have to do that for you."

The short, soft man looked up at Vince through watery eyes. He was still coughing and couldn't speak.

"George, you're in deep shit. I don't want to take you back in the alley, but if I have to, you know I will." The guy wasn't bad, just stupid. He should know better than to be in the kind of trouble he was in, and Vince felt sorry for him. But not much.

"Vince, I, I've got thirty bucks. If I don't bring it home the wife's gonna kill me."

Vince slumped for a moment. He was good at acting the tough guy, maybe he got it from all the movies he watched, but it took effort. "That's not enough. You're about to get it at both ends, George, the wife and me."

"Wait, wait, Vince, maybe we can work something out."

Vince waved a fist in front of his face to shut him up. "That's what we did last week. And the week before and the couple of weeks before that. The Luccas are done making deals, George. They're not the patient type. Finish your drink and we'll go for a walk."

"Jeez, Vince, wait, I, you, you can have my car. You can hold onto it until I come up with the dough. That oughta be worth at least the six hundred."

The car wasn't worth anything like that. It was a beat-up old Ford coupe that might go for a couple of hundred if it was nicely polished and parked in the dark when the buyer took a look. Problem was, the car plus thirty bucks still wasn't enough. The jerk was wearing a watch, but it was a crappy Timex. His wedding ring didn't look like much either. Maybe the Luccas'd think a good beating was worth another hundred.

George was never going to be good for the rest of the money no matter what happened. Sooner or later the Luccas would have to write off the debt, which Vince knew wasn't going to happen. Or have Vince kill the guy, which was a line he wasn't willing to cross. Roughing up a mope was fine with Vince, he understood the necessity. It was business. But offing a guy? Vince didn't really much care if George lived or died, but leave him out of it. Once he did that there'd be no going back. The Luccas would own him, forever. He'd be stuck doing whatever the hell they wanted him to. So long as he was making money for them and didn't do anything they could hold over him, he was his own man, mostly.

"Hand over the keys, George."

The soft guy smiled. "Thanks, Vin." He handed them over.

"And the thirty bucks."

He lost his smile. "Gee, Vin, can't I? You know, the wife, she's gonna . . ."

Vince didn't smile. "No, you can't, George. Fork it over."

He pulled out his wallet and took out two tens and two fives, carefully, with two fingers like he was handling something hot. "How'm I gonna get home, Vin? You gonna give me a ride?"

Vince was getting happier by the moment about having to pound on the guy. "No, George, you're gonna have to figure out how to get home on your own. We're going out to your piece-of-shit car, you're gonna give me the registration and sign over the pink slip if you've got it."

He could drag George into the alley once the paperwork was done. There wasn't much sense in letting the guy know what was coming next. It'd just make him harder to handle.

The car was parked in the alley. That was perfect. It was even more of a heap than Vince had remembered. That wasn't so good.

"Damn, George, look at this thing. It's not worth a hundred fifty bucks."

"It runs good, really it does, Vince. You'll see. It just needs some detail work, that's all, really."

"Shut up and get me the papers."

George fished the registration and the pink slip out of the glove box. He must've been expecting something like this. Who the hell drives around with their pink slip?

"Sign the car over, George."

"Vince, can't you just hold onto this stuff? Let me have the car back when I get you the money?"

"No, George, I can't. This shit barely covers the vig. I'm gonna have a hell of a time convincing the Luccas not to take it out on me."

"But Vince, I—"

The little guy didn't see the solid right that took the wind out of him. He doubled over, his eyes going bleary, tears squirting. Vince looked down at him in disgust. His fist had sunk so deep into the blubbery gut that he was amazed it came back out so easily. He waited for George to catch his breath.

The stupe finally straightened up.

"Sign it over and you don't have to get hit again." Of course he was going to get hit again, and worse, but for the moment Vince needed him conscious and cooperative.

George's hand shook like he had the palsy when he signed the pink slip. Vince angled the paper toward a dim streetlight to make sure the signature was legible. The idiot had signed the car over to him. He'd have to go down to Motor Vehicles, register it, then sign it over to the Luccas or whoever they wanted him to. They weren't going to be happy about the delay. They weren't going to be happy about any of this. He might even have to take a beating of his own. He folded the papers and put them in his jacket pocket. George was walking away toward the street.

"Hold up a minute, George. We're not done."

George turned left into the first punch. His nose popped, exploding blood off to the right. A follow-up left in the ear turned George's head the other way, putting his jaw right where Vince wanted it for an uppercut. On his way down Vince gave him a quick couple of shots to the ribs. He thought he could hear one crack.

George fell whimpering and gasping next to the right rear tire of a new Caddy. Vince sank a shoe deep into his belly. This time he did have trouble getting it out, the lump doubled up on it. It took another kick to straighten him out and get his foot back.

George's head made an inviting target, but Vince didn't want to kill him. He was nearly mad enough to, but not so mad that he didn't know it was a bad idea. He levered the guy over on his back and gave him a hard stomp on his stomach. Air rushed out of his mouth and he went slack; not dead slack, just unconscious.

There wasn't any sense beating on a guy who didn't know it, so Vince paused to catch his breath. George's head lolled just behind the Caddy's tire. Almost gently, Vince moved it out of the way. He stepped back to look at the limp man on the ground. He bent down again and pulled on an arm, laid one of his hands where it'd get run over if he didn't come to in time and the Caddy's driver didn't notice him. That was George's tough luck.

Vince eased behind the wheel of George's piece-of-shit Ford. He'd take it somewhere and stash it. Then he'd have to come back for his car. It was becoming a lousy night. Vince turned the key and pulled out of the alley onto the Avenue. At least George hadn't been lying, the car seemed to run pretty good.

If only there hadn't been a bad taillight. He'd made it about twenty blocks up the Avenue and was looking for a spot to park so he could find the next guy on his list: a two-bit movie producer with a sideline making nudies and a bad slots habit who usually held down a stool at the bar in the Alabam. A car started to pull away from the curb, just across the street and a little up in front of the Downbeat, and he stopped to wait and take its place. That's when the red light and the short squeak of a siren got his attention.

Vince wasn't sure if it was meant for him or not, so he pulled into the spot as he'd meant to, turned off the car but waited to see what the cops would do. What they did was move up next to the back of his car, leave their red light flashing, and get out. One moved to the sidewalk, slowly walked up to the rear passenger-side window, and stood there. The other came up to Vince's side and motioned him to roll down the window. He blinded Vince with a flashlight, then moved the beam down and around, over Vince, onto the seats of the car, before bringing it back up into his eyes.

"You got a taillight out."

That was a relief. It was a bother, but what cop's gonna give him too much grief over that? Still, fucking George. Vince hoped he didn't move his hand in time.

"Yeah? Okay. Sure, I'll get it fixed. Can you get that light out of my eyes? It's working too well."

The cop didn't like that. "You got a mouth. And you look a little familiar. I seen you somewhere before? Somewhere I shouldn't?"

Vince wasn't unknown to the local station house. They knew who he worked for. He'd had his share of scrapes, nothing too serious but enough that when something ugly was going down they'd pick him up sometimes to see if they could sweat something, anything out of him. He knew he was small potatoes, but rousting guys like him was one way the cops could squeeze his bosses for more money, favors, or just to let them know who was really in charge without having to get tripped up in the mess of tangling with the big guys head-on.

"Get out of the car. Hands on the roof, back to the street." The other cop moved up to the front window, his hand resting on his holster.

A whole lot of things Vince wanted to say ran through his head, but even with the whites and coffee still percolating his blood, he knew better than to say any of them. Keeping his hands in sight he slowly opened the door, got out of the car, and did as he was told.

He could hear the music spilling out the door of the Downbeat. The club was owned by that Jew in Hollywood, the well-dressed one, Cohen. Above Earl, above the Lucca brothers, he was Vince's real boss. The band sounded crazy. Hopheads most likely. The bass rattled the windows. What was their name? Some of Vince's friends were nuts over them, said they were the future. He sure as shit hoped not. Stars of Swing, that was it. Some guy named Charlie was the dope fiend on the bass. The girls were crazy over him. No explaining that.

The cop turned him just enough to run the light over Vince's face, collar, and the front of his shirt. He took a step back and put his hand on his holster. "What's this? Looks like blood."

Shit, fucking George again. Vince should have checked himself over after pounding on him. "Cut myself shaving. Guess I was in a hurry to get out and didn't notice to change shirts."

The cop just nodded and told his partner to check out the car. The other cop opened the passenger door and got in, ran his flashlight around the bottom of the seats, then opened the glove box. He pulled out the pink slip and looked it over. "This your car? When'd you buy it?"

The slip was typed out to George but signed over to Vince. He didn't know what George was going to do, maybe go to the cops, maybe his wife'd make him do it, maybe someone would find him. Better not to put himself and George in the same place tonight. "A few days ago. It's a piece of shit but it runs. Sorry I didn't notice the taillight."

The cop shined his light back into the box and came out with a folded piece of paper. He carefully unfolded it, shined his light on it, and held it up so that the cop next to Vince could see. "What've we got here?"

The cop shoved Vince hard up against the car and pushed into the back of one of his knees with his knee. "Put your hands behind your back."

Vince did and was cuffed, quick and tight. "What the fuck? What'd I do? Told you I'd get the light fixed."

The cop moved him to the open driver's window, pushed his head down to it so he could look inside and see what the other cop was holding. Shit, George, fucking George, what the hell? Vince hated that shit. It was for losers.

The other cop started tossing the car, looking it all over as the cop with Vince steered him toward the prowl car. "You know reefer's illegal, pal, even just a little, a felony rap, even on the Avenue."

Vince snorted. Mary Jane? Two reefers. That was all. There wouldn't be more. George didn't have the money or the connections. And it was all over the Avenue, all the time, and for the most part no one gave a shit, not so long as it was a white guy caught holding.

"Okay, fellas, you got me. It ain't much of nothin'. You let trouble like this slide all the time. You know who I work for, right? I'll get the light fixed, you can take the reefer, I don't smoke that shit anyhow. And I'll make sure you get taken care of soon as I get a little ahead."

He was looking into the eyes of the cop when he said it and

missed seeing the knee coming up toward his groin. He could still hear the cop, though, once he was on the ground breathing hard to try to get through it.

"That's resisting arrest and attempted bribery, shitbag."

The reek of vomit and piss in the tank wasn't helping Vince's pains. His crotch had settled into a slow dull throb, but his hips, stomach, and shoulders ached hard where he had "fallen" onto the booking cop's billy while he was being processed. The whites and coffee still working their way through his veins weren't help-ing either. Where was a real drink when he needed one?

And what was it with so many guys in the holding tank? He saw someone he knew a little across the cell and slowly picked his way over. "Hey, Tom, what'd they nab you for?"

"Hey, Vince. A bullshit B&E. The ex's place, trying to get my radio back. Used to be my place. Cops knew it too. You?"

"A little reefer, on the back of a busted taillight. What's going on? Why the crowd?"

"I hear it's come down from on high. Clean up the Avenue. Some radio preacher's got his hooks into the deputy mayor's wife and now we're paying for it. And it's not like the locals mind. They're just going to hop on board figuring they can use it to raise the going rates on leaving things be."

Another guy had moved into Vince's seat on the bench and he wasn't up to the rumble it would take to clear him out. He found a spot on the concrete to try to mull over the possibilities.

They weren't good. Normally Earl would have him out in no time. And he'd stay out. The whole ruckus would disappear. But it would cost him. Palms would be greased, strings pulled, favors called in, and Vince'd be in deeper hock to Earl and the Luccas than the schmos he regularly had to brace on their behalf. Though it wouldn't be anything he couldn't work off in a few good months.

But this might be different. Vince was small fry, he knew that.

And so long as the little guys didn't cost too much, didn't rock the boat, didn't stir up shit for the bigger fish, and brought in more than they took out, all was right with the world. A little trouble every so often, taken care of easily with something the Luccas could scrape out of his cut of things, no problem. It was like any company, just business.

Vince understood the politicians and the high-ranking cops and even the cops on the beat weren't earning their keep by being stupid. The way to lean on the Luccas was to raise their cost of doing business. They weren't ever going to shut down, everyone knew that. They didn't even want to. The "legit" guys were like everybody else, they wanted to gamble, they wanted dope, they wanted women, and they wanted their slice, a fat slice, of the money being made from that.

And the soft part of the Luccas' business was guys like Vince. Give enough grief to the little guys and it was one of the very rare times that shit could defy gravity and roll uphill. This was going to be expensive, a lot more expensive than usual. And by the time the internal ball of shit rolled back down from the Luccas to Earl and got to Vince, it would gain a whole lot of weight and pick up a mighty head of steam. He'd be theirs, forever, for whatever the fuck they wanted him for. And there were some things he didn't want to do, wasn't sure he could do if it came down to it. And if the Luccas owned a guy, "no" was a very dangerous word.

The whole thing gave him the kind of pain that was a lot harder to deal with than a knee in the crotch or falling onto a cop's billy ever could. His head hurt, throbbing at his temples, pushing on his eyes. His gut churned in a way that made the club-shaped bruise on his stomach seem like a nice bit of decoration by comparison.

Fucking George. Even under the circumstances they probably couldn't have pulled him in over the taillight. Sooner or later they'd have to give him his call. Then what was he gonna do?

He could call his mom. His mom, his hardworking, dumped-by-his-pop, dragged-down-sad, miserable mom. She'd scrape up the bail somehow, he was her boy. And then there'd be some lazy-ass public defender who'd just be another piece of shit he was going to be flattened by. He'd be sent down, hard, maybe for years. And the Luccas could still get to him inside, still own him, or at least a big piece of him. If he was lucky and kept his trap shut tight, did his time and got out, maybe they'd leave him alone after that. Maybe not.

He squeezed his eyes shut, tried to will his ears closed; anything to not feel the wet, anxious stink of the caged men all around him. Anything to avoid having the walls press closer in on him, to keep the barred ceiling and harsh lights from crushing him.

"Lasker, you got your call."

The guard cuffed his hands in front of him, led him stumbling down what felt like a very long, bright-lit linoleum-and-plaster hall to the pay phone. He had to borrow the nickel.

HAINT IN THE WINDOW

BY TANANARIVE DUE

Leimert Park Village

T hey walked in with a gale of authority, the bells on the door jangling with ferocity that made you jump and feel guilty even if you'd only spent the morning arranging to rent chairs for next week's Terry McMillan book signing. Darryl noted their flanking formation—one on one side, one on the other—as they eased inside the bookstore, their hands never far from their waistbands. Fingers never far from their triggers. Maybe that was how they had moved when they served in Afghanistan, or wherever else they had moved on the lookout for targets.

Darryl had noticed the uniforms through the window long before the door opened, but he kept his eyes down on his seating chart just the same, as if they hadn't shaken those bells loud enough to wake the dead. Fucking security guards. A salt-and-pepper team like *Lethal Weapon*. Or *48 Hrs*. In *his* store with such an imperious air. (His store except on the deed, anyway.)

"Sir?"

When Darryl looked up, the Black security guard, who was closest, smiled an irritated smile, worse than a frown. The white one kept a distance as if he were waiting for Darryl to pull out a sawed-off from underneath his counter: his head tilted slightly down, eyes angled upward. Meant to look scary, maybe, but he was only five eight, so Darryl, who was six feet, wasn't scared. They looked like they were serving a warrant. Darryl had to remind himself they weren't really cops. And that he'd never been served a warrant in his life. He managed a damn bookstore.

"Yeah," Darryl finally answered when he figured they had waited long enough.

"A couple was mugged down at the intersection today."

Darryl waited for the part that had something to do with him.

The white security guard went on, trying to enlist Darryl's indignation: "New residents at the Gardens?" *The Gardens.* Darryl almost laughed at the nickname for the former eyesore he'd walked past his whole life. Residents had been begging for a new paint job for twenty years, but new paint only came with the re-opening. The evictions.

"We're keeping an eye out for a Black male," the white one said.

I'll let you know if I see him. It took all of Darryl's restraint not to say it aloud. He did say it with his eyes, though. The Black security guard glanced away, getting the joke.

The song "Fuck the Security Guards" from Rusty Cundieff's *Fear of a Black Hat* was in Darryl's Friday-night mix, which he played late when there were fewer children in the store. It would be so easy to punch on the sound system and let it blast. Security guards were cops without the training or even imaginary ideals, and a whole gang of them had been hired to patrol the shopping center where Sankofa was nestled since the renovated apartment building across the street began leasing at three times the price. Leimert Gardens, the landlord called the complex now, although it had no garden and the bougainvillea flowers wrapped around the fence had turned brown and died years ago. Darryl had seen these two rent-a-cops before through his picture window at the counter, their necks swiveling as they marched up and down the strip like the street was under occupation. Darryl hoped that the sun was burning them up in those black uniforms that made them look like SS.

"About your height and weight," the white security guard said without irony. The brother still didn't meet Darryl's eyes. "If you see anyone . . ."

"If I see *me?*" Darryl said. "Sure. I'll give you a call. You got a card?" He held out his hand. The white security guard was confused by his juxtaposition of sarcasm and willingness. He finally reached into his front pocket, behind his badge, and pulled out a business card: *South LA Security—established 2016.* But now his minor irritation had bloomed to anger that turned his earlobes red. When he leaned forward, he stared into Darryl's eyes almost like a lover—and that was when Darryl *knew.*

Darryl's grandmother had called it his Third Eye, claiming it was his birthright. Darryl knew things that were unspoken sometimes, whispers of premonitions. His stomach always knotted when he brushed against knowledge that was none of his business, but he'd learned to use the feeling to avoid problems when he interviewed job candidates or suffered through first dates that wouldn't lead anywhere except where he'd already been. This time, the feeling was even stronger: the knotting, but also a *burning.*

This guy was bad news, a violent bully. Okay, maybe he didn't need a premonition to guess that, but Darryl knew this particular man—RICK, his name tag said, no last name offered—was a security guard because he couldn't qualify for LAPD, which was a true testament to his instability. And he deeply craved an excuse to hurt a smart-ass like Darryl Martin Jones. To kill someone, if he could get away with it—just to see what it might feel like. Even his smile looked like a trap ready to spring. Darryl pulled his hand back, hesitating to take the card. He wanted no ties to Rick.

"You've got a great view of the street here," the Black one said. "Maybe you'll see someone you don't know? Someone who doesn't belong?"

The door jangled again, and this time a white couple walked inside, maybe in their late twenties, both in hiking sandals and cargo shorts, their toes bare. On an adventure together. They hesitated at the sight of the security guards, but after a quick assessment they decided the space was safe. Darryl noticed how the woman drew her arms around her oversized purse.

"Do you have any children's books?" she asked Darryl. "Picture books?"

Darryl pointed to the colorful corner display at the front of the store with the child-sized plastic play table. Bright red. Truly impossible to miss. But because his desk was so prominent across from the door, he was the concierge from the moment customers walked inside—no need to look for themselves. "Picture books up front. Young adult's near the back. Let me know if you're looking for something specific."

"Great!" the woman chirped. She seemed to notice how tightly she was clutching her bag and let it fall limp to her hip. "Just looking for something for my niece for Black History Month. This is a beautiful store."

"Thank you," Darryl said, his eyes back on the white security guard. He realized he had never taken the business card, which the guard still held out within his reach. He hated the part of himself that felt more at ease with white witnesses nearby. He even put on a show for them. "And we serve beautiful customers. In a beautiful neighborhood."

Darryl took the security guard's card. From Rick's icy smile, he hadn't liked waiting.

Darryl hoped they wouldn't come by the store again. But the knot in his stomach, still stewing, told him they probably would—Rick would, at least. Darryl was pretty sure of that.

That day the security guards came inside was the first time Darryl saw the haint.

A less watchful manager might not have noticed, but that wasn't Darryl, so he saw right away: two books were face out in Protest & Revolution. Instead of the newly published books by UCLA professors he was trying to promote, the two books facing out were

Franz Fanon's *The Wretched of the Earth* and *The Autobiography of Malcolm X*. He had read both of them in high school, his first and favorites. Truthfully, they usually *were* facing out—but not today. Except they *were*. He hadn't seen a customer in that section in the hour since he'd propped up the other books, so no one else could have done it. And the two books he'd chosen were on the floor. Facedown. As if the two books in their place had popped out on their own and knocked down the upstart competition.

Darryl wasn't a haint-believing kind of brother, so that's not where his head went first. He told himself that he must not have noticed one of the customers rearrange his shelf for whatever entitled reason—maybe a *"well, actually"* commentary on which books deserved to be in the section and which didn't—and Darryl was muttering about it under his breath for the rest of the day because *the fucking nerve*. The thing was, the only customers who had been in his store since he arranged those shelves were two white dudes who had gone straight to Biography and then ambled over to the *New York Times* best sellers, and then the new section at the front where he kept most of his books by white authors, decorated with big enough posters to be seen from the store window: Colson Whitehead, yes, but also the usual suspects: Stephen King, James Patterson, John Grisham, and Gillian Flynn. Whitenip for casual passersby who weren't drawn to the kente cloth and *Essence* best sellers that took up most of the window space.

For the first year after the Gardens opened up, newly renovated, three times the price for a one-bedroom, he'd delayed stocking anything except Black and brown authors as usual. But he had to admit that his sales had gone up almost 20 percent since he added the new section. Maybe more, if he were honest. His old customers were moving on and out, and his new customers wanted to treat him like a Barnes & Noble despite the sign clearly marked *Sankofa Books & Gifts* outside. Even if they didn't speak any languages from Ghana, where Sankofa meant to go back and retrieve what was lost, they should be able to tell it meant *Black*.

Darryl had studied enough sales trends to predict that if he had a time machine, he might not recognize Sankofa in five years—assuming it was still here—just like he already didn't recognize the rest of the street. The books and shelves might still be here, but the spirit of the place could be gone.

Like everything. Like everyone.

Darryl never planned to run a bookstore. He'd noticed how hard Mrs. Richardson was working as he strolled the aisles and vowed that he would never be seduced by a love so fickle. Too many empty seats when the visiting author deserved a stadium. Hardcover books too expensive for customers to afford. He promised himself he would not be swayed by the whine of Coltrane's sax hypnotizing him from the speaker in the top corner of the east wall. Not by boxes of greeting cards adorned with the blazing colors of Harlem Renaissance artists: Jacob Lawrence. Romare Bearden. Loïs Mailou Jones. Not by hand-painted placards posted to announce the myriad sections, each more glorious than the last: Protest & Revolution and Biographies, of course, but also Science Fiction. Mystery & Thriller. Romance. Comics & Graphic Novels. Each aisle a world unto itself, his mother's favorite weekend spot, God rest her soul. *Lemme take you to school so you'll see what they won't teach you*, Mama used to say, and they would each disappear into Sankofa as the hours passed outside. Sankofa was the sun on its venerated street in South Central and everything else was in its orbit. Or so Darryl thought.

Sankofa was not only a fortress from erasure, it had been a citadel during the fires. In 1992, when a jury in Los Angeles proclaimed that a Black man's plight was worth less than a dog's (since his neighbor had gotten jail time for beating his dog, unlike those cops who beat Rodney King for the world to see), the strip mall across the street had gone up in flames while Mrs. Richardson opened her doors to anyone who needed to sob or rant, or both, behind the safety of her bookshelves. Fruit of Islam guarded the doors, but even if they hadn't, Darryl's father and his Uncle Boo—both high school football coaches—would have joined any dozen other men or women to protect Sankofa and its treasures. Smoke rose east, west, north, and south of Sankofa, but not a single page in the bookstore burned.

When Mrs. Richardson offered Darryl a job after school when he was fifteen, it seemed harmless enough. Why not earn his movie and comic book money organizing the boxes, stacking books on shelves, and—after a couple of months of building trust—running the register when Mrs. Richardson had more than one customer, so she could hover and make suggestions? He'd imagined himself becoming a writer, so a bookstore felt like a natural incubator. If he were honest with himself—and honesty was harder to come by now that he was nearly forty—his days working at Sankofa had been some of the happiest of his life.

The problem was, he'd fixed the store, the street, the neighborhood, in time, as if they would always be the way he remembered. But in the Afrofuturism section, Octavia E. Butler had written, "The only lasting truth is Change" in *Parable of the Sower* for all the world to see, so that fallacious thinking was nobody's fault but his. *Everything* changed. The South Central LA he'd grown up in had been different in his grandmother's time, when it was mostly white. His grandfather used to say that the coyotes and mountain lions and bears that sometimes ventured from the hills were only a reminder that this land had never belonged to humans, period.

The Only Lasting Truth indeed.

Darryl first thought the word *ghost* the day the boxes tumbled down in the storeroom. The store was empty when he heard the noise, and the cramped storeroom, which housed the bathroom, didn't have a door to outside. (How many times had the more celebrated authors complained that there was no rear door to sneak into past the crowd?) This was about a week after the wrong book covers had been turned out, which he'd pretty much forgotten, even when the other strange things started happening. Always when he was alone.

On Tuesday, the blinds over the picture window unfurled even though no one touched the pull string. The right half fell until it nearly touched the floor, but the left half got caught midway up, a leering eye. *That* was a first. Then the Barack Obama book cover he'd hung on the wall was on the floor when he opened the store Wednesday morning, the plastic frame cracked, Obama's face grinning sideways at him. By then, it was three strange occurrences in as many days, and he'd begun to wonder if someone was sabotaging him on purpose. Low-key.

Then the storeroom. Darryl had part-time helpers who came in after school like he had—although, frankly, they lacked both drive and pride in their work—so Darryl checked the stability of every box himself even if he didn't stack them. Hardcovers could get bent up in the box, and returning was a hassle, so he ran a tight storeroom. When he heard the crash, he thought a vagrant had snuck in to find a quiet place to sleep . . . and instead, he found all six boxes from the top of the wire shelf on the east wall tumbled down to the concrete, one of them bashed open and spilling Stephen King paperbacks.

"Hey! Who's back here?" he called out with extra bass in his voice, picking up his broom, because, again, he wasn't a "ghosty" kind of brother and the only hauntings he'd heard about were in old houses. Grudgingly, he remembered the security guards' visit and talk of a local mugger, so he thought maybe his store was a target: he couldn't guess the angle of knocking down boxes in the storeroom, but it *could* be a ploy to get him away from the register. He tried to keep one eye on his desk through the doorway, but the storeroom had a lot of narrow aisles to cover, so eventually his desk was no longer in sight as he peeked around corners.

No one. The storeroom was empty. He was about to try to figure out what else could have made the boxes fall when the bathroom door slammed itself shut. The slam was a loud CRACK like a gunshot that made him jump inside his clothes. The doorknob rattled like it might fall off, then abruptly fell still.

"Hey!" Darryl called with far less bass this time, more like a petulant child. "Get your ass out here and get the hell out of my store!"

The door didn't move. The doorknob didn't so much as tremble.

Darryl never kept a gun in his store. He had his dad's old Glock at home, a memento more than protection, but it wasn't with him now. The notion of an armed bookseller didn't sit well with him, felt like an oxymoron, so all he had in his trembling hand was a broom handle as he approached the bathroom door. "Come on. No one's gonna hurt you!" he said, trying to sound folksy and empathetic. Sometimes desperate people only wanted five dollars, or a sandwich. "You need somethin' I can get you, brother?" (Sexist to assume it was a man, he knew, but whoever it was would have to be pretty tall to reach those boxes on the top shelf. And strong enough to pull them down.)

Stillness and silence.

Darryl knew that most store owners would call the police, but not on his damn watch. And he wouldn't call those security guards either. He used the hashtag *#abolitionnow* on his Twitter, so this was how a world without policing would look like. People would need to deal with their own damn problems instead of expecting somebody to come help them.

"All right, then. One . . . two . . ."

He didn't wait for *three*. He turned the knob and kicked the door open so hard that he tore a foot-sized hole in the wood, which apparently was hollow inside. *Shit*.

No one was in the bathroom, which was only as big as a broom closet, with no windows, so its emptiness sat in plain view. One gray-white toilet, water low as usual. A sink with a rust trail in the basin from the faucet left dripping over the years. The mirror with a triangle-sized crack in one corner. An old *Devil in a Blue Dress* movie poster featuring Denzel. Empty.

"What . . ." Darryl said aloud to his reflection in the mirror, ". . . the fuck?"

That was the first time the word came to his mind: *I've got a damn ghost.* His grandfather would have called it a haint or a spook. Whatever the word for it, his experiences in the past couple of days finally made sense.

"Well, I'll be damned," he said.

And just maybe, he thought, he was.

The Spirituality section gave him clues but no real answers. Yet he'd pieced together enough from ghost stories and horror movies to figure out that any haint going to the trouble of being noticed by human eyes must have a message. But what? And, more importantly, *whose* message?

He thought first of Mrs. Richardson's husband, Calvin, who had died of a heart attack behind this very desk back in 2005, but why would he bother coming back after all these years? (All he'd talked about was getting *away* from the burdens of Sankofa, so it was hard to imagine him returning now.) Same for Calvin Jr., who had never shown much interest in the store before he OD'd on painkillers in 2010. Documentary filmmaker St. Clair Bourne had spent hours at a time visiting Sankofa before he died after brain surgery in 2007, but wouldn't he be more likely to haunt a movie theater, his beloved medium? Muhammad Ali had done a signing and called the store "the greatest" years ago, though believing it was Ali's ghost was plain wishful thinking. Like, damn, Ali could haunt anywhere in the world. Same with so many of the others:

Prince had surprised him one day and bought a couple hundred dollars' worth of music biographies, but wouldn't Prince haunt a recording studio instead? Or, better yet, a keyboard? Could it be E. Lynn Harris, gone so soon in 2009? Or Eric Jerome Dickey, who'd broken his readers' hearts when he passed away in 2021?

And sister Octavia. Octavia E. Butler had done a book signing for *Fledgling* only months before she died, on Halloween night, no less. He'd almost sprung for an overflow space but decided to let the customers sit close to each other for the experience. They'd been shoulder to shoulder, beyond standing room only. Some had sat on the floor. Every time Octavia had spoken with her deep, wise timbre, the room had been so silent it might as well be empty. Her books could be grim, yet she'd smiled all through that night. Octavia *might* be haunting the store, he thought, so he put an asterisk by her name. She just might.

But how many other customers had died since Darryl started working here when he was fifteen, their hair graying, walk slowing, persistent coughs shaking stooping shoulders, breaths wheezing under the weight of cigarettes, heart conditions, and diabetes? Three dozen, easily. And those were just the ones whose names he remembered, whose faces had graced the aisles with laughter and smiles and "What you got for me today?" That wasn't counting the ones who had just moved away, and that was a kind of death too, so why not?

The more Darryl tried to think of whose ghost might be haunting Sankofa, the more he realized it was a long-ass list. His parents were gone, killed by a drunk driver on Crenshaw when he was thirty. His mother might be the haunting type, but she would never intentionally knock over boxes of books; that was sacrilege. And why nearly twenty years later? His Aunt Lucy and Uncle Boo. His cousin Ray. Dead, all of them. They were ghosts haunting him even when they didn't make themselves known. But would they follow him to Sankofa?

All he knew was that this haunting felt deeply personal. The haint *knew* him, and well. The *Autobiography of Malcolm X* was a good guess, but Fanon too? When he'd read them the same year, back to back? No way that was random. Only his father knew that—maybe. But his father would never have knocked down the Obama poster, not enough to hurt it. They'd had long arguments over what Obama was and wasn't doing for Black people, and his father had been Obama to the bone. If anything, Dad would have sat the poster in Darryl's office chair.

Darryl wrote down as many names as he remembered. Tried calling out a few. But no answer came, not even the sound of a flapping page. The more names he called out to the silence, the more a cold loneliness wrapped itself around Darryl's chest, the feeling he sometimes tried to drink away with half a bottle of wine after work, when there was nothing else for his hands and mind to do except remember that, once upon a time, he'd planned a bigger life. He couldn't remember the last time he'd even pretended to write.

Old folks called dead people who came back *haints*, but what was the word for those, like him, who had been left behind?

Darryl was close to telling himself he'd imagined everything when he saw the haint in the window. He?—She?—was standing just below the giant golden script of the backward *S* in *Sankofa* on the glass. At first he thought it was someone standing outside, obscured in a blaze of sunlight, but it was a reflection as if someone were standing *inside* the store. No one else was with him, not on a Tuesday afternoon when it wasn't Black History Month. About six feet tall. Dark skin. Darryl couldn't make out the facial features, but the figure's bulk standing there looked as real as the life-sized Michelle Obama cutout posed beside his desk.

Darryl couldn't read the expression on the blurry face, though the eyes were staring straight at him. The stare felt ominous, so dispassionate and yet . . . so urgent. All moisture left Darryl's mouth. For the first time in his life, he rubbed his eyes like people do in movies to make sure they're not hallucinating. He wasn't. The haint was still in the window when he opened his eyes.

"Who . . ." Darryl cleared his throat, since the word was buried in nervous phlegm. "Who are you? What's your name? What do you want?" The questions running through his mind for days spilled from his mouth.

The haint only stared from the window, reflecting . . . no one.

"Why are you here? Tell me what you want me to—"

Bells jangled, and for one glorious, endless breath, Darryl was sure the haint was communicating in a musical language from another plane—until the front door opened and a customer wandered in. (Only the door chimes! The disappointment was *real*.) She was a blond-haired white woman in a sundress and wide-brimmed hat like a Hollywood starlet. A tourist, obviously. Her nose was sunburned bright red.

"Excuse me . . . can you recommend a good beach read?" She pointed to the new names in his window display. "How about Stephen King?"

Darryl had glanced away for only an instant, yet of course the haint was gone the next time he looked. Rage coursed through him, but he swallowed it away. Would rage bring the haint back? Bridge the gulf between the living and the dead? The present and the past?

For horror fans, Darryl usually recommended Victor LaValle instead, or Octavia's *Fledgling*, or that anthology *Sycorax's Daughters* with horror by all of those fierce sisters, but instead he only said blandly, "Which one? I think I've got 'em all."

"Right?" she laughed. Her laugh was a knife twist, though he didn't have time to explain the long story about how Sankofa was supposed to be.

He pointed her toward his *New York Times* best sellers section.

She bought two King books and didn't blink at the price. At the register, she chatted about how she was staying in an Airbnb at the Gardens after flying in from Phoenix for a pitch meeting and how the neighborhood was *so* convenient to everything in LA. Darryl barely heard her. He was thinking about how Mrs. Richardson rarely visited in person after she broke her hip last December, and how she would barely recognize her own store now. And how maybe it was time for him to find another job. Another city, even. Another life.

Darryl stared at the window looking for his haint the rest of the day.

The next morning, every book from the shelves lay across the floor in a sea. Darryl stood in the doorway staring at the spectacle for a full two minutes, nearly in tears. Then he went inside, locked the door, and kept the CLOSED sign turned out. He definitely wouldn't be selling any of Stephen King's books today. Or anyone else's.

He almost called the security service—the card was still propped by his register as an inside joke to himself—but he didn't want to invite those two assholes near him again, especially not that itchy one. Besides, the more he looked around, the more he realized it couldn't be the work of vandals.

The evidence was all around him. The door had been locked. No windows broken. Nothing taken from the register. It was as if Sankofa had suffered its own private earthquake, the books shaken away while everything else was left upright. No part of it looked natural.

And the scene felt angry. An attack. A taunt. For the first time, Darryl felt afraid of the haint. (But he definitely didn't want the haint to know that.)

"Oh yeah?" Darryl said. "*Fuck you.* This is my store, not yours. What else you got?"

His knees were tense, ready to spring him under his desk in case the haint *did* have something else. (As he thought about it, a haint might have a hell of a lot else.) Yet the store was still and silent, just like the storeroom before the door slammed.

"You want me to leave? Is that it?" Darryl said. "*You're* the one who needs to leave. Get out of here! I better not see you again. Leave me alone!"

Darryl didn't go to many horror movies because the characters could be so dumb, but he wondered why more people in movies didn't just tell the ghost to fuck off. *Because that would be a short-ass movie,* he decided. But that was his plan. And if establishing dominance wasn't enough, he'd bring in that new tarot reader from down the street to make the banishing more official. "Mess up *my* store like this?" he said as he went shelf by shelf, replacing the fallen books one at a time, setting the ones with bent covers aside, a growing pile. "You just fucked *all* the way up."

He impressed himself with his tough talk, decided he wasn't scared, but then a soul food cookbook in trade paperback teetering on a shelf behind him fell to the floor, and he screamed like a high school girl. And then laughed at himself. And then . . . yeah, maybe he cried a little too. Or a lot. All of those Black books scattered in disarray on the floor, the bare shelves looking eager for a new adventure, made Darryl want to curl up in a corner. The store felt closer to the truth today than it had in a long time. Mrs. Richardson said she could barely make rent in the past couple of years. How long before he would be packing up Sankofa anyway? Should he even bother reshelving the books?

But over time, as he filled the shelves aisle by aisle, the despairing feeling was replaced by resolve. Excitement, even. He'd always wanted to move the Science Fiction section closer to the Mystery & Thiller section, and add a dedicated Horror section, and suddenly he had the freedom to recreate the store the way he'd wanted to, no longer bound by Mrs. Richardson's years of habit. By the end of the day, he'd filled all of the shelves except the *New York Times* best sellers section. No way he'd put those back. Now he finally had room for the Young Adult section he'd been dreaming of: rows of Black and brown boys and girls who were wizards. Vampires. Basketball champions. They were anything they damn well pleased.

What was that line from the baseball movie? *If you build it, they will come.*

The tourists could buy Rivers Solomon and Nnedi Okorafor and Attica Locke and Steven Barnes and Nikki Giovanni and Toni Morrison too. They just had to learn. Someone could stay behind and teach them. Then mail orders, which were picking up since he hired someone to update the store's website, could take care of the rest.

Maybe that was what the haint was trying to tell him. Make the store *his.*

Darryl was so excited that he climbed inside the window display to start ripping down the posters and signs he had put up to try to catch the newcomers' eyes. More than he remembered, actually—an entire side of the display, including the prime corner. Gillian Flynn was dope, but why was she in the window at Sankofa when she could be celebrated anywhere?

Darryl didn't hear the commotion until it was practically in his ear, the shout of a woman who sounded like Big Hat with the sun-broiled nose. "Maybe he went that way?" More of a question than a comment, and Darryl heard stampeding feet from around the corner.

When his attention slipped, his foot followed. He landed against the plate glass hard enough to make him think he might fall through and be shredded. But only a small shard of glass in the center fell out, a sparkling diamond in fading sunlight, and the spiderweb of cracks seemed to cradle him as he tried to straighten himself up.

The white security guard was amped up on imagination and anger when he turned the corner, his gun already aimed, looking for something to shoot. Darryl winced as soon as he saw him, expecting a gunfire blast. But it didn't come at first.

The security guard squinted against the window's glaring dusk light to glance inside the window at the *New York Times* best sellers still scattered across the floor. He noted the CLOSED sign on the door. Then his eyes came back to the man who'd broken the glass—still standing inside the store window. Darryl saw him decide what to do.

"Freeze!" the security guard yelled, because he'd seen it on TV so often, but he didn't wait for Darryl to freeze. Didn't seem to care that Darryl's only motion was raising his hands.

Just before the gunshot—the first one—Darryl noticed a figure reflected in the glass, too far away to be him—and yet, it *was* him. The same eyes he'd seen from behind his desk now stared at him up close with an expression that seemed to say: *Do you get it now, brother?*

Grandmama had always said he had a touch of the psychic. He'd had a feeling about this security guard from the moment he saw him. And he still hadn't read the signs.

"Well, I'll be goddamned—" Darryl started to say.

Then the bullets came. One. Two. Three.

"He works there!" a woman's voice screamed from somewhere far away.

Before the brief flash of pain turned to a silent soup, Darryl had time to vow that he would haunt the fuck out of whatever they built where Sankofa used to be.

Just you wait.

I AM YOJIMBO

BY Naomi Hirahara

Kokusai Theatre

On the last day of the Kokusai Theatre on Crenshaw, Eric Montgomery's boss, Sab, told him that he could keep anything in the lost and found.

"Go to town," Sab said. His back had become bent over the years, as if two decades in a dark theater had shriveled his body.

"Okay, boss." Eric tried to sound grateful but he knew what was in that lost and found box. Actually, calling Sab "boss" was being too generous because Eric wasn't technically paid. He was fourteen and, according to child labor laws, needed a parent to sign off on a work permit. And no one in his family was going to approve of him working at a Japanese movie house in the neighborhood. If he was going to spend his extra time there, that was his choice and not theirs.

"It's a sickness," his mother, Jessie, said to her husband, Hal. She adjusted the cat's-eye glasses that brushed against the curls of her relaxed hair in an attempt to look like Phylicia Rashad. Why would her youngest son be so obsessed with Japan?

"What, you think that you're part Oriental or something?" Hal had spent two years fighting in Vietnam. He had seen things that he would never share with his family.

Hal was the one, ironically, who had taken Eric and his older brothers to the Kokusai to watch a screening of Akira Kurosawa's classic *The Seven Samurai*.

Eric, who was sitting next to his father and middle brother, had been mesmerized by the black-and-white images of the kimono-

clad warriors brandishing swords. A small Japanese town popu-
lated by old people was being overrun with thugs. It was up to
a ragtag group of samurai, including a man who posed as a warrior but wasn't officially one. That character was played by actor
Toshiro Mifune, whom Eric later saw multiple times after "working" with Sab at the Kokusai. His favorite Mifune movie was *Yojimbo*, in which the Japanese star played a masterless samurai and
bodyguard for hire.

It was at a screening of *Yojimbo* that Eric thought he saw his
father's favorite Laker, Kareem, and mentioned it later at the dinner table.

"You crazy," the middle brother said.

"Are you sure it wasn't Mel Ware?" the oldest brother asked.
Mel was the local star athlete at Dorsey High School.

"I know the difference between Kareem and Mel," Eric
snapped back.

"Oh, you know Eric and his night vision," the middle one said.

"Whooo, whooo, whooo," both brothers let out owl noises,
and laughed at Eric's expense. It was easy to do, the youngest one
separated from the other two by an entire war. He was odd; he
didn't fit in with other boys. He didn't play basketball or football
and instead of taping posters of rap stars or athletes on his side of
his bedroom, he put up images of Bruce Lee and Mifune.

Eric wanted to go to the local Japanese-language school on
Jefferson and 12th Avenue near Saki Liquor. Every Saturday, he
saw young Japanese Americans being dropped off and picked up
in Toyota Corollas and Honda Accords from places probably miles
away from the Crenshaw area. He didn't care if he would be the
only Black kid in those bare classrooms. All he cared about was
learning the code, the Bushido code that would set him free.

He heard a little about Bushido from Charlie, a Japanese man
originally from a place called Terminal Island. He was a gardener
who drove a beat-up brown Chevrolet pickup truck. He installed

metal pipes in its bed to hold his tools—a gas-powered blower, rakes, edger, and an extra coil of green hose. Charlie had weather-beaten skin as dark as his truck and tufts of severe hair resembling the steel wool Eric's mother used to clean dirty pans.

Charlie was Sab's friend and he didn't care about child labor laws, either. On Saturday mornings, he'd occasionally pick up Eric to accompany him to do an uncomplicated but vigorous job like collecting hedge clippings on an estate in Leimert Park.

"Bushido is like, you never shame your family. Your name is everything. You show honor until death," Charlie said one Saturday before he pulled the cord to start his blower.

A week before the closure of the Kokusai, Charlie treated him to a bowl of won ton saimin at Holiday Bowl, a landmark building that reminded Eric of a large boat gliding along Crenshaw Boulevard. The huge orange neon sign, BOWL, towered over the structure, the neighborhood's replacement for the sun.

"Two saimin, yeah?" The waitress was small, but her arms were strong, expertly balancing the two steaming bowls on her tray. Eric couldn't tell the ages of the Japanese. The waitress could have easily been either his mother's or his grandmother's age. At the next table were an older couple that Eric recognized from their Four Square church. And at the table after that were some students in UCLA gear.

"Don't let it go cold." Charlie was already slurping up the noodles with his plastic chopsticks, a few drops of soup broth spilling onto the Formica surface. "Use fork, okay? That's why Doris brought that for you."

Eric had wanted to try the chopsticks after watching Mifune devour rice with his, but he listened to Charlie and picked up the fork. The noodles kept slipping off and Charlie admonished him, "Use spoon too," referring to a plastic ladle that Eric had seen in Chinese restaurants.

Guiding a slippery wonton onto the ladle, he was finally able to take a bite. He had never eaten anything quite so delicious. "I wonder if the samurai ate this," he said.

Charlie laughed, making sounds from the back of the throat. He didn't confirm or refute Eric's musings. Truth was, he had no idea but he would like to imagine that they were eating the meal of warriors.

And now, finally, the day Eric was dreading. The Kokusai Theatre was closing on the day before Halloween, 1986. Sab explained that there weren't enough Japanese living in the neighborhood anymore. He hoped to reopen in Little Tokyo, but he wasn't sure if it would happen.

Eric couldn't be a part of a Little Tokyo incarnation of the Kokusai. He could be a part of this up to now because it was on his home turf.

"Pick up the trash after the final screening. One last time. Moe will be coming to wipe the floor down." Sab didn't seem particularly sad about the closure of his operation.

Eric stood in back of the theater and listlessly watched the last offering, *Lost in the Wilderness*. The movie was about a Japanese mountain climber who was the first man to reach the North Pole by himself. No fight scenes and half of the story was about the man's wife, stuck at home.

There were only about twenty people in the theater, which was actually more than usual on a weeknight.

In the back row near the door, there was a low rumble of voices that got louder and louder. Eric couldn't understand the argument because it, like the movie, was in Japanese. Two men were fighting and before Eric could let his boss know, Sab burst in with the janitor, Moe, who sometimes played security guard.

"You, out!" Sab yelled.

Before they could collect themselves, Moe ushered the men out of their seats.

Eric, captivated by the men more than the movie, went out the other door to follow their activities in the lobby. One was a clean-cut Asian man wearing a fresh-pressed collared shirt and a sports jacket. The other one was smaller with wild, angry eyes. For a full second those eyes met Eric's. He averted his gaze, hoping not to draw attention to himself. But it was too late. Both men were pushed out the door by Moe and they stalked off in different directions.

The lights went up shortly afterward, with a few of the white moviegoers clapping to commemorate the Kokusai Theatre's long history in the neighborhood. Several of the Japanese customers stayed back to offer their appreciation to Sab.

Eric rolled the trash can down the aisle and picked up strewn popcorn containers and empty giant drink cups. He started from the front row and worked himself to the back. When he got there, his foot stepped on something hard. Eric looked down at a black plastic bag. Inside were two VHS tapes, unidentified aside from Japanese writing on the labels stuck on the spines.

He rolled the trash can back to the lobby and pulled out the battered lost and found box that was stored behind the counter. Inside were a green sweater, a set of keys from five months ago, and three pairs of sunglasses. Eric was about to drop the VHS tapes into the box but then stopped himself. Sab had said that he could keep anything he wanted in the lost and found. He chose a pair of oversized tortoise-framed glasses and held onto the bag of VHS tapes. Even though it was dark, he wore the sunglasses and stuck the bag in his jacket as he retrieved his bike from storage and went out the back door.

Later that night, Eric snuck out of his bed when everyone was sleeping and carefully pushed in one of the videotapes in their VHS machine in the living room. On the TV he was shocked by what he saw. He had seen women's boobies in *Hustler* magazines that boys brought to junior high school but he had never seen what this man was doing to the woman's body with his burning cigarette, first to her nipples and then—

He heard his father stumble in the hallway en route to the bathroom. His heart pounding, Eric quickly ejected the tape and placed it inside his pajama bottom to cover his erection.

The next day was Halloween, but of course the Montgomerys wouldn't be celebrating it in any way. Instead they walked to church for Friday-night service, Bibles clutched in their hands. Eric didn't complain about missing out on any parties or trick-or-treating (even though he was too old for it, a few in his class still went out). He felt sick to his stomach about what he had seen on that videotape. It looked like real tears were rolling down the woman's cheeks, her lopsided mouth crying out for the man to stop it.

While Eric sat in the sanctuary, he prayed for Jesus to erase those images from his mind. But even when he closed his eyes, he didn't picture his Savior, but the pale naked body of the woman.

On Sunday, there was more church. Hal noticed that his youngest son had seemed subdued the last couple of days, and announced after service that he was taking the family to the coffee shop at Holiday Bowl for a late breakfast. Jessie was surprised but thankful to have a break from cooking for four ravenous males. She worked as a nurse three nights a week and was exhausted.

It wasn't Doris who served them today, but a younger woman with long black hair tied back in a ponytail. Everyone in the Montgomery party ordered grits and bacon with their eggs, except for Eric. No, he went for his rice and Portuguese sausage. Nobody teased him that morning because they were too hungry to care.

Heading to the restroom before his family left the bowling alley's coffee shop, Eric saw the woman at a table in the back. He thought that it was perhaps Satan playing tricks on him. But the woman in the video . . . he recognized her drawn face with a wide mouth that tended to lean right when she spoke. Eric stopped dead in his tracks on the carpet and someone behind him almost crashed into him. "Boy, watch it," said an old Black man.

Eric kept walking but snuck a look before he turned for the restroom. He was shocked. Her companion was the Asian man— the clean-cut one that looked like a cop.

As he took a piss at the urinal, he thought to himself, *What is she doing with him? Is she in some kind of trouble?*

He washed his hands with a puff of soap as his mother taught him, and there he decided. He would do what he could to help the woman.

He returned to his parents, who had already left the table to pay the bill at the cash register. "I'll walk home," he told them. His older brothers were off to meet up with friends.

"Suit yourself," his father said.

The man got into a shiny Buick, while the woman took to the sidewalk, walking south.

This was meant to be, Eric thought, and slowed his usual pace to trail the woman. About three blocks down, she entered a mall and walked into a women's clothing store. Eric noticed that she was wearing a name tag and realized that she worked there.

He lingered at a rack in the corner. He couldn't even pretend that he was interested in any of the clothing, which was bright and oversized, nothing his own mother would wear. The Japanese woman, carrying a bunch of jackets on hangers in the loop of her fingers, was now one rack away from him. There were no other customers in the store.

"Kon-nichi-wa." He bowed slightly in front of her.

The woman, whose name tag identified her as *Kanako*, narrowed her eyes. "Stop following me."

"You speak English." He was amazed.

"Fuck you."

Kanako's crudeness caused him to step back, almost falling into some blazers with enormous shoulder pads.

A group of five women entered the store, immediately filling the space with a frenetic, nervous energy. It was definitely time to leave.

Did Kanako notice him from the Holiday Bowl? Eric wondered as he walked outside. When did his presence enter her consciousness?

Eric was riding his bike later that afternoon when he noticed several black-and-whites were parked around the Kokusai Theatre. A crowd had gathered to check out the commotion. Eric walked his bike to the front where Charlie was standing. Yellow crime tape hung loosely over the open glass doors.

"What happened?"

"You shouldn't be here," Charlie said.

Out in the parking lot, Sab was talking to police officers. And then other men, pulling down the crime tape, emerged from inside wheeling a gurney with a covered body. The large body weighed down the bed and one of the men seemed to be holding one of the arms in place as they eased it into the coroner's vehicle.

Sab, who didn't notice Eric's presence, approached Charlie after speaking to the cops. "He was shot in the head. They think it happened on Thursday night after he was cleaning up."

"Robbery?"

Sab shook his head. His eyes were even more bloodshot than usual. "I had all the money. Why in the hell would anyone want to kill Moe?"

Beyond the fluttering yellow tape, Eric saw the lost and found box on its side, the green sweater strewn on the floor. That box had been behind the counter, next to a large plastic container of popcorn kernels. Why would it be out like that? There was only one reason. Someone was looking for something.

When Eric got home, he felt nauseous. His brothers always teased him that he was the least street-smart boy in Crenshaw, but he knew that Moe's murder was related to what he was hiding in between his mattress and their bedroom wall. Whoever killed Moe wanted those tapes.

The next day, Eric was walking home from Audubon Junior High School when a black car idled up beside him. He tried to ignore it but the car stayed on his heels like a hungry cat.

He glanced over to see that the driver was the angry Asian man from the theater. His heart pounding, Eric whipped around the corner, only to have the man jump out of his car to chase after him.

"Don't make me run." The man grabbed the collar of Eric's jacket with his right hand, revealing, with his left, the handle of a knife in a leather case stuck between his lean stomach and pants. Eric noticed that the man was missing part of his pinky finger. He knew what that meant from watching the movie *Battles without Honor and Humanity*. This man was a real-life yakuza.

"How did you find me?"

"The janitor told me where you went to school."

Moe sold him out? Eric couldn't believe it.

"I think you have something of mine," the gangster said.

There was no use denying it. "I'll give them back to you."

The yakuza grinned and began pulling him toward the car.

"No, I have to get them. Meet me at the Japanese senior center."

"Where?"

"The senior center. Right on Jefferson."

"Oh, you mean Seinan?" The guy seemed impressed that Eric would even know such a place existed. "In an hour then. You don't want me to come to your house, right?"

After running all the way home, Eric pulled out the plastic bag from between his mattress and the wall and stuffed it inside his jacket. Their black Labrador barked from behind the metal fence. Eric got back on his bike and wondered if this would be the last time he would see his dog.

When he arrived at the nondescript building, the gangster was already there in his black car. It was almost five and most of the seniors had left for the day.

As soon as he stepped off his bicycle, the man was out of his car and practically pulling Eric behind a wall near the doorway of the center. Eric felt the air leave his lungs. He imagined the knife slicing into his stomach or neck. He hadn't even thought of bringing any weapon with him, as he hadn't been able to figure out how to use his nunchucks yet. His oldest brother did have a switchblade from Tijuana that he had been hiding in his under-wear drawer. *Oh, why didn't I think of bringing that?* Eric wondered.

"Hey, whatsu happenin' here." Hearing that familiar voice al-most made Eric cry. Charlie was much older than this gangster, but he was tough. Eric remembered hearing that he had boxed with Filipinos on Terminal Island. During World War II, the govern-ment had emptied the man-made island and sent Charlie barefoot to Bismarck, North Dakota. "Dis young man is my helper. You have any problems with him, you gotta problem with me."

Eric unzipped his jacket and the black bag fell to the ground. The gangster scooped it up like a raven grabbing its prey. He had what he had come for.

"If they aren't in 100 percent good condition, you'll hear from me again," the yakuza said, before disappearing into his black car and driving off.

Eric was so shaken that he couldn't even speak. Charlie pulled the accordion security gates closed in front of the glass door and fastened them together with a padlock, then turned back to Eric. "You be careful who you spend time with. You don't want to end up like Moe."

Afterward, instead of going straight home, Eric cruised on his bicycle down Crenshaw. He felt heartsick about releasing the videos into the hands of the yakuza. Where would they end up next?

As he rode his bike by, he scanned the clothing store, barely able to see above the racks. And there, the small head of the woman.

He quietly approached Kanako. "I had to give your tapes away," he confessed.

Her eyes widened. "I'm going to take my break now," she called out to a Black coworker. She gestured for him to follow her onto the floor of the mall in the front of an athletic shoe store.

"Now what did you say?" She folded her arms over her blouse, covering her name tag.

"I worked at the Kokusai Theatre. A man left some videotapes on the last day we were open."

"You stupid kid. Why did you have to poke your head into this?"

Eric was confused. His mind tried to follow what the woman was saying. So she knew?

"You shouldn't have gotten involved," she said, the right side of her mouth drooping slightly.

How could he not? He was destined to be her protector. Didn't she understand?

"How old are you, anyway?" Kanako studied him for the first time and Eric's face grew hot.

"Fourteen."

"You're about two years older than my kid."

Eric was dumbstruck. He couldn't imagine Kanako being a mother of someone his age.

The woman's posture softened, absorbing his surprise. She focused on his *Yojimbo* T-shirt that he'd purchased from a man selling bootleg shirts from the trunk of his car in the parking lot of the Kokusai Theatre. "You need to be more like him in his movies," she said. "Mifune really didn't give a damn about anyone."

With that, she returned to the clothing store. Eric was paralyzed. Was Kanako right? Was Mifune just like an animal in *Yojimbo*, scratching his balls through his kimono? But Eric remembered the movie's final scene: Mifune tearing through the gangsters' bodies with the sword of a dead man. And a short knife—that's what he used to stab the arm of the ringleader. Mifune had restored peace to that village. Whether Kanako believed it or not, the bodyguard was the hero.

Eric could have called the cops, but what would they do? Interrogate him, and then he'd be in hot water with his parents. As soon as he got home, he found the hidden switchblade underneath a pair of his brother's Jockey briefs. He slipped it in his pants pocket and rode his bike back to the empty parking lot of the Kokusai Theatre. In the shadow of the building, he practiced flipping open the switchblade and slashing it toward an invisible enemy. If the yakuza ever came back around his neighborhood again, Eric Montgomery would be ready.

MAE'S FAMILY DINING

BY PENNY MICKELBURY

Slauson Avenue

M ae Hillaire worked six days a week, ten to twelve hours a day, every day except the days before and the days of Thanksgiving, Christmas, New Year's, and her birthday. Most days she didn't mind because where she worked was the restaurant she owned—Mae's Family Dining—and the place was always packed because the food was always good and she was always too busy to think about anything but the work. So while she usually didn't mind the long hours and long days and hard work, on days like today she hated every second of it and edged one step closer to her periodically threatened retirement.

The hoots and catcalls signaled the arrival of three of her regulars who also were performers at the Night Life club. Never sure whether to call them female impersonators or drag queens, Mae called them by the names they called themselves, and right now it was Etta James throwing gasoline on the fire.

"That ain't what you was sayin' last night, Deacon Robinson!"

Mae hurried over to the table where Alvin Robinson was cowering beneath Etta's glare. "Etta, please come and sit down."

"He's a hypocrite, Miss Mae, callin' me all kinda names in here and sayin' all kinda other things in the club at night!"

"Be careful how you talk to my customers, Alvin."

"They ought not to be in here with decent people!" the deacon fumed with righteous indignation.

"Nightclubs let church deacons come in, so I can let nightclub performers come in here," Mae said, and led Etta to the table where her companions were seated and signaled for water and menus. "Y'all know there's nothin' I can do about hypocrites and you also know I won't let nobody abuse you. But y'all got to behave yourselves!" And she left them amid giggles and a chorus of *Yes ma'am, Miss Maes.*

She'd barely resumed her seat at her station before another ruckus erupted on the other side of the dining room. "Who y'all think you s'posed to be in them stupid hats and military fatigues and boots?" Only one person talked so loud. She got up wearily and walked to the other side of the room.

"Augustus Jackson, you leave them boys alone! And if you can't leave 'em alone, then just leave! Get outta here!"

"You got no cause to talk to me like that, Mae!"

"And you got no cause to talk to them boys like you was, Gus! You got no right to call them names. They come in here to eat just like you do. Ain't no difference."

Gus Jackson stood up tall and straight and it was an impressive sight from behind: He was six feet, four inches of hard muscle earned from years of lifting and moving everything that came and went through the Port of Los Angeles. Everything, that is, the union boys didn't want to bother with and left for the colored men to handle. The view from the front, though? A belly that entered a room five minutes before the rest of Gus, but he came by it honestly: He ate at Mae's every day and he always ate two dinners at a time, followed by two desserts, followed by a night of heavy drinking. Today it was liver and onions with sides of rice and gravy, black-eyed peas and rice, and yeast rolls, then the baked chicken with sweet potatoes, macaroni and cheese, collard greens, and cornbread. The desserts would be cobbler and cake. "There's a big damn difference, Mae!" he bellowed. Too bad his vocal cords weren't in his gut—they'd be squeezed shut by now.

He took a few steps toward the back of the room and the table where five Black Panthers sat. Mae approached from the other direction. She liked these boys. They were very respectful, always, and she had noticed that their presence spelled increased security outside. They nodded at her. They ignored Gus, which infuriated him.

"They oughta be over in Vietnam like the rest of our boys—"

One of the Panthers started to stand but two of the others restrained him. They all looked at Mae. Everyone in the restaurant was looking at Mae. "Please go sit down and finish eating, Gus."

"I wore the uniform and fought for this country, just like your husband did—"

"You leave my husband outta this."

"These boys oughta be doing the same thing."

"Like your son, Gus? Is your son in Vietnam?" It was a low blow and Mae knew it but didn't care. She was past caring. Today. Perhaps tomorrow she'd care about hurting someone, but today she didn't. She watched Gus sag and deflate and shuffle back to his table where his two desserts waited. She sagged and deflated internally but walked briskly back to her cash register station, exchanging smiles and nods and handshakes with patrons on the way. She knew most of these people, and just as she knew who patronized the Night Life club listening to the risqué, raunchy patter of Redd Foxx and Richard Pryor, and enjoying Sir Lady Java and the other female impersonators, she knew which men were WWII and Korean War vets. She knew whose sons were in Vietnam. And she knew who Gus Junior had robbed, sometimes at gunpoint, to get money for his drugs because his parents had put him out of their house: he'd robbed them once too often. Then Velma Jackson put Gus Senior out after he came home drunk one time too many, pushing her past the breaking point. And some of these people in here were pushing her the same way, especially the holier-than-thou church people. She'd had enough of stone casting.

She walked to the front of the room. "A lot of y'all in here owe me money. You eat your fill but say you can't pay and ask will I wait till next payday or the next one or the one after that. I don't call you names and I don't embarrass you in front of people. So here's my new rule: no more name-calling and no more sitting in judgment of other people. And if you don't like the people who eat here, then you can eat elsewhere."

Mae Hillaire didn't need the newspapers and the television to tell her that the world was changing fast. She saw the proof every day. In the people who came in, yes, but also in the clothes they wore and the things they talked about and the food they ate . . . or didn't eat: more and more people didn't eat pork, and quite a few didn't eat meat at all, so Mae added more vegetables to the daily menu and more fish a couple days a week. But perhaps the biggest change wasn't a visible or tangible one, it was the change happening within Negroes. Or Black people, as the young people preferred—demanded—to be called. She thought about the Louisiana countryside where she grew up and wondered how her relatives and friends and neighbors reacted to being called *Black* these days. When she was a child that five-letter word was worse than a four-letter one and an invitation to fight.

Mae thought a lot about what the young people were saying and doing, and she wished she could discuss it with Samuel. Damn that loudmouth Gus Jackson! She didn't need him talking about Samuel, not when and where she couldn't weep for his loss if she needed to, and she almost always needed to, even after the passage of six years. She'd miss him after sixty years. Maybe if she wasn't in this restaurant all day, every day—*their* restaurant. It bore her name but opening it was his idea. Ten years ago this month in a little storefront place on Vernon Avenue. He'd truly be proud of what his germ of an idea had grown into—three times the space here on Slauson near Denker, the Southern Pacific Railroad tracks on the north side of the street visible through her picture window.

* * *

"Look like you girls gon' get outta here early today," Dave Hebert chortled as he burst into the kitchen. "Y'all done cooked up all them chickens already! Melvin said we'll be sold out when y'all finish fryin' up these ones." He didn't look at them as he spoke. As usual, he was too intent on transferring the money from the cloth sack he carried to the metal box he kept in the storage closet.

Mae finished battering and flouring the last of the chickens and Delilah grabbed up the big metal bowl of chicken pieces like it was one of her children, hauled it over to the stove where Sarah stood; the two women had chicken sizzling in the hot grease before Mae got all the flour off her hands. The three of them would literally run out of the back door as soon as they could. They couldn't escape the hot, stinking kitchen fast enough. Mae was about to dump the flour into the garbage barrel when Dave emerged from the closet folding the empty cloth bag.

"What the hell you doin', Mae? Don't be throwin' that flour away!"

"I used this flour for three days—"

"And you'll use it for three more!"

"—and it's time to change that grease too," Mae continued. "It's starting to smell rancid, and the chicken will start to taste rancid—"

"Y'all don't throw nothin' away till I say so, you understand me?"

"Yessir, Mr. Dave," Delilah and Sarah said in unison.

Mae shrugged and nodded. She was damned if she'd ever call him Mr. Dave or say yessir to him. She took off and folded her apron.

"Y'all go on and get outta here. Mae can finish cookin' the chicken while I talk to her."

Delilah and Sarah folded their aprons and placed them beside Mae's, gave her a nod, and exited the screen door into the alley. Mae put her apron back on and rolled down her sleeves: she'd rather be hot and sweating than have blister burns up and down her arms. Delilah and Sarah easily worked the three-deep, cast-iron skillets filled with hot grease and sizzling chicken while Mae got the chicken ready. Not so easy a task for one woman working alone.

"Everybody say this the best fried chicken in South Central, and that's 'cause of them seasonings you use," Dave said. He was way too close—directly behind her. If she had to back up out of the way of popping grease, she'd knock right into him.

"I'm glad people like the chicken," Mae said. She knew she had to say something.

"What seasonings you use?"

"Family recipe."

"You use it in my place on my chicken, it's my recipe."

She turned several pieces of chicken in the skillet on the front burner and two hot grease balls hit her in the face. She backed up fast, almost knocking Dave on his ass. She grabbed a cloth from her apron pocket and dabbed at her face, praying it wouldn't blister. She turned all the chicken, constantly moving up and back, keeping Dave at a distance.

"You always been above yourself," he snarled. "Runnin' off to join the women's army during the war, comin' back wit' a college-boy soldier, then runnin' away from Loosiana to California, like y'all was too good to stay home."

Mae didn't speak. She also didn't heave one of the kettles of hot grease and chicken at him, which is what she wanted to do. "I can't give you my recipe," is what she said, not looking at him, and still figuring out how she could throw hot grease at him without burning herself.

"You gon' bring me that recipe t'morra, you smart-mouth nigger bitch, or I'm gon' kill you and your college boy, you hear me? And you know how you better answer me!"

When he was mad all the cracker Cajun poured from Dave's mouth faster than he could speak the words, and only somebody from Louisiana who'd grown up listening to the patois could understand it. Mae kept her back to him, kept turning the chicken. She'd be damned and burning in hell before she ever uttered the words *Yessir, Mr. Dave.* She was preparing for the hot-grease shower they'd both take when Melvin Gibson saved them.

He burst into the kitchen and stopped short. "Where the hell is everybody? I got a line out front waitin' to order! How many chickens is cookin' and when they gon' be ready?"

Paying customers. Money. The only things that could grab Dave's attention. "I sent Delilah and Sarah home early and Mae's finishin' these last five. They almost ready. Come on, Melvin, let's go sell 'em 'fore the people change they minds."

Dave pushed past Melvin and out the swinging door: White man in front, colored man bringing up the rear. Melvin shot Mae a worried look, then followed. Mae ladled all the chicken out of the skillets, not caring whether it was fully cooked. She wouldn't be in the kitchen when Dave returned, and she knew he'd take his time enjoying the fact that he was the only white man with a business on this part of Central Avenue in the Black part of Los Angeles, and that he sold the best fried chicken. All the help were colored, as were all the customers, but there were no tables and chairs for them to sit and eat the best fried chicken on this part of Central Avenue.

Mae folded her apron and put it on the shelf in the storage closet, grabbed her purse, and was about to flee when she noticed Dave's money box sitting open on the shelf. She hesitated only briefly before scooping it up, piling the three folded aprons in its place, and running into the alley, going the wrong way so she wouldn't have to pass in front of the Chicken Coop—that's what Dave called the place.

She walked four blocks out of her way before she could catch a bus that would take her home. She stopped in a liquor store and got a big paper bag so she didn't look so awkward carrying the money box—the *heavy* money box.

Samuel heard her coming up the stairs and met her, taking the big bag, and he was about to hug her until he took a close look at her face. He pulled her into their rented room and quickly closed the door. "What's the matter, Mae?"

She sighed deeply and they stood in the middle of the floor squeezing each other for a long moment. Finally Mae spoke: "Dave Hebert, the bastard."

He held her at arm's length. "What happened, Mae? You call him a bastard and quit?"

"Worse than that, Samuel."

His eyes widened. "Did you hit him with something, knock him out?" Then his expression changed. "Did he do something to you, Mae? Did he put his hands on you?"

"No, Samuel. No, I promise you."

"What then, Mae? What could you do that's so bad you had to run?"

"I stole his money, Samuel. All of it."

He looked confused so Mae pointed to the liquor store bag, which heightened his confusion. He released her and opened the bag that he'd placed on the dining table. He lifted the metal box, then opened it.

"Great God Almighty! How much money is in here, Mae?"

"I don't know how much but it's all he's got. He don't trust banks."

Samuel looked all around the room, as if he expected Dave Hebert to materialize. He rushed over to the door and opened it, looked out, then slammed it shut and locked it. "Does he know where you live?"

Mae scoffed, "He'd have to give a damn about me to know where I live, which he doesn't, so no, he doesn't."

"What about the other cooks—what's their names?—Delilah and what's the other one's name?"

"Sarah, and she knows where I live 'cause she lives on Normandie and we usually ride the bus home together—"

"Did she see you take this box?"

Mae was shaking her head, then quickly explained the events that led to her becoming a thief. She explained that Melvin Gibson was the only one there with Dave, and that he would leave when the last piece of chicken was sold. Dave would lock the front door and turn out the lights, then he'd come into the kitchen to add the cash from the final sales to his box. "Then he'll tear up the kitchen looking for it even though he'll know it's gone—"

"Then he'll come looking for you. We gotta clear outta here right now, Mae."

"And go where, Samuel?"

"I don't know, but pack your things—NO! Leave all this old, wore-out stuff. I'll take my work boots and clothes and you just take your personal things—"

"I got to wash the grease stink off me first, Samuel, and outta my hair. I can't go nowhere smellin' like this."

"All right, but hurry up, Mae!"

She ran into the tiny bathroom that wasn't really a bathroom but just a corner of a room with pipes from the floor below delivering water with barely any pressure. Maybe wherever they were going would have a real bathroom.

Samuel had changed into his one nice suit of clothes and shined shoes when she came out of the shower, and he had her one nice dress laid out on the bed, along with the underwear, stockings, and shoes she wore with the dress. She brought their deodorant, toothbrushes, toothpaste, and shampoo from the bathroom and Samuel tossed it all into a plastic bag, which he put into their one suitcase, where he'd packed his work clothes and boots, and hurried to the door with it. Mae had never dressed so quickly.

"We look like we're going someplace special, Samuel," she said, a bit of excitement creeping into her voice to join the dread.

"Maybe we are, Mae, but for sure it's the first time we went somewhere with more than eight or nine dollars in our pockets."

"I never stole nothin' before, Samuel." That admission killed all the excitement.

"Me neither." His head dropped and his big shoulders slumped and they stood at the door, Samuel's hand on the knob.

"I don't think he knows where to find us, but if he finds us, he will kill us. He won't even think about it."

Samuel turned the knob and opened the door, then quickly closed it and hurried to the bed with the suitcase. "Gimme your purse, Mae," he said, and he stuffed it full of money from Dave Hebert's cashbox. "No matter what, don't open this purse," he said as he snapped it shut. Then he put some bills in his wallet, folded some and put them in his pants pocket, closed the suitcase, and took them back to the door. This time they left. It was still light out, and still warm, though the cool air was coming in from the ocean. Samuel put the suitcase into the trunk of their beat-up '55 Ford Fairlane and covered it with blankets and put a toolbox on top. Then they got in the car and drove. Mae didn't ask where they were going and Samuel didn't say. They were both the kind of people who could get lost in their own thoughts, people who didn't mind quiet, in fact preferring it over idle chatter and random noise.

Mae watched the street signs as they drove and knew enough to understand that they were driving west, away from Central Avenue, but she wasn't sure where exactly they were. Then Samuel turned off the busy, wide street and onto streets lined with small, pretty houses, and there were colored people in all the yards and on all the porches. Samuel stopped in front of one of them. There were no people outside the house that needed painting and the yard with raggedy grass and wilted flowers. Mae looked the question at her husband.

"Fella I work with lives here, Gus Jackson. Him and his wife both from Texas."

Mae frowned. "I never heard you mention him."

"That's 'cause I don't much like him, and you won't neither. He talks too much, outtalks everybody and knows everything. Loud and wrong is Gus. He's a fool is what he is."

"Then why are we here, Samuel?"

"They got an apartment up over the garage that till a couple of weeks ago some family was living in, and Gus couldn't stop talkin' about how glad he was when they moved on—"

"Maybe somebody else has moved in since then."

"Gus woulda said. He couldn't keep his mouth shut about something like that." Samuel opened the car door. "Come on, my girl."

Mae opened her door, got out of the car, and joined Samuel on the walk up the cracked cement walkway to the front door, which opened before they could knock.

"I thought that was you, Sammy! What brings you to my door?"

Gus Jackson was as big as he was loud, but he didn't open the door any wider and he didn't invite them in.

"This is my wife, Mae—"

"What y'all doin' here, Sammy?"

Nobody called Samuel *Sammy*, and Mae was waiting for her husband to say that when the mass that was Gus got shoved aside and a woman half his size took his place in the now wide-open doorway. "I'm Velma Jackson. How're y'all this evenin'?"

"Fine, thank you, Miss Velma," Mae said, extending her hand. "We're Mae and Samuel Hillaire. Samuel works at the port with Gus and we came to see if you'd rent us that apartment over top of your garage."

The Jacksons looked surprised, then Gus looked nasty. "Why? You get put outta where you was livin'?"

Mae grabbed Samuel's arm before he hit Gus. "No, we didn't get put out but we left in a hurry 'cause I quit my job, walked out without a word 'cause I got tired of that mean, nasty cracker I worked for, and we were afraid he'd come lookin' for me. So we just left."

"Come in and sit down," Velma said.

"What did your boss do that made you quit?" Gus demanded to know, and when she told them, he exclaimed, "That place on Central Avenue, the Chicken Coop? That's the best fried chicken I ever ate!"

"When did you eat it, Gus, 'cause I've never had any."

The man really was a fool! He launched into some elaborate lie, taking no notice of the look Velma was giving him, when she cut him off, explaining that the place above the garage was in no shape to be rented because Gus's cousins all but destroyed it.

"That ain't no way to talk about my people, Velma."

"But it was all right for you to ask Mae and Samuel if they got put out from where they lived? And your people *did* tear it up. But I might know 'bout a place—"

"What place?" Gus was snarling now.

Velma, ignoring him, told them about a place on Normandie, around the corner from the beauty parlor where she worked: two stores, side by side, were just closed by the owners who'd lived upstairs and recently moved to someplace called the Inland Empire.

"Try not to talk to the husband. He don't like colored people and don't mind lettin' you know, but the wife—her name is Elaine—she's all right. At least she's better than him."

Mae and Samuel stood up and headed for the front door. "Thank you so much, Miss Velma," Mae said.

"Yes, ma'am, we really appreciate you taking the time to help us," Samuel said, shaking her hand.

"We'll be sure to let you know where we end up, and we'll have you to dinner when we get settled somewhere."

Velma hugged Mae. "Will you cook that fried chicken?"

They easily found the side-by-side stores Velma told them about.

Samuel pulled up to the curb and parked behind a Ford station wagon that a woman was loading with boxes piled on the sidewalk. She saw them and began speaking before they were all the way out of the car.

"We're closed," she called out without looking at them.

"We know," Mae said. "Miss Velma told us."

The woman stopped loading the station wagon and peered at them. "Velma from the beauty parlor?"

Mae nodded. "You must be Elaine. We're Mae and Samuel Hillaire and Velma thought your upstairs apartment might be for rent."

"She's such a nice person. Always thinking of someone else." Elaine wiped her hands on her pants and took a step toward them. "We have some people who want to buy the stores, and if they do, they want that apartment. But please tell Velma I appreciate her thinking of us."

"We'll tell her," Mae said, and began to follow Samuel back to the car, when Elaine announced, "I might know someone with a house to rent a few blocks away."

Mae and Samuel were at her side so fast she took a step backward, fear in her eyes.

"We're not here to hurt you, Elaine," Mae said. "I thought you knew that."

Elaine hung her head for a brief moment, then gave them furtive glances. "Would y'all mind goin' to sit in your car while I head inside to call Jimmy Miller and tell him you might want to rent his house?"

Mae and Samuel quickly returned to the Ford while Elaine just as quickly entered the first of the two buildings. "People might get the wrong idea they see us standing outside," Samuel said sourly.

"I think it's her husband she's worried about," Mae said. "She don't want him seeing her talking to us."

Samuel didn't have time to reply before the woman was back.

She thrust a piece of paper at Mae. "Jimmy Miller is at his house waitin' on you. I wish y'all good luck," and then she was back to loading boxes into the back of the Country Squire with such intensity that it almost felt as if she'd never paused to talk to them at all. She didn't look their way and when Samuel pulled away from the curb, the Hillaires didn't look back at her.

They pulled up in front of Jimmy Miller's house moments later. It was eight blocks away on 39th, a quiet street lined on both sides with small, neat houses, very much like Gus and Velma Jackson's 54th Street. Samuel was about to park when a lanky, almost bald white man came out of the house and gestured for them to pull into the driveway. They did and got out of the car, figuring it was safe to do so.

"Elaine told me y'all was on the way," the man said, and Samuel shook the hand that was offered. "I'm Jimmy Miller."

"We're Mae and Samuel Hillaire. Pleased to meet you, Mr. Miller, and we appreciate you seeing us."

"I just hope y'all like my house. Come on inside and take a look."

Mae and Samuel looked at each other, then at Jimmy Miller, or at his back because his long legs already had him up the walkway, onto the porch, and at the front door, which he swung open, then stood aside to let them go in first. Three steps in, they knew they wanted to live in this house. It was practically empty and it was spotless—the walls gleamed white and the hardwood floor shone. They could see straight through to the kitchen where there was a stove and refrigerator, and in a room beyond that, a table and two chairs.

"We already know we want to rent your house, Mr. Miller, but what do you want to know about us?" Samuel asked.

"You were in the war, weren't you, son?"

"We both were," Samuel said, and Miller's eyes got wide. He turned them on Mae.

"You were in the Women's Army Corps?"

"Yes sir, I was."

"Where did you serve and what did you do?"

"In France. I was a mechanic first, then an ambulance driver."

"And where did you serve, Mr. Hillaire?"

"In the Pacific."

Jimmy Miller closed his eyes and took a couple of deep breaths. "We saw some things, didn't we, Mr. Hillaire?"

"Yes sir, we did," Samuel replied, and briefly closed his own eyes. When he opened them Jimmy Miller was smiling. A real smile, not one of the phony ones. He told them how much the rent was and they gave him three months' worth on the spot. He promised to return in a couple of days with the lease. "I hope y'all like livin' in this house as much as I did," and he gave them a ring of keys, "'specially you, Miss Mae, 'cause my Mildred never did like it. Never did like California. She left, and now I got to go too, back to Mississippi." He looked as miserable as Mae would if she had to return to Louisiana.

Mae clutched the keys until her hand hurt and didn't release them while Samuel drove to a store on Vermont where they purchased enough of what they'd need to spend a first night in their new home. They didn't talk because they couldn't. Would Jimmy Miller play a cruel joke on them? Were they both in the same dream?

They hurried back to the place they now called home, locked and bolted the doors, went into the big bathroom, got into the tub, and counted Dave Hebert's money. Mae began shaking her head almost immediately. "No way on God's green earth he earned all this money. You know that Louisiana Fish Market down the other end of Central? His family owns it and they fired him 'cause he didn't come to work half the time and he was drunk when he did go."

"Then where'd he get almost five thousand dollars, Mae?"

"Gambling or stealing," she answered, and Samuel knew she was right, and they both felt a bit less guilty for taking this money. Not good about taking it, just less guilty.

"We should open our own business, Mae."

"Say what, Samuel?"

"A café. Where you'll fry up the best chicken in town and I'll make the best red beans and rice."

The new menu at Mae's Family Dining was a big hit, especially the vegetable plate and the new vegetable selections to accompany the new meat selections: baked and fried chicken and fish, beef and pork ribs, beef and turkey meatloaf, fried and smothered pork chops. Once a week, offerings of lasagna, beef, and pork ribs always sold out. So did the daily favorites macaroni and cheese, collard greens, and sweet potato casserole and soufflé, and the red beans and rice. Gone from the menu were liver and onions and oxtails. Three complaints about the discontinued items and dozens of compliments on the new menu, and the dessert menu drew nothing but praise: chocolate, coconut, and lemon layer cake, apple and peach cobbler, and nut brownies.

Customers also appreciated the newly installed air-conditioning, maybe more than the new menu, and the combination of the two created a totally unexpected problem for Mae—having to ask people to leave once they'd finished and paid for their food because there was a line of people outside waiting to get in.

"Whoever heard of too much success, Mae?" Velma Jackson, who had become a good friend, enjoyed Mae's unusual predicament even as she helped her navigate it.

Mae had put up signs all around the room and notices in the menus so nobody could claim ignorance:

DEAR VALUED CUSTOMERS,
YOU HAVE MADE US SO SUCCESSFUL THAT PEO-

*PLE ARE IN LINE OUTSIDE WAITING TO GET IN.
SO WHEN YOU HAVE FINISHED EATING, PLEASE
LET WAITING (AND HUNGRY!) CUSTOMERS
HAVE YOUR TABLE.
THANK YOU,
MAE HILLAIRE*

So while no one ever claimed ignorance of the notice, quite
a few simply ignored it. That's where Velma stepped in. She pa-
trolled the room, stopping at tables that had been cleared but
where people sat talking and enjoying the cool air. Velma would
point at the wall of glass that fronted Mae's. "All those people are
hungry and hot too, and Miss Mae would appreciate your good
manners by letting some other people sit at this table."

One afternoon the door swung open with way too much force,
and two LAPD cops strode in, both of them white. Silence descended. The larger of the two cops looked around. "Somebody
needs to get up so we can sit down, then somebody needs to bring
us some menus."

Mae stood up slowly. First she closed the front door, then she
fronted the cops. "There's a line of people waiting to get in—"

"We don't stand in no line, and I ain't gon' say it again: somebody get up so we can sit down."

Two customers hurried forward, Dinah Washington and
Eartha Kitt, and each of them grabbed one of the cops by an arm
and delivered an award-winning performance.

"You can share my table, lover boy," Eartha Kitt growled, "if
you let me sit on your lap."

"And I'll make a difference in your night, baby," Dinah Washington cooed, "I promise."

The cops snatched their arms away and glowered at Mae.
"You don't get it, do you, lady? We don't stand in line and we don't
pay to eat. So whoever you are—"

"I'm the lady who owns this place and I don't give away free food. This is a business, not a hobby, and the line for a table is outside." She didn't care how mad the two men were getting. She hated cops and wasn't afraid to let them know. What could they do, kill her?

"I heard y'all supposed to protect and serve," Dinah challenged. "Is that right?" She looked around the room where every eye was on her, a familiar experience and she was enjoying it. "Anybody ever been protected by the cops?"

"I got real protected coming home from work one night last month. Matter of fact, I was so protected I couldn't go back to work for a week!" a man called out.

"I got protected like that once," another man declared.

"But I ain't never had one of 'em serve me," a woman said in a mocking, plaintive tone.

The shorter of the two cops reached for his gun, but Etta James, who had joined her colleagues, grabbed his arm. "Don't you want to tell Mama all about it instead of shootin' somebody?"

"I'm sorry you hate LA so much, darlin'."

"I don't hate it, Samuel—how could I? I'm here with you."

"But you don't really like it here, Mae, I know you don't."

Mae held both his large, rough hands in hers. Squeezed them tightly as she looked all around their carefully tended backyard with its fruit trees and the barbecue pit that Samuel had built, and across the yard to the house: their perfect, beautiful home that was everything Mae had dreamed of—and more. The only thing missing was children, and they had accepted that there would be no kids for them and that was all right. Really, it was. They had each other. "I do not ever want to go back to Louisiana, Samuel. I don't even like remembering what it was like to live there. Being here is like being in some kind of . . ."

"Magic land?"

Mae grinned at him. He loved LA and she didn't want to do or say anything to spoil that feeling. "Someplace where you can get in the water and ain't no gators? I guess that is magic. But I wish I had a wand to wave—I'd warm up that water for sure!"

"No doubt about it, the Pacific Ocean is some kinda cold water. Up here anyway."

Mae remembered the stories he's told her about his service in the South Pacific during the war. "Is it warmer down by Mexico?"

Samuel brightened. "You wanna visit Mexico? Why?"

"The one thing I hoped and prayed for when we left Louisiana and came here was that we were leaving evil white folks behind, but they just as mean and evil here, 'specially the police. And that's true everywhere in this country, Samuel. All the colored newspapers and magazines from all over everywhere—New York and Chicago and Washington, DC, and Atlanta and Detroit— evil, mean, nasty white folks doin' what they was doin' in Louisiana: hatin' us to death." She looked about to cry. "Are there white folks in Mexico?"

Samuel almost wished they never had to leave the safety and serenity of their backyard but recognized the thought for the foolish wishful thinking that it was. They needed to leave this very minute so he could prepare for his monthly poker game.

They were upstairs above the restaurant. It was a large room— part of it used for storage and the rest held a fully stocked bar, a poker table, a television set, and a radio. Samuel didn't spend much time here because he preferred being home with Mae, but several of his friends enjoyed the room even though they had to bring their own booze.

"I hope Eddie Lloyd makes it today," Mae said. "The cops had him pulled over on Florence this morning."

"Probably 'cause of that brand-new Cadillac. You know how they hate that, a colored man with a new car, 'specially a Cadillac."

Eddie was indeed the first to arrive. "Mae, Samuel, how're y'all doing? Ruthie said to tell you hey."

"How's Ruthie?" Mae asked.

"She's fine."

"How're you doin', Eddie?"

"Fine, thanks, Samuel. Tell the truth, I was a little outta sorts this morning, but I'm fine now."

A steady flow of heavy male feet ended all conversation until all six poker players were present, then a general exchange of pleasantries lasted until they had drinks and snacks and their usual places at the table. Mae bid them good night and retired to the combination bedroom–sitting room next door. She could have gone home but Samuel liked for her to stay, and while she knew that he appreciated her presence and having her ride home with him, he also used her presence to end the games that dragged on too long. She drifted off to sleep while reading.

Mae jerked awake. She thought she heard feet on the stairs, but now fully awake she heard only Jerry Taylor's silly laugh and Samuel's challenge to put up or shut up. Mae picked up her book, found her place, and resumed reading *Brown Girl, Brownstones*. She decided she wanted to visit New York City before Mexico.

Pounding footsteps woke her again and this time there were loud voices—Samuel's and white men. She quietly crept to the door and peeked into the main room. Two cops! They had their guns pointed at the five colored men around the table. Five men, not six. Eddie Lloyd was gone. So it must have been his footsteps she'd heard earlier.

"I said put the money in a bag, nigger. I'm not gon' ask you again. And I mean ALL of it, all three hundred dollars."

Samuel stood up but he didn't collect the money. He looked at Eddie's vacant seat, then at the cops. "You think it's all right to break in my place and steal from me?"

"We didn't break in, smart-ass," one of the cops said.

"That's 'cause Eddie left the door unlocked," Samuel said. "He set us up. That's how you knew how much money would be in the pot."

"You talk too damn much," the cop said, and without another word he pointed his gun at Samuel and fired.

"One of you get a bag and put the money in it and the rest of you get out before you can't," said the other cop.

Jerry Taylor told his friends to leave then went behind the bar where he knew there would be empty paper bags. He brought one to the poker table and gathered all the money. He was weeping when he finished. He gave the bag of cash to one of the cops, then started to lean over Samuel.

"You're going too, Sambo. Can't leave no eyewitnesses."

Mae was shaking. She'd read a story in the *Sentinel* about some rogue cops out of the 77th who robbed colored businesses. The beauty parlor where Velma Jackson worked was one of them, but the woman who owned it had a slot in the wall by her station where she dropped most of her money, leaving only enough in the register to make change. When the cops came to rob her one Saturday night after closing they netted about twenty bucks. They didn't believe that's all a colored shop had after a busy Saturday, but they couldn't prove otherwise and the woman's husband was outside in the car leaning on the horn.

And here were two cops come to rob Samuel. She grabbed her .45—like everybody in Louisiana, she had a gun because snakes and gators didn't need an invitation to visit.

Jerry was dragging his feet and the cop who'd shot Samuel hit him on the back of the head with the butt of his gun. Jerry tripped down a few steps before gaining his balance and hurrying down the final few steps and out the door. Oh God, she wanted to kill them! She raised the pistol and fired into the ceiling.

The roar in the narrow stairwell was deafening. Both cops fired at her but missed, then dashed out onto the street. Mae hurried down and locked and bolted the door, then knelt down beside Samuel. He was gone—she knew that. The filthy cop shot him in the heart. He probably died immediately and for that she was glad. No suffering for her Samuel. She's the one who'd suffer now. Forever. But she should be dead too! If only the cops had taken the time to aim, she would be. Then they'd both be dead. There was no one to miss them, so what did it matter?

The phone kept ringing and someone kept pounding on the door. She struggled to her feet and shuffled to the stairs. Good thing there was a railing to hold on to. She stood at the door, listening.

"It's me, Mae. Jerry. Open the door. Please."

Mae slid the bolt back, then turned the lock and opened the door a crack. Jerry was there, and behind him, A.C. Jennings, the lawyer. She knew who he was, his picture was in the *Sentinel* so often.

"I don't need a lawyer," she said when she was back down on the floor, sitting beside Samuel, his head in her lap. "Unless you can make that cop pay for murdering my husband."

Jennings explained that calling the police to report her husband's murder by an LAPD officer would bring dozens of them to this place—where they'd find evidence of illegal activity including gambling, prostitution, narcotics, along with "proof" that her husband was killed because he assaulted a police officer. They would take possession of this building, close the restaurant, "and maybe even seize your home."

Mae was too stunned to speak. She just kept watching Jennings, as if he'd walk back his words. Instead, he said, "Your husband died suddenly of a heart attack, Mrs. Hillaire. His good friend Jerry Taylor, an accountant at Golden State Mutual, was present, and is helping you with the details for his funeral.

"But what about the law, Mr. Jennings?"

"The law does not protect us."

"Then what do you do?"

"I keep good people like you from making bad mistakes. Now please, Mrs. Hillaire, we need to get this room cleaned up—"

"Why, damnit! Why?"

"In case those cops come back or send others. There will be nothing to see." He asked if she knew why Eddie Lloyd helped the cops rob the poker game.

"He was mad 'cause Samuel wouldn't sell his hot dogs here. He argued that people wanted a hot dog with chili as much as a fried chicken or fish dinner, but Samuel said no."

The lawyer was thinking so hard the gears in his brain were grinding. He knew everyone in South Central, whether they knew him or not, and he knew Eddie Lloyd had two hot dog stands— one on Florence and one in Watts. "I wonder if the cops came for Eddie's stands and he made a deal—"

"He'd keep his money and give 'em ours," Jerry said bitterly.

Jennings didn't argue the point. He asked Mae to change out of her blood-soaked dress, shower, and put on clean clothes. Mae, looking sad and lost, clutched her dress with both hands.

"Bernice can help you, Mae," Jerry said gently.

Mae hadn't seen Bernice arrive but was thankful for her presence and followed her into the bedroom, where she took Mae's bloody dress then helped her into the shower. Bernice was the head cook at Mae's Family Dining and she took charge here with the easy competence that she used to run the restaurant kitchen. While Mae showered, Bernice watched men from the funeral home carefully but quickly wrap and remove Samuel's body, and then the lawyer's cleaning crew got rid of every trace of blood. They'd brought pillowcases to collect everything that needed to be disposed of, including Mae's .45. The cleaning crew even dug the bullets out of the staircase walls.

When Mae Hillaire returned to find Samuel gone, she screamed his name and fainted.

* * *

"I can't hardly believe it, Mae! You're really stepping away from the daily operation of this place?" Velma looked skeptical, impressed, and a little bit proud. She admired her friend as much as she liked her, and the feelings were mutual. Velma had endured a lot in the last few years and she'd not only survived but she seemed stronger.

First she had nursed Gus through what appeared to be every possible kind of sickness, which required him to move back into their home. When he'd finally had to go into the hospital, Velma was at his side until the end. Mae never saw her shed a tear until A.C. Jennings gave her the details of Gus's will, which had come as a complete surprise: the house and car now belonged to her, as did the proceeds of two Golden State Life Insurance policies she never knew he had. Tears first leaked from her eyes, then flowed unchecked, accompanied by deep, racking sobs. Mae held her friend.

Jennings, who seemed to have an endless supply of neat, white handkerchiefs, produced them one after the other, until Velma was cried out. She drank the glass of water he gave her, then she apologized.

"You got nothing to apologize for, Velma," Mae had said.

"Don't y'all misunderstand me, I'm glad he's gone. I just wish I could ask him why I had to wait till he was dead to learn that he gave a damn about me!" She pointed at the file on the lawyer's desk. "I never knew about none of this! He always told me his business wasn't none of *my* business, then, when he was dying, he kept wanting to talk about growing up in Texas. Not one kind word for me."

"Maybe he didn't know how to speak kind words, Mrs. Jackson," Jennings had said, passing the file across the desk. "Here's the deed to your house, the title to your car, the life insurance check—all in your name—and Mr. Jackson's death certificate, and this is all *your* business."

* * *

Mae looked across the table at Velma, remembering that day at the lawyer's office. They hadn't spoken of it until now. "How do you know this is the right time to walk away, Mae? What makes this the right time? After all, you've been free for a long time, not like me." With the death of her son in a prison yard fight a year ago, Velma now was completely free. She knew that Gus Jr. had been charged with murdering a man named Dave Hebert, but Mae doubted that she recalled him as the man Mae and Samuel had run away from all those years ago, if they'd even mentioned his name. In a confrontation described as "stupid as shit" by witnesses, a staggering-drunk Hebert had waved a knife at a high-as-a-kite Gus Jackson Jr. and threateded to kill him unless he told where the fried chicken lady was. He'd slashed Gus to show he was serious. The sight of his own gushing blood had killed Gus's high and he tackled Hebert and stabbed the man with his own knife, killing him. Witnesses said it was self-defense, and Mae had hired A.C. Jennings to prove it, but what the DA saw was that a Black man had killed a white one. What was the white man doing there, Jennings had asked the jury, but the DA got the question dismissed so no one knew how close Dave Hebert had come to finding the fried chicken lady and Mae didn't think Velma realized that Dave Hebert's yelling was more than just the crazy talk of a drunk.

Mae sighed. Maybe it was time—not just to release her hold on Mae's Family Dining but to release her closely held worries too. "It's about the eights, Velma. The eighth month and years ending in eight: Samuel and I left Louisiana in August 1948. That cop murdered Samuel in August 1958. And it's now August 1968—"

"Has something happened, Mae?" Velma looked frightened.

"No, no," Mae said. "It's just . . . I'm still not over Dr. King's murder. It still upsets my stomach like it was yesterday. So . . . a four-month and an eight-year. Kind of a balance . . ."

"What will you do with your time?" Velma was surprised when Mae laughed.

"I have discovered the Los Angeles Public Library. If I read two books a day, I still couldn't read all the books by and about Negroes!" Mae sounded like a little kid in her excitement. "And so many of the librarians are colored women . . . Negro women . . . Black women, and they help you find books to read! I wish Samuel was here, he would love going to the library. But we didn't know about libraries, and we didn't have time for that anyway. And it's not just one library, Velma, there's a bunch of 'em and we can go to whatever one we want!"

"But you can't read all day, every day," Velma said.

"I think maybe I could. But I don't have to 'cause I'm learning how to swim. And there's more than one pool too! Can you swim, Velma?"

Horrified by the thought, Velma said the only thing she did in water was bathe, and she refused to even consider the suggestion that she join Mae for a lesson. "Besides, the water is too deep."

"Velma, the water is three feet deep at the shallow end of the pool. Only people who know how to swim go to the deep end," Mae explained, but Velma wasn't listening and Mae knew when to quit. She watched Bernice work the room—she was a pro, no doubt about it, and the place would be in good hands with Bernice, her sisters, and their daughters in charge. Mae knew she was doing the right thing.

"Miss Mae, Miss Mae, come here quick!" The summons came from the front door and both Mae and Bernice ran toward the trouble.

"Oh dear Lord!" Bernice exclaimed when she saw the beaten and bloody body of Etta James being supported between Eartha Kitt and Dinah Washington.

"Side door," Mae said.

"I'll go unlock it," Bernice said, and ran through the kitchen and up the stairs into the main room, then down the interior stairs to open the door.

"Velma, call Dr. Harris and tell him I said to please come quickly and to use the side door."

Getting the unconscious Etta up the steep stairs was difficult, but should anyone doubt it, Eartha and Dinah were men despite the gowned and jeweled brilliance of the show they put on every night, in secret now since a recent law had made female-impersonation shows illegal.

Mae hadn't been in this staircase since the night Samuel was murdered and the memory made her dizzy. "What happened?"

"That cop. The one whose arm she grabbed to keep him from shooting you that time," Dinah said, and Mae had to hold the edge of the bar to keep her balance. Not someone else hurt protecting her!

"I am so sorry—"

"You got nothin' to be sorry for, Miss Mae," Eartha said. "It's that damn cop. He come runnin' outta that liquor store up the block and we didn't see him in time." She added that his partner never showed up.

"And people were in line? They saw this?"

"Don't worry 'bout it, Mae," Bernice said. "I'll handle things outside." She headed for the steps, beckoning Eartha to follow, just as Velma hurried up the stairs, followed by the doctor.

The doctor greeted Mae, then went into the bedroom to look at Etta. "Good God! I'm gonna have to remove the clothes, you know that, right?" Dinah nodded. "And I'm gonna need hot water, lots of it, and lots of towels and some clean sheets." He peered at Dinah. "You can help me, everybody else can leave."

"Should we stay up here just in case?" Velma asked, and Mae asked if she'd help Dinah do whatever the doctor needed.

Mae was too busy inside her own head. One of the undercover venues for female-impersonator performances was not far away, at 21st and Vernon, and they'd probably gone for dinner before their show. But what was the cop doing there alone? Mae had too many thoughts in her brain.

I jinxed myself. It's acting like the eighth month of an eight-year after all, was one of them, followed by an old, old thought: *What if I hadn't stolen Dave Hebert's money?* And as happened every time she had that thought, she heard her Grandpa Oliver's voice: *If a frog had a glass ass, it'd break every time he jumped.*

DEATH OF A SIDEMAN

BY GARY PHILLIPS

Exposition Park

T he old man wore ratty sneakers, a kaftan with various food and unidentified stains on it, and a fedora at a jaunty angle on his bald head. He also had a snow-white brush mustache. In his head he was John Travolta from that opening scene in *Saturday Night Fever* gliding with a dancer's grace along the city sidewalk.

"I'm staying alive, goddamnit," he said, loudly and proudly. "Staying alive, yeah," he sang off-key.

Other pedestrians gawked at this presumed refugee from a retirement home passing by them on this sunny morning. A few took his picture or a brief video clip with their smartphones and wondered how he'd gotten loose from his keepers. One empathetic soul dialed 311. Another considered calling the police but didn't. For even though the elderly gent was white, they figured that given his agitated state he might come to harm, though the odds were in his favor he'd be treated professionally.

"Can I get a witness?" the old man said jocularly, spreading his arms wide as if he were a pastor welcoming his flock. He encountered a young man and woman walking side by side from the opposite direction, laughing and talking and unaware of his presence until they nearly collided with him as he abruptly stopped in their path. "I mean, damn," he said, swaying and doing a 360 on the sidewalk.

"Mister, is there somebody I can call for you?" the women asked softly. She was tall, with stylish basketball shorts and a nose ring.

The old man stood alert as if a soldier snapping to at the appearance of a superior officer. "I regret to say we are powerless to act in cases of oral-genital intimacy, unless it has in some way interfered with interstate commerce. Or words to that effect," he guffawed.

"Time to go," the young woman's companion said. The two breezed around him.

He watched them for a moment then stepped into the roadway, heedless of the traffic. A motorcyclist had to act fast to avoid hitting him.

"Get out of the street, you fuckin' idiot!" the rider swore as he roared past.

The old man doffed his hat to the receding figure and machine, his back to oncoming vehicles. A truck's brakes screeched and several cars jerked to a stop.

"And away we go," the old man said, smiling. He managed to make it to the other side of the street and continued on. Rounding a corner, he spotted a group of people lined up for a table at a popular neighborhood café. He stopped again as if also lining up for brunch. Several regarded him and muttered. He simply stood there swaying and humming, though occasionally he'd wander over to patrons sitting at outside tables, invading their space. He would then return to the line. Finally, the owner of the restaurant came outside to talk to him. He was a heavyset, middle-aged man with a head of thick hair.

"Sir, I need to ask you to move along," the owner began. "You're making some of my customers uncomfortable. Do you know where you should be? I can call an Uber for you. Happy to pay for the ride, okay?"

The old man fixed the owner with a quizzical look. "I need to be among them, don't you see? Left to their own devices, who knows what devilment they'll be up to? This is for their good too, understand?"

"And where is this place you need to be among them?"

"Ha," the older man replied, wagging a finger at the owner. He backed away and headed farther down the block.

"I tried." The owner held his hands aloft and went back inside his establishment.

The wanderer took several more turns and was now nearing a residential area. In this section of the sidewalk, the serpentine roots of a large tree had caused a portion of the concrete to rise and buckle. The old man's feet got tangled and over he went, landing face-first on the sidewalk. He gashed his head but was still alive. A bystander saw what happened and hurried over to help.

"Hold on, I'm calling an ambulance."

The old man groaned and rolled onto his back, gazing up at the sky. His breathing was labored but his face was untroubled.

The helpful bystander knelt beside him. "You have any ID? Somebody I can call for you?"

"Yes," the old man answered, "put in a station-to-station call and find out all their also known as . . . ases." He giggled.

"I'm sorry, what?"

The fallen man began to tap out a phrase in Morse code on the concrete with his index finger. Three other people had also gathered around and though they noticed his finger moving, they assumed it was a spasmodic response to his fall. An ambulance soon arrived, and after his head wound was attended to, he was carefully loaded onto a stretcher, a neck brace having been snapped in place as well.

The phrase he'd been tapping out was *Reason frees us from fear*. He would last three more days, tapping out the phrase all the while, and succumb to complications arising from an unforeseen heart attack in the hospital. On a ventilator, his eyes fluttered open seconds before death as he stared at an image only he could see.

"The angel of death is here. And just my luck, she looks like Angela Davis." He chuckled, coughed up phlegm and blood in his throat, and expired. The words he'd been tapping out were inscribed on his headstone along with his name and birth and death dates. It was among several sayings the ninety-four-year-old man was known for uttering over the years. In the following days, that and other details of Jonah Montgomery Rikemann's colorful life were related in print and by newscasters and pundits across the airwaves.

Magrady sat off to one side in the World Stage, bopping his head as the quartet grooved. There was a piano player, an upright bass player, a drummer, and his friend Tyrone "Ty" Banshall on the sax. They'd been improvising but had dropped into a Paul Desmond number, "Feeling Blue." After that they played several more compositions and finished off the night with a tripped-out, jazzed-up instrumental rendition of Jimi Hendrix's "Voodoo Child."

Amid the applause, Magrady came over to his friend. "That was wild, man." He stuck out his hand and the saxophonist shook it vigorously.

"Glad to see you made it out, brother," Banshall said. "It's been a minute, like the kids say."

"Well, it is past my bedtime. But y'all knocked it out the park."

"Not to brag but I think we did."

"This is Horace," Banshall said, introducing the drummer, a stout man with gray at his temples. "This is Magrady. We were in 'Nam at the same time."

"No shit."

"Pleasure," Magrady said, shaking the drummer's hand. "Me and Ty weren't in the same unit but a lot of us bloods hung out together away from the bush."

Magrady looked like a beer truck driver, the hair bristled close on his head mostly snow these days, clean-shaven and neat in jeans and a buttoned-down shirt. His windbreaker was draped on the back of the folding chair he'd been sitting on.

Banshall, tall and lanky, was taking his sax apart to put in its padded case as the piano player came over. This individual was a medium-built Black man decades younger than both of the other two, who were in their sixties. He wore stylish glasses and trendy sneakers.

"You were in the stratosphere tonight," the younger man said, grinning at the saxophonist. The drummer had walked off to talk to someone else.

"Just following you, youngster. Lee Sorrells, meet Magrady, he was all Sergeant Fury and shit over there."

"Mostly shit," Magrady said, the emotion flat in his voice.

"Good to meet you," Lee said. He and Magrady also shook hands. "See you Friday, Ty," he added with a nod to the saxophonist.

"For sure," Banshall answered. Then to Magrady he said, "Gimme a ride to the crib and I'll buy you a drink." He made a face. "Damn, sorry, man. Old habit."

Magrady was some years sober. "Ain't no thing. I can have tap water with an ice cube."

"I think I have a bottle of fruity seltzer," his friend quipped.

The two left the World Stage, exiting onto the wide expanse of Degnan. Shops such as Hot and Cool Café and Eso Won Bookstore lined the next block of the boulevard. As Magrady and Banshall headed south away from the stores, they saw a man and woman in yoga gear each riding a hybrid unicycle-tricycle. The bikes had one large front tire and the two rear ones were canted outward for balance. They each had a seat and pedals but no handlebar. The two expertly maneuvered about.

Magrady and Banshall neared the recently refurbished Leimert Park Plaza which fronted the main throughfare of Crenshaw. The coming of a metro train signaled an uneasy development of the area. Riding in on those rails was gentrification, which often as not meant displacement. The two also passed several pup tents and lean-tos made from cardboard and scrap, evidence of the city's ever-present homeless population.

The two arrived at Magrady's car, a twenty-year-old PT Cruiser with a rebuilt engine and faded fake-wood paneling on its sides and rear hatch.

"Haven't seen one of these in a month of Sundays," Banshall remarked.

"Haven't had a car in that long either," Magrady replied as he unlocked the passenger-side door for his friend. "Even a goofy one like this." The bus and occasional biking had been his modes of transportation for years.

"I ain't complaining."

Banshall put his case on the backseat as Magrady went around to the driver's side. Off they went to Budlong near 35th Place, not too far west of USC. Banshall lived in what was called a neoclassical wood-sided fourplex built in another era. Back then it would have been called a rooming house. It was set among several humble abodes with well-tended lawns, some with security bars on doors and windows. Magrady found a parking space at the curb in front.

Banshall yawned, working a kink out of his neck. "Remember when this would have been the time we'd be hitting our stride in Soul Alley?" This had been a section of the then-called Saigon of nightclubs and joints where Black GIs hung out. A fleeting relief from the toils of war and antagonisms with their fellow white soldiers on base.

"Man," Magrady said, shaking his head, "I once got so high there in the Three Clicks that I saw Ho Chi Minh floating through the ceiling with a deck of cards. Bobby Seale showed up and we played Spades."

They chuckled and headed inside. Upstairs Banshall unlocked the door and, stepping inside, set his keys on a small table with a vase on it. His rooms were comfortable and tidy. There were photos and framed posters here and there chronicling his years in the music business. While not always a headliner, he'd put out a few albums of his own, and worked steady as a session man and a sideman on various tours, including ones with Herbie Hancock and various rock stars. There was also evidence of his playing gigs for causes ranging from police accountability to when Jesse Jackson ran for president in the '80s.

"It's okay if I drink in front of you?" Banshall asked. He shrugged off his sport coat and draped it on the arm of his couch. "Damn, don't mean to sound like a lush."

"Yeah, pretty sure I can resist temptation."

After Banshall poured a glass of orange juice for Magrady and for himself a Jameson, neat, the two sat in padded chairs. On the sound system he'd put on KKJZ, the jazz station out of Long Beach. The volume was set low.

Magrady said, leaning forward, "Here's to the long, bumpy road we've been on."

"And what lies ahead." They clinked glasses and each took a sip.

"You remember that chick Tempest?" Magrady said.

"Of course, fine as wine, as we used to say. What made you think of her?"

Magrady pointed at something on the end of the mantle. "That's from when we met her."

Banshall blinked at the rectangular object as if seeing it for the first time. He got up, staring at it as if it came from another dimension, and plucked it off the mantle.

"What?" Magrady said.

Banshall looked over at him, frowning. "I didn't know I still had this."

"You must have forgot, old-timer."

"I guess so." Banshall laughed nervously, setting it back on the mantle. "Hey, how about I make us a couple of sandwiches? Got some fresh smoked turkey."

"Sounds right."

Before he went into the kitchen, Banshall picked up his glass and drained it.

Magrady settled back listening to a Mose Allison number, half dozing.

"You want mustard on your sandwich?"

Magrady opened his eyes to see the saxophonist standing in the doorway to the kitchen holding a butter knife smeared yellow at the tip. A pained look contorted his face. He took a step back into the other room.

"Ty," Magrady called out, rising from the chair.

"What about that mustard, huh?" The words slurred out of Banshall's mouth as he fell to his knees. The knife slipped from his twitching fingers.

Magrady crossed the room in long strides to reach him, taking a knee. "Lie back, man, I'm calling 911."

"Sure, great." Banshall's voice was wispy and fragile.

Magrady made the call, then tossed his phone aside and applied CPR. He compressed Banshall's chest, stopping, then repeating the action. Long ago, when he gotten clean, again, he'd taken a course at one of the Narcotics Anonymous conferences he'd attended. Magrady also tried mouth-to-mouth as he'd been instructed. Soon, hearing muffled footfalls rushing up the carpeted stairs, he went to the door to let the paramedics in. It was a male and female team and they rushed in with a stretcher and their kit.

"I tried to resuscitate him but he doesn't seem responsive."

"Thank you. We got this."

The two went to work on Banshall. To his face they strapped an oxygen mask attached to a small tank. After several minutes the woman rose.

"I'm afraid he's gone," she said flatly.

"Damn."

"Is this your place?"

"No, his. I was visiting."

Sometime later Magrady went back to his home, a converted garage turned into what the city called an ADU—additional dwelling unit. This one had been redone legally, though he'd lived in his share of bootleg units and on the street too. Undressed and teeth brushed, Magrady sat on the edge of his compact bed in his boxers and undershirt. Lost in the fog of Banshall's demise, he worked Icy Hot liniment onto his knee.

Three days later he was in a strategy meeting with his boss, Janis Bonilla, at Urban Advocacy where he was an organizer, when the police came looking for him.

"That's a cop," he said to Bonilla. Her compact office had a window overlooking the main floor.

"He looks like any other bureaucrat from Building and Safety," she said.

"He's probably here for me."

"Something I should know, Magrady?" Hardly anyone called him by his first name.

The newcomer was dressed in a suit, light-blue shirt, and colorful tie. He removed wire-framed sunglasses from his bronzed face. He was Japanese American and maybe early fifties, Magrady estimated. The man was talking to one of the other organizers, Jessica Alvaringa. She in turn knocked on the office door, which was already open.

"Yo," Bonilla called out.

"He's LAPD and would like to talk to you," Jessica said to Magrady.

"Thanks, Jess," Magrady said, already up. "Okay to use the conference room?" he asked Bonilla.

"Sure."

Magrady went over to the detective and told him who he was.

"Yes sir, I'm Aaron Tsuji with the LAPD."

"This about Ty Banshall's death?"

"Where can we talk?"

"This way."

Magrady led him along a hallway and they went into the conference room, sitting opposite one another.

"What is it about Ty's death that's so odd?" Magrady asked.

"What makes you say that?"

"You're robbery-homicide and about the only thing Ty had of value was his sax."

"You've been in trouble with the law before, have you, Mr. Magrady?"

"I'm sure you looked me up before coming over here."

"You and the deceased served in Vietnam."

"We did but weren't in the same unit."

Tsuji let that sink in. "Can you tell me about the other night?"

"Not a problem." Magrady related the events matter-of-factly, then added, "He was dead by the time the paramedics arrived. Ty wasn't beaten, shot, or stabbed. And you being here means it wasn't just a heart attack." He paused. "Was Ty poisoned?"

Tsuji allowed no reaction onto his face but a gleam flickered in his eyes. "Why don't we go over to the station and see if we can clear this up."

"Arrest me and I'll go."

"You don't seem to be too upset about Mr. Banshall's murder."

"I've seen death in the jungle and on the streets, Mr. Tsuji. I've been near enough to it that she's kissed me on the cheek once or twice. Me and Ty were friends but not ace boon coons, if you dig what I'm sayin'. Until I heard from him about the jam session, I didn't even know he'd come back to town. Apparently he'd been here for a while."

"Why is it you didn't drink that night?"

"I'm an alcoholic and a drug fiend."

Tsuji stared at Magrady for several beats, then stood, extracted one of his business cards, and placed it on the table. As Magrady had assumed, he worked out of the Southwest Division.

"Let me know if you think of anything."

"I will."

Tsuji headed toward the door. "I'll probably be back in touch." Magrady resisted making a sarcastic remark as the plain-clothesman left. He remained sitting. The booze had probably been poisoned, thus the question about why he hadn't taken a drink. It wasn't a virgin bottle of Jameson, Magrady had noticed the night before. He also figured they'd pulled his prints from the glass he'd used, and spoken with the EMTs.

"Well?" Janice Bonilla stood in the doorway.

He told her what was up.

"Why do you think he would be poisoned? Some old beef?"

"It has to be," Magrady said. "Far as I know, Ty made some good money but he blew through it a lifetime ago. I mean, except I guess for some royalty payments now and then, he probably only had Social Security."

"Maybe like Robert Johnson, it was a love triangle."

"Sheet, at his age? A jealous boyfriend did him in?" Or so went the legend about the demise of the famed bluesman.

Bonilla snorted. "Who you tellin', playboy?" She knew he had a lady friend named Angie Baine who was older than him. She was a former B movie starlet who'd been in films such as *Wolfman A-Go-Go* and *The Atomic Eye.* "About a month ago in Rosemead this great-grandmother stuck a knife in the back of her old man as he was playing Scrabble in the facility they lived in 'cause he was ending their relationship. And she was in her eighties."

"Okay, could be," Magrady conceded. "That cop Tsuji will sort it out or not. I'ma get to the tenants' meeting."

"See you later," she said.

Several days after the planning meeting, Magrady drove past the rear of a laundromat where a few compact nylon tents and other forms of precarious shelter were arrayed. He parked near his destination, joining Bonilla and Alvaringa, along with various community members and organizers from two allied organizations. They were there doing a direct action in front of a house on Budlong near the intersection of Jefferson.

"This is not the way we solve homelessness in this city, by making more homeless." Bonilla was talking into a portable mic attached to a speaker. "This won't do displacing a hardworking single mother and her two children over a matter than can easily be resolved. *Needs* to be resolved."

Yells of support issued from the gathered, more than seventy people standing on the lawn facing the speaker. Several police cars rolled into view and parked haphazardly in the street. The officers joined the media who were also present. The family Bonilla was referring to had been evicted from the house, a rental. Not for failure to pay but over what in a higher-income area would have been a minor infraction: an unauthorized repair. But the rental company, a national outfit called Demizro which owned various units in South LA, knew the mother was a housing activist and wanted to make an example. A lot of the housing stock they owned had been acquired during the last economic downturn.

Bonilla continued, "We have to stand up to the likes of Demizro and their mercenary methods. People have a right to shelter just as they have a right to food and water."

"Hell yes!" went up the cry. Fists pumped the air and placards were held aloft.

"Whose streets? *Our* streets!" echoed from the protesters.

The cops spread out in a semicircle around the crowd. Two sergeants were among them, one on either end. There were also a few people wearing light-green caps standing around. These were lawyers—legal observers. If there was an attempt to occupy the premises, the cops would have cause to move in. As it was, they still might declare this an unlawful assembly.

"Hey, Magrady," said a man in one of the light-green caps. He wore a plaid shirt and jeans.

"Mark, how's it going?" They shook hands.

"Same old, same old." Mark Josephs was white, in his forties, pleasant-looking with a pockmarked jawline. He was a surfer and civil litigator who'd won a handful of significant cases against the LAPD over the years. "How come there's a detective over there mad-dogging us?"

Magrady had noticed a silver-colored Chrysler arrive on the periphery with Tsuji behind the wheel. "He's here to rattle me." He explained why.

"Huh," Josephs said. "Let me know if you need my help."

"I will, thanks."

Josephs joined two other legal observers talking to one of the sergeants. The protesters were now out on the sidewalk and that, too—obstructing a public right-of-way—could be used by the cops to vamp on them, Magrady reflected. He threaded his way through the gathered as more speakers came to the mic. At one point the uniforms pressed their semicircle tighter, seemingly trying to prod everyone onto the lawn. Magrady and the others tensed. The person at the mic kept talking but everyone's eyes were on the police. At some imperceptible signal, the officers took a few steps back and everyone exhaled.

Eventually the event wound down, the collective release of energy like air escaping a balloon. Bonilla was being interviewed by a radio reporter outlining their next steps in the fight to keep the family's home. This involved putting pressure on specific members of the Demizro board.

Hands in his pockets, standing at the curb as people left, Magrady saw that Tsuji was gone as well. It suddenly occurred to him that Banshall probably didn't have any immediate family in town. He knew his friend had been married but he recalled the wife had died a few years ago. And as far as he knew, the jazzman didn't have any children. He wasn't sure how long the county morgue would hold onto his body. If unclaimed, it would eventually be cremated to save space. Since it was still an open investigation, it would probably be Tsuji who would inform the coroner to release the body.

Back at the Urban Advocacy office, Magrady used one of their real estate databases to look up information on the fourplex where Banshall had lived. He discovered that the owner didn't live there and the other units were all occupied by tenants. The police might have put up their warning tape on Banshall's door or maybe not. He did recall, however, that the main entry door was kept locked. He smiled, realizing he was working himself into how to get into the dead man's apartment. He couldn't exactly say why, but did anyone deserve to die alone? A B&E was out of the question. The front door was heavy and sturdy and the windows on the ground floor were barred. Imagine if Tsuji threw him in lockup for trying to force his way in? He'd look guilty as hell. Not that he gave a shit. He wondered if he called the owner pretending to want to rent the now-vacant apartment, how might that go? Magrady supposed that like a vampire, he was going to have to be invited inside.

The next day before sunup, Magrady sat in his car keeping watch on the fourplex. He saw a man leave the place around seven thirty that morning and a woman leave at ten past nine. The man walked along the street and turned the corner. The woman got into a car. That left the occupant of the third apartment. Maybe they worked from home. What kind of ruse could he try to gain entry? He sat and waited. Magrady had planned and had brought along a sandwich, but despite jonesing for it, no coffee. The latter an effort to not have to pee, at least not frequently. A little before eleven, an older woman exited the premises. She had on a straw sun hat and pulled one of those adjustable rolling carts old folks used to take their groceries home from the supermarket. She stood in front and soon a cab, a Prius, pulled up. The driver got out, collapsed her cart, and put it in the hatchback. She got in the rear. Off they went.

Nearly an hour and a half later the older lady returned in another cab. As the driver helped her get unloaded, Magrady came up.

"Ma'am, sorry to bother you, but does Ty Banshall live here? He's a saxophone player." He held up his phone. "We had an appointment today about an upcoming gig, but he's not answering."

"Oh my, I guess you haven't heard." She was a walnut-colored woman who looked to be in her seventies. She reminded him of those ladies who did the volunteer work at the church of his youth.

"What's that?" He took hold of her cart to take it up the front steps onto the porch. He nodded at the cabdriver, who nodded back and returned to his car.

"The way I understand it, they had to carry him out of here feet first the other evening. He died."

"That's terrible."

"Yes, I'm so sorry. He was a nice man. Told me his stories like playing in Count Basie's band." She'd unlocked the front door and pushed it open. Magrady followed her into the vestibule, hauling the cart up and over the doorway's frame. She occupied one of the ground-floor dwellings.

"Well," he said, "thank you for your time."

"Of course. No bother. Sure will miss him."

"Me too." Magrady turned back toward the entrance. She was rolling her cart inside her place, closing the door. Magrady didn't want her hearing him go up the stairs, arousing suspicion. At the main doorway he placed a waded-up piece of paper in the door-jamb cavity where the lock would catch, then closed the front door, faking like he was leaving for good. He returned to his car to retrieve a hammer and chisel. These he placed in a paper bag along with some cheap cotton gloves he'd bought to make it less obvious he was carrying the amateur burglary kit. He sat behind the steering wheel, listening to a podcast debunking conspiracy theories.

After another forty minutes he went up the steps, unlatched the front door, and moved inside. He heard muffled voices through the closed door of the older woman's apartment—she was watching her stories on TV.

Up the stairs he went. At Banshall's door there was no X of crime scene tape. The door was locked. Gloves on, he inserted the chisel between the door and the jamb. Three quick raps of the hammer on the head of the chisel, and the door popped opened. Magrady paused then stepped inside, closing the door quietly behind him. Fortunately, these rooms were not above the older woman's place. For a moment he felt disoriented, viewing the main room in the light, knowing the recent inhabitant was never to return.

He glanced around, not sure what he was looking for, though he supposed he should try to find a next of kin. But the medical examiner's office would do that as a matter of course. Yet it seemed impersonal if he didn't also try. There were a couple of framed photos on the mantle, including one with Banshall in a sport coat with his arm around the shoulders of a woman in a mink coat. Both were smiling.

Staring at his dead friend's face, he could tell it had been taken a few years ago. Should he try to find the woman? He picked up the frame and slipped the photo free. Nothing was written on the back.

Before putting the picture back together, he took a shot of it with his phone's camera. He picked up the black wooden rectangle also on the mantle. The thing that seemed to puzzle Banshall by its presence. Magrady had one just like this. It was a commemorative gift given to those who'd worked on a successful political campaign more than twenty-five years earlier. What went down on and after April 29, 1992, were etched memories. The days-long conflagration had jumped off at the intersection of Florence and Normandie. Everyone had been tuned in to their TVs or radios as the not-guilty verdicts were announced that afternoon for the four LAPD officers who beat the living hell out of Rodney King after a chase-and-stop in the San Fernando Valley. The two passengers in his car untouched. In those days there were no smartphones with cameras to chronicle police violence, Magrady reflected. On that evening, it was grainy images captured via a video camera operated by a plumber from his apartment's balcony. He'd been awakened by the commotion from below.

The memento Magrady held had been handed out by a grateful candidate who'd won a city council seat, running on a platform of neighborhood empowerment zones and racial reconciliation several years after '92. It had been a contentious race. Banshall had headlined a benefit concert to fundraise for the campaign. The singer had been a woman calling herself Tempest. Magrady had been one of several in charge of the canvassing, the door knocking. Tsuji must have searched the apartment once he got the tox report from the coroner. The detective must have also talked to the musicians who last played with Banshall that night at the World Stage. That might have been another way in which he'd zeroed in on Magrady. But who had Banshall run up against since coming back to town?

Banshall had a good number of vinyl LPs arranged on a shelf in the tidy dining room. Magrady sifted through these but no hidden treasure map fell out. Frustrated and feeling aimless, he was hesitant to leave but he was getting nowhere. Well, he reasoned, he'd try to hunt down the woman, though he had a feeling that was going to be a dead end. Magrady poked about some more but nothing jumped out at him.

When he stepped outside the apartment, he heard the main front door opening. For a blink he froze but knew he had to feign being nonchalant. He descended the stairs as the woman he'd seen in the morning started up them.

"How you doing?" he said, angling past her with his paper bag.

She glared at him but didn't say anything as she ascended. He didn't think she took him for a cop. But she was going to notice the broken in door any second. It wouldn't latch and that was noticeable.

"Hey," she called out.

Magrady quickened his pace through the entrance and out onto the walkway. Hopefully she wasn't packing. He jogged as best he could, bad knee and all, over to his car to get away from there.

Later that night, not having had a visit from the law, Magrady leafed through the contents of a large ten-by-twelve gray envelope of mementos. If he couldn't find out who poisoned Banshall or who might claim his body, he could at least revisit parts of a past they shared. There was a Polaroid of a young, thinner him in the Three Clicks in uniform, a Vietnamese "B girl" sitting on his knee. They were obviously both tipsy. Another picture showed Banshall blowing the sax on the club's tiny stage accompanied by a guitarist and a drummer, the musicians also in uniform. Hard to believe any of them had been that young.

Magrady kept sifting through the items in no particular order. There was a letter his daughter Esther had written him years ago, begging him to get clean. He was glad they were no longer estranged these days. He scanned some newspaper clippings from the city council campaign, finding his name mentioned in an article from the *Sentinel*, LA's Black newsweekly. But it was an article from the *Los Angeles Times* that he fixed on. It was an interview with the candidate, Tina Chalmers, and she was talking about the death of one of the architects of the gang truce between the Crips and Bloods. This had been an effort begun before April 29 but had gotten traction when it came into effect afterward. The truce eventually broke down, but Chalmers was talking about its merits and the need to redouble that sort of effort.

"Tony Blow does not need to have died in vain," Chalmers was quoted as saying.

Tony Blow was the street name for a reformed gangbanger who'd been killed. He was controversial as he was the face of the gang truce, even being interviewed on national news. But it was also alleged he was under investigation by the FBI for drugs and guns. Magrady couldn't remember his real name. He got on his laptop and found a pertinent article about his death. Blow was found shot to death in a rear house on 76th Street off an alley. His murder was unsolved at the time of the article, though believed to have been gang related. Magrady did more checking and it seemed the murder was still open now, decades later. He returned to the original article. Toward the end of the piece, he found Blow's real name. Then he read it again to make sure.

"I felt no particular emotion about poisoning him. It was just one of those things," he said, a slight smile on his composed face. "The more it stayed on my mind, though, the more it seemed I should do something about it. He was my father after all. When I knew he was gonna bring the quartet over after our opening night for a little celebration, it all came together."

Magrady stood in his windbreaker before Lee Sorrells, who sat at a piano. They were in a half-lit space, the back room of McDade's Wholesale Beauty and Fixture Supply on Avalon Boulevard. Sorrells had an arrangement with the owner and this was where he rehearsed. The space was sparsely furnished, only one other chair and a mini fridge on the concrete floor. High up in the rear wall were three barred windows overlooking an alley. This provided what light there was.

Sorrells thunked a key. "You talk to that detective?"

"No." Magrady sat down in a chair angled toward the piano. "What am I gonna tell 'em?"

"I'm Tony Blow's son."

The murdered gang truce leader's real name was Anthony Sorrells. When Magrady had read that, he recalled Banshall's introduction of the members of his quartet.

"It could be a coincidence," Magrady said. "The last name. But he died violently and now Ty gets murdered."

The younger Sorrells plinked several keys.

Magrady continued: "Anyway, those supposed coincidences itched at me. I got to thinking about Tony Blow back in the day. I'd met hm a couple of times, a charismatic dude. He had real potential."

The son looked at him evenly.

"Of course, there were also the rumors about him."

The pianist remained motionless behind his instrument. "So you got online and went down the rabbit hole about my dad."

"Some of that," Magrady admitted. That's how he'd learned about the passing of J.M. Rikemann. Among his achievements, he'd been one of the FBI supervisors overseeing COINTELPRO, the counterintelligence operation to destroy the Black Panthers and make sure Martin Luther King Jr. would not become the Black messiah. Magrady also recalled Daryl Gates, the chief of the LAPD in the '90s who had his own counterintelligence unit, the Organized Crime Intelligence Division. Several of its officers had infiltrated leftist groups and spied on local elected officials.

The younger man went on looking at him blankly.

Magrady said, "Being old school, I wanted print. I know about this archive in the hood, the Southern California Library. It was started by some Reds," he chuckled. "The library has all kinds of books on the labor movement, Chicano liberation, and so on. Naturally, there's several books they have there about '92. One of them examined the gang truce and its aftermath. The woman who wrote the book talked about this white guy named Rikemann."

That seemed to catch Sorrells's attention.

"She stated that in the '90s, Rikemann, after leaving the FBI and stints in the Reagan and Bush White Houses, was a kind of disruption consultant to law enforcement. An imperialist for hire, she wrote."

Sorrells snorted. "He confessed to me, Magrady. Ty knew who I was. Kept tabs on me over the years, he said. When he came back to town, he finally wanted to come clean, atone. He sought me out specifically for this last gig." He paused, regarding the older man. "I guess age makes you think about setting the record straight before it's too late."

"It does. Why did Ty kill your father?"

Sorrells's laughter reminded Magrady of Christopher Lee as Dracula. "From what Ty said, he had Rikemann's bootheel on his neck once upon a time."

Magrady wound back to Soul Alley. "Smack. Ty knew a few cats who got into dope over there, using and selling. But I don't remember him ever being on the needle."

"He wasn't. Back in the States, this Rikemann had him by the balls on a federal rap. Not for using but for importing. Instead of putting him away, Rikemann got him to snitch on the civil rights activities he was involved in."

"There's a statute of limitation for a drug bust," Magrady noted.

"Ty didn't want his past being exposed," Sorrells said. "At least not back when my dad found out about him."

"How did your father find out?"

"Rikemann put the squeeze on Ty, threatening to expose him. That motherfucker was paying attention to what was going down after '92 and didn't want my dad becoming what he and his kind feared the most: a new Malcolm X. From gangster to Black leader."

"Ty was supposed to see if Tony Blow would go for the okey-doke," Magrady said.

"Yeah, but he was changing, according to my mom, about to tell all, like who was part of the coke pipeline he profited from. My mom knew he'd been trying to get a book deal."

"Damn. So Rikemann supplied your dad?"

"Who better to sell the drugs helping to keep us down than a War on Drugs warrior?"

"From the Golden Triangle to Colombian marching powder," Magrady said.

Sorrells leaned back from the piano. "Now what, you gonna avenge your buddy the sellout?"

"I don't really know," Magrady stammered. "Shouldn't I?"

Sorrells rose. Magrady remained sitting, a hand in his jacket pocket.

Rikemann's memoir, which he'd written in longhand, was published about a year after he died. In those pages he named names and made startling allegations further fueling conspiracy theories about intelligence agencies up to no good in the nation's inner cities.

PART III

THE WORLD IS A GHETTO

SABOR A MI

BY ROBERTO LOVATO

Slauson Park

R oque "Rocky" Anaya bobs his head to the mellow beats of melancholy and sweet bolero love songs blaring inside his beat-up Toyota. The rain pelting the windshield blurs his view of the crime scene across the street, on the soccer field in Slauson Park on 54th Street near the corner of Compton Avenue. He closes his eyes, as if in meditation, giving the war veteran–turned-detective a vulnerability he never displays in public. Rocky's confident that, at one a.m., nobody will mess with him while he does his music thing. This despite the popular perception of the Alameda corridor neighborhoods in South Central as a "gang-infested" industrial wasteland with pockets of Black and Brown people living in between factories, warehouses, and empty lots.

The sight of Rocky doing his music thing would lead any late-night passerby to think he's either jacking off or in a trance. Like what the Salvadoran and Guatemalan feligréses experience weekly speaking in tongues in their crowded Iglesia de Dios Pentecostal la Resurrección church across the street.

Nobody would guess what he's actually doing: deciding whether he really wants to investigate the murder of a Salvadoran man hacked to death with a machete across the street from la Resurrección. Neither would they believe that he's up at this late hour on a hot August night figuring things out while listening to, of all things, "Sabor a Mi," a sultry bolero classic loved for decades by generations of local lowriders, young and old people across Latin America, the Caribbean, and the Latino United

States. And even his closest friends don't know he's listening to the music to ponder the savage murder of Arnulfo Cartagena, a man he's known since their childhood in the Barrio Santa Cruz slum in prewar El Salvador.

Lyrics fill his head and body as he ponders the possibilities and pitfalls associated with the tiny country of titanic sorrows named for the Savior.

If you deny my presence in your life, it would be enough to hug you and talk . . .

Fuck. Why the fuck am I here? he wondered. My goddamn stomach's bloating like I've been dead for three or four days.

Rocky's jaw tightens.

He's fine occasionally doing Jack's "Latino" cases—finding migrants kidnapped by cartels, figuring out if "disappeared" means "dead," surveilling Hollywood hotshots, surveilling cheating spouses, corporations doing dirty work in Latin America or the Latino United States, investigating links between local power brokers and narcos, etc. But this Salvadoran shit is the last thing he wants to investigate.

Despite Rocky's resistance to the assignment from his boss, longtime LA private detective Jack Palomino, memories of Arnulfo—the murdered man and him as barefoot boys hiding between the tin walls, playing ladrón librado as they took turns being cop and crook with other kids—roll in the movie screen of his mind.

Poor cerote, he thinks, never stopped believing he and the social movements could change this fabulously corrupt system. I used to believe that shit. No más. You died for another grand causa, left in the middle of the green grass of Slauson Park. Tied up like that, you must've looked like the saint the public made you, the "Peacemaker," out to be.

He smiles. They can believe what they want, but I remember

how the "Peacemaker" learned his trade—as a "terorista" fighting a war against a fascist military dictatorship.

The photos he saw from the crime scene he just visited—Arnulfo's nose hacked off, his arms tied behind his back and gashed, and his head ready to fall off with another chop—run through his head.

Of my life, I give my best
I'm so poor, what else can I give?

Even as kids, Arnulfo was charismatic. He was a guy able to get others to do stuff, including Rocky. He was also a fucking blowhard—a young blowhard who became an adult media hound for his causas. But he *was* an effective organizer, he knew how to conspirar like we were taught. Ego or not, he died with that Jedi belief: Revolucíon. He didn't deserve to die, especially not like this, like one of the escuadrones de la muerte death squad killings from back when they were fighting the fascistas of the Salvadoran government.

He looked eastward, toward the gigantic projects stuck between the warehouses and small factories that LA's powers that be squeezed into the eastern part of South Central. Slauson Park, where Arnulfo was killed, stands out as a green patch in the gray and black lines of concrete, prison stripes coloring the satellite maps of South LA. Different parts of the scenery—the tropical rain, lots overrun with weeds and graffiti, la Resurrección church, the industrial warehouses and small factories, railroad tracks, the general browning of South LA—give Arnulfo's machete murder a sultry, sad Salvadoran feel. Sometimes, LA itself feels very Salvadoreño, a dark, ugly feeling Rocky rejects as if it were a gun in his gut. But the comparison is limited. War is war. Even during the worst of the '92 riots here, weeks and months in LA never came close to a single day of absolute terror in El Salvador.

"Sabor a Mí" seduces Rocky back into detective mode.

"There are lots of people who have wanted to kill Arnulfo," he says out loud. He really was *that* good of an organizer, one who, as they say in good Salvadoran, knew how to touch los guevos del tigre. Arnulfo's touched a lot of tiger balls.

Pero tú llevas también sabor a mi . . .

Rocky rockets through the mental Rolodex of possible suspects besides Guardado, the guy they have in custody: smaller cliques of MS-13 or 18th Street gangs opposed to the gang truce he was organizing; the Mexican Mafia or Crips or Bloods wanting to foment and grow with continued violence; the escuadrones de la muerte that have operated in LA since the '80s and still carry a big ax—or machete—to grind.

He grits his teeth and shakes his head at the thought of how the cops are compounding the problem. The cops hated Arnulfo too. His loud, articulate, and passionate—and very public—calls to "abolish the police" as part of the larger movement guaranteed the cops were celebrating his death. Arnulfo's prominence also guaranteed that the cops would do little to nothing to investigate the circumstances surrounding his murder.

The real question, he thought, is who wanted to kill the peace by killing the Peacemaker?

This was Jack's brilliant idea, he says to himself, the disheveled but brilliant old-school Italian Jew version of Columbo. Jack's old friends from Comite Esperanza, a Salvadoran advocacy organization Rocky volunteered at years ago, approached him with Arnulfo's case. Jack has always been solidario. Like good Salvadorans, they don't buy the official story.

Fucking Jack figured Rocky'd dive headfirst into this case because he went back years with Arnulfo. Jack figured wrong. He's not so into it. Rocky's gonna let Jack know he should find someone else as soon as possible. This isn't good for him.

The deeper sources of Rocky's Salvadoran malaise are known only to him, but have something to do with his relationship to the music. Whatever the sources, there, between the lines of these sublime bolero songs, is something else: the sweet-and-sour secrets of the better life left to him by his parents, two extremely poor Salvadorans who danced and struggled their way through a Great Depression and other calamities that made Steinbeck's *Grapes of Wrath* look like a wine festival. Whatever the relationship between his parents' music, the malaise, and his preternatural ability to connect dots that are invisible to most, Rocky keeps it deep in himself, like it's a plan to attack the Ilopango airport from clandestine safe houses in San Salvador during the war. But as mysterious as the madness in his detective method is, it is effective enough to keep Jack giving him work.

Rocky turns back to the case, his closed eyes and the sultry sweetness of El Chicano's version of "Sabor a Mi" making him look like he's serenading his ex-wife or one of the other women he never managed to stay in a relationship with beyond a few years. Except Marivel. His head moves as if he's painting a circle with it.

Our souls got closer, so much
So, that I keep your taste
Like you too carry
The taste of me . . .

Rocky's lover seems to be the crime itself. While a mystery even to him, his alchemical method involves transforming the rhythms and lyrics into an incantation, a spell that makes the background music the fuel for his analytical and emotional processes.

Rocky, an avid reader and quick study, hears a connection between the lyrics "*I keep your taste like you carry the taste of me*" and Locard's Exchange Principle, a forensic theory he learned about from Jack, a former professor of Romance literature at Berkeley back when.

Locard's Principle, the foundation of forensics and detection, is premised on a simple but powerful idea Rocky adores, one that feels, for him, like the bridge between the love of poetry and science he learned in El Salvador before the war collapsed everything: every crime leaves a bit of itself on the criminal, and criminals also leave a part of themselves at the scene of the crime. This is what Rocky hears and feels in "Sabor a Mi."

At one level, the physical evidence of the crime would indicate that the accused killer, Pablo Guardado, did in fact leave a lot of his sabor at the Slauson Park scene. Serena, a very smart and buxom Chicana LAPD clerk Rocky once dated, managed to sneak a look at the case file. She let him know that the evidence includes hair samples, DNA, fingerprints, and other materials gathered by LA's less-than-finest, all matching with Guardado. And, of course, the bloody machete the cops say Guardado bought at Liborio's market in Mid-City.

Despite (or probably *because* of) their especially sloppy work, the LAPD wrapped the case up in a neat package, putting the responsibility squarely on Guardado, a thirty-five-year-old former member of the LAPD's favorite group of "terrorists," MS-13. Before finding salvation in Jesús, Guardado, the former "Smiley," was an MS shot caller–turned–born again believer bro and pastor. Being "saved" is, more often than not, the only way to escape la vida loca. Prior to his salvation, Guardado was hard as hard can be, leading the Hoover Street Locos, an MS-13 clique whose intrepid actions and violence were legendary. Prior to his arrest, everything looked like Guardado was trying to follow Saint Paul and Buddhist saint Milarepa's path from murderous violence to holy redemption. Maybe not.

More than two weeks after Rocky attended the joint LAPD and DA press conference in the park, a taste of the shitshow remains.

Qué yo guardo tu sabor, como tú llevas también
Sabor a mi . . .

Pigs at the trough, he thinks. These motherfuckers take Salvadoran and other gangs as slop to feed their fucking law enforment careers at any cost. Every other word at that ridiculous press conference in the park was "terrorist," the police chief reassuring everyone that he would do "whatever necessary to stop these barbaric criminals terrorizing the community." The mayor adopting that smug, self-righteous tone about how "terror won't stop the people of Los Angeles" and other shit like that. Terrorist tu madre, cerotes.

Even the white supremacist president and his attorney general mentioned Arnulfo's murder in a glitzy Oval Office press conference last week, complete with "most wanted" pictures of the tattooed faces of gang members, even though most Salvadoran gangs stopped sporting facial tattoos more than ten years ago. The president's presser also included maps of the US with big red flags where MS-13 was alleged to operate.

Terror, Rocky thinks, I'll show you terror, cerotes. I grew up hearing that fucking word thrown around El Salvador like it was holy water at a baptism or burial. Terrorist students. Terrorist priests and nuns. Terrorist guerrillas. You think this is terror? I can take them back to lugares donde asustan, the places that really scare, places that make the worst of South Central LA look like the *Baywatch* episodes Arnulfo and me used to watch as kids in El Salvador and think it was the real LA.

Rocky considers Paul Yagoda the worst of the pigs. Yagoda is an undersheriff running to be the LA County sheriff. Recalling the Italian-suited, well-coiffed Yagoda as he droned on at the press conference about "getting to the root of the terrorist gang problem" makes Rocky want to vomit. The sensation worsens at the thought of the candidate's TV commercials featuring him speaking directly at the camera while Latino kids play in the background, saying, "Our kids' safety comes first. I'll fight the gangs and other threats for them, and for you."

Weeks before the murder, Yagoda was put on the spot during a debate. One of the moderators asked him about tattoos he's alleged to have, tattoos of a Viking with a .357, the logo of the Norsmen, a white supremacist gang that's operating within the LAPD. Yagoda admitted to having the tattoo, but not to any affiliation with the Norsemen.

On top of everything else, the whole thing seems off to Rocky. To begin with, he calculates, the gangs haven't resorted to killings with machetes since the early days, when Arnulfo and he worked at the refugee comite in Pico Union. The only ones who keep talking about maras and machetes are the media and politicians who also use outdated images of tattoo-faced gangs. The kids used to buy the machetes at Liborio's market less to terrorize people than because they couldn't afford the AKs, Uzis, and other weapons favored by the Mexican Mafia and the other gangs that operated south and east of here. Why would anybody want to resurrect the machete decades later?

We Salvadoreños know how that "terrorista" takes on its own life when there's no opposition to it. It will continue to rule like a king, unless somebody gets in its way. Somebody wanted to kill the peace by killing Arnulfo. The question is, who benefits from continued war? Arnulfo's murder threatens everything he spent his thirty-plus years in LA building.

The thought of these hypocritical pigs is too much to bear. Fuck it, he decides, I'll take the case. I may not share Arnulfo's dreamy *Star Wars* Jedi code in the causa, but I will investigate.

They've got this thing wrapped up too nicely in the material realm. Seems like this Guardado kid did do it, but the evidence is nonetheless questionable. The killing of Arnulfo in the middle of the park, the use of the machete—it's all staged, but not by a Salvadoran director. The script doesn't feel like a Salvadoran wrote it either. He needs to find a witness.

For the next week, Rocky keeps coming to the same spot at the same late hours, parking his car, listening to boleros, in the hopes of finding a witness, a clue, something that will confirm what the music led his gut to believe about the questionable circumstances surrounding Arnulfo's murder. Then one night, looking in the direction of Slauson Park, he notices a young male leaving the rec center building off the basketball court.

Holy shit, he thinks, it's after midnight! Before Rocky can start his Toyota, the kid speeds off in an old Chevy.

The next day Rocky returns to the rec center to ask about the guy. He's greeted by a young man and woman. They're dressed in the blue-and-white shirts of the Parks and Rec department. He quickly sizes them up and concludes that their demeanor, physical appearance, and especially the way the woman uses her mouth to point, indicate Salvadoran ancestry.

"What say you, young compatriotas?"

"Compatriotas?" the young woman replies.

"Yes," Rocky says, "I notice you're sporting the national colors and figured we're compatriots."

The two young people laugh. Rocky knows it's nice to be recognized as Salvadoran, a people who live in anonymity, oppression, the culture of secrecy imposed by a country with a long history of military dictatorship, and, in the US, the faceless nothing of being "Latino."

"My name's Rocky," he says. "I'm a private eye looking into the murder of Arnulfo Cartagena. I'm sure you've been asked about this before."

"Yeah, the cops questioned us once," the young man says. "But that was it."

214 // South Central Noir

"So, you're a real detective and Salvadoran?" the woman asks.

"Yes," he says, and shows them his license. He looks at the posters of Che Guevara and the Salvadoran poet Roque Dalton in the corner of the rec office. "You know that we had detectives in El Salvador, including in the Frente?"

"You were in the FMLN?"

"Yes. We had compañeros who, in addition to being guerrilleros, were doing counterintelligence work."

"You mean like chasing spies and infiltres?" the increasingly excited young man says.

"Yes, and there were many compañeras who did the work too. We also investigated crimes among members of the Frente—you know, rape, beatings, and even killings committed by some of our soldiers."

"Wow. You were a guerrillero detective!" says the young woman. "That's sooo cool."

"So, what can you tell me about the people who use the gym at night?"

"Well," the young man says, "the main people who use it are basketball players, mostly young guys playing pickup games and this one team that uses it once a week. Them and the church group from across the street that practices music here Mondays and Thursdays."

"Church group?"

"They bring guitars, an electric drum set, a bass, and singers."

"Who leads the band?"

"The guitar player. I think his name is Alfonso, a guy with a bunch of tattoos. I think he was in a gang. He's the one we gave the keys to because they asked permission to stay late. And, you know, they're in a church and they've always been respectful."

Rocky heads to the church, acting like a feligrés, one of the faithful looking to reconnect with God after backsliding. Sure enough, he quickly locates Alfonso Mejia. He and the other band members use the space at night to rehearse songs of redemption with the blood of Christ.

Rocky had confirmed with local Salvadoran sources that Alfonso's a former gang member, now part of the ministry of the church targeting at-risk youth for salvation. He also found out who led him out of the gang and into God: Pablo Guardado, the accused murderer. Guardado had actually led the ministry targeting gang kids in South LA. He himself was a kind of peacemaker. What would lead him to go back to la vida loca? Rocky wondered. Maybe he never left it and remained connected. Many a homie has.

Rocky parks on Compton Avenue, on the same side as la Resurrección. It is about twelve thirty in the morning when the young band members open the door. Rocky steps out of his car.

"Alfonso?"

"Who's asking?"

"I'm Roque Anaya, private investigator. Folks at the Comite Esperanza asked my firm to look into the murder of Arnulfo Cartagena. I just want to ask you some—"

"Nah, bro. I ain't got nothin to say to you," the young church member says. "I'm not in that world anymore and already spoke with the police."

"Which world?"

"Never mind."

"The gang world. Actually, I'm told you're still in la vida loca, using the tithes the faithful give you each week to buy one of God's gifts: crack. Word is you're like those Catholic curas who preach beautiful by day and party hard as hell by night."

"What the fuck, ey? Who's tellin you this shit?"

"People who have a lot more stuff to tell me, they say, stuff I can share with your wife, your friends in the congregation . . . and Homeland Security."

"Fuck them—and fuck you."

"Okay. I'm gonna give you a break and let you cool off and think about what you can and can't tell me. I'd hate for your baby to graduate from elementary school without seeing his dad there." Rocky had discovered that Mejia has a newborn son, a redeeming force without equal in the world of Salvadoran migrant gangs.

The young tiger's balls have been touched. He adopts a pensive posture before speaking again. Rocky knows that deportation can often mean death to young Salvadorans. It also means not seeing their families. He knows precisely how to squeeze Salvadorans, many of whom live under the boot of being undocumented because the US government never recognized how it created a refugee and migration problem when it backed the fascist military dictatorships for all those years. Rocky doesn't like using this lever, but needs to if he wants to get to the bottom of Arnulfo's murder.

"Okay, okay," Mejia says. "Look, I can't talk right now. All I can tell you is that it involved escuadrones." With that, the young man hurries to his Chevy and speeds away.

Escuadrones? Rocky says to himself, as he stands in the park pondering the possibility that Salvadoran death squads have indeed been resurrected to kill Arnulfo and frame Guardado. He wrestles with sudden feelings of anger and fear. He's at a loss, but is humble enough to know when he needs help. So he leaves the park to go seek the assistance of the wizard of LA detectives, his boss, Jack Palomino.

Rocky walks up the stairs of Jack's house on Silver Lake. The previous night's rain has left a glitter on the sidewalk of the posh neighborhood.

Jack had put in the time and earned the house and his stellar reputation. A former hippie-professor, Jack Palomino started doing private investigation with a San Francisco–based firm founded in the early '70s by a motley crew of poets, philosophers, scientists,

Vietnam veterans, lawyers, journalists, former strippers, techies, and literary scholars. It distinguished itself as much for its effectiveness as for the funky backgrounds, swashbuckling swagger, and the unorthodox methods of its founding members. Among such methods were using guns only as a last measure, conducting extensive research, and gaining deep cultural knowledge surrounding the objects of investigation.

One member of the firm was clued in to the computer revolution rising out of Silicon Valley and expanded the art and science of secret recordings with miniature reel-to-reel tape recorders. On the social front, the firm did for private investigating what Sly Stone did for both soul and psychedelic music: employed women and Black people along with whites. The firm was antiauthoritarian, fueled by sticking it to the Man.

Rocky liked that Jack's new firm was also dedicated to taking on leftist causas. Jack had moved to LA in the late '70s and had done detective work for both God and the Devil, conducting investigations for the Black Panthers, Harvey Weinstein, former president Bill Clinton, and others. He offered Rocky a job as an apprentice investigator after he first migrated from El Salvador during the war. Rocky had been painting the man's home/office when Jack somehow noticed that he "had some skills" and hired him. Jack's politics, along with his brilliance and the opportunity to do interesting and good-paying work, persuaded Rocky to resurrect the investigative skills he had learned as a counterintelligence officer in the FMLN. And though he didn't understand Rocky's musical methods, Jack loved the lyrical aspect of Rocky's approach.

The two men greet each other in the usual joking way before getting straight to the business of murder.

"The real question here, Jack, is who killed the peace?"

"What do you mean?"

"Arnulfo was a leader in negotiating gang truces. He's been doing it since just after the war ended in '92, the same year gangs started escalating violence. He's been working between MS-13 and 18th Street since then and has facilitated conversations between Crips, Bloods, and the Salvadoran gangs."

"Where did this happen?"

"In Slauson Park, near the corner of Compton and 54th. That's where I've been staking out."

"Compton and 54th? Are you sure?"

"Yeah. What's the big deal?"

"That's the corner of 1466 East 54th. Do you know what happened there in 1974?"

"No. I was a ten-year-old living in El Salvador, Jack. How the fuck would I know?"

"That's the address of the hideout of the Symbionese Liberation Army."

"Who?"

"Some called them the first domestic terrorist group in the United States. I was hired by Patty Hearst's family to help find her, and that's where the cops had a shootout with them. The cops ended up burning the house down. It was national news. The shootout was one of the earliest examples of copaganda, a commercial for the new, more militarized police units that were starting to appear: Special Weapons and Tactics, or SWAT. The cops used the SLA to justify bringing in heavy artillery, tanks, and other stuff that is 'normal' today."

"This sounds like El Salvador," Rocky says, "constantly looking for communists, subversivos, and other terroristas to justify the militarization of communities."

"Yep. You need terrorists to keep police budgets fat."

"Fuck. Arnulfo was one of the loudest voices calling to demilitarize and defund LA's police force."

"But how do death squads fit in when they have what sounds like pretty solid evidence pointing to Guardado? Why not accept their results?"

"That whole killing-with-a-machete shit feels fake."

"So who do you think did this?"

"Cops are looking at it from a typical US perspective, when what you need is a Salvadoran lens. I tracked down this kid, a young ex–gang member in the church Guardado belonged to. I found out he's involved in some small-time illicit shit, cornered him, got him to give up some info. He's scared. Told me it was the escuadrones."

"Death squads?"

"Yes."

"Didn't the death squads operate in tandem with the military, the police, and other security forces in El Salvador?"

"Uh, yeah, Jack. What's your point?"

"Something I've learned over the years is that there are people who don't like to have their hands bloodied with murders, people who use others to do their dirty work."

"Hmmm. So the death squads might be working for someone?"

"Who knows? But it's something to consider, if you're Salvadoran sense is that Guardado was set up to kill Arnulfo."

"I gotta go speak to Guardado."

Rocky waits in the long visitors' line at the hulking, labyrinthine LA County jail. The line is overwhelmingly made up of Latino and Black women and children going to see loved ones being warehoused by the government. After an hour and a half, Rocky finally steps into the glass-plated room to meet the murder suspect.

Guardado looks Rocky over as he strolls gangster-style to his seat in front of the glass. The evangelical minister is nowhere in sight. "You're that guerrillero detective that used to hang at Casa Esperanza, right?"

"Yes," Rocky says. "I knew your uncles from the movement."

"Yeah, my tíos gave everything for that causa, and what do they have to show for it? Ni mierda."

"No argument from me," Rocky responds, as his stomach tightens. "This whole situation smells funny to me."

"Funny? Funny how?"

"They're saying you went and bought a machete at Liborio's to kill Arnulfo."

"And?"

"And that's not how your homies in the gangs kill people anymore. Come on. You know that, you know MS and 18th have graduated to where their weapons of choice are revolvers or the occasional semiautomatic. Killing Arnulfo with a machete feels out of synch with where Salvadorans are now, including the gangs."

"So fucking what, ey? What difference does that make to me? I'm fucked and gonna be put away for the rest of my life."

"Yeah, but what about *your* story?"

"My story?"

"Yeah, you know. The way people remember you and what you did. You were on your way to heaven before all this. I want to understand why you returned to hell."

Guardado stays silent.

"Look, I've been checking out your case and have a hunch about it."

"Yeah? What's that?"

"That you were working with somebody to kill Arnulfo," says Rocky.

"Somebody like who?"

"I dunno. The escuadrones de la muerte, maybe? Who even operated in LA, until a few years ago."

"Well, Mr. Guerrillero Detective, that seems like a smart theory. Too bad it's wrong. Look, man, you're right. For my family's sake, I ain't never gonna tell you or anyone else anything. But I will say that there's someone else, someone who wants to terrorize people. Though they don't sport gang or death squad outfits."

"And what kind of outfits do they wear?"

"El de la chota. Take it easy, terrorista." Guardado turns around and leaves his side of the glass-plated room.

Holy shit, Rocky thinks as he walks back to the parking lot. The fucking cops in the gangs are the ones who put Guardado up to this murder in order to shut Arnulfo up and send a message to those who want to "abolish the police." Fuck, fuck, fuck. Mejia was talking about the escuadrones like he was in El Salvador, where the police and military *were* the escuadrones, the terroristas.

Rocky drives back to South Central and parks his car on Compton. He plays "Sabor a Mi" and thinks about telling Yagoda that he knows what his cop gang buddies did. But this terrorist thing is bigger than Yagoda and him. Rocky will listen to what the boleros tell him about diving into this bottomless pit of lies and corruption, murder and cover-ups.

"Sabor a Mi" begins again.

IF FOUND PLEASE RETURN TO ABIGAIL SERNA 158 3/4 E MLK BLVD

BY DÉSIRÉE ZAMORANO

Martin Luther King Jr. Boulevard

My school counselor said that I have to do this. She said she wouldn't, ever, read what I wrote. She added: not that she didn't want to know what was going on in my head, it was just rude to assume someone could read the words you had just written. She would need my permission.

Her name is Ms. Cifuentes and she's glaring at the two boys in the back who are mumbling to each other. I know why I'm here, but I'm not sure why they are.

Ms. Cifuentes seems to always have a bunch of us come see her, though we're not in her office, which is tiny. Today we're in an area of the cafeteria not far from where a bunch of other kids are messing around in the after-school program. That's where kids pretend to work on their homework and people pretend to help them. What is real are the snacks that are handed out. I've tried to sign up a couple of times for that, but they looked me up and said my grades were too good for that.

Too good for free apples and string cheese? What's up with that?

I am not thinking about my grades right now. I'm thinking about Ms. Cifuentes. She's old, not as old as my mom, but she must be thirty at least. She wears black plastic glass frames that end up on the tip of her nose. She could be super pretty, if she wore makeup. If I had a face like that I'd fill in my eyebrows, do a cat's-eye and a cherry lip.

It's almost like she doesn't care. That worries me in adults. What made them stop caring?

My problem, and this isn't official, is that I care too much. That's not word for word what Ms. C said, but it does have something to do with why I'm here, scrawling my pencil across pages in a cheap composition book.

Everything here at the Accelerated School is cheap. When I was a kid—I mean, when I was younger—I knew LA had a lot of rich people, so why weren't there any rich people in our school? And why was our elementary school so dang poor we had busted swings and shit that nobody was allowed on so it was roped off, which posed a whole new set of challenges?

It wasn't until I got older that I found out the rich have their own schools. Wow. What a setup, right? I found this out recently, when our pathetic, bony, no-talent volleyball team, of which I am a member, set off with our PE teacher, Mrs. Jones, in her scuffed and smelly minivan, the kind of minivan Carmela's mom drives. We teased her about it being so old. Carmela just sniffed at us, "At least she has a car, she's not taking the bus!" That shut us up cuz all our moms take the bus.

Although we all felt it was rude of Carmela to point that out.

In any case, we drove through hills that were greener than anything I'd seen before. Why was our neighborhood so parched and dry? Even in elementary there was only concrete and maybe a little sand underneath the roped-off swings.

You might think I'd seen LA on TV, and wealthy places and green hills, but we all know just because something's on TV or in the movies doesn't make it real. *Fast & Furious*, right? My mom loves those films and it just makes me laugh.

We drove up through all these green hills with a view of the beach. Straight up. Green hills, beach, blue skies. The most expensive houses I'd ever seen in real life, imagine all the expensive stuff inside, and *not one of them* had bars on the windows.

Where I'm from all of our windows have bars. I realized I was in a completely different part of the world. Even the air smelled better.

We shuffled out of Mrs. Jones's beat-up van and went to a school gym where the floor had been waxed and polished so hard it was glowing. The walls looked freshly painted. There weren't a lot of people in the stands, something I should have been grateful for, but I could see the stands looked brand new. This gym didn't stink of cafeteria food and sweat and yelling teachers. This gym smelled of money. And I was gagging on it.

Right across the net from us were four girls who looked like Amazons in training, and eight more standing by for their time at the net. I swear to God each of them was two heads taller than Annette, our captain, our star, our tallest member.

The weird thing was, after we lost game after game after game, I don't think any one of us felt humiliated. Nah, a volleyball game against rich girls in the most beautiful school we'd ever been to? Nah. We, or at least I, realized we lived in a parallel universe. An entire world lived not too far away, somewhere bright and shiny.

After the game Mrs. Jones pulled into a beach parking lot and set us off down the beach. She'd even packed Subway sandwiches and chips and drinks in a cooler. I didn't think about it until right now, writing it down, but it probably cost her something. I hope I said thank you. Now I'm worried that I didn't.

Which, full circle, the writing down is what I'm supposed to be doing here, and *not* the overthinking. Ms. Cifuentes gave me a stern talk, said that I was overthinking things, and overthinking was gonna freeze me and make me unhappy.

I have a theory that plenty of other things make me unhappy, but I didn't want to disagree with Ms. Cifuentes and risk her not talking to me.

She told me to write down everything that I was overthinking, fifteen minutes a day, and somehow, like magic (she didn't say that, I'm drawing an inference, as my English teacher, Mrs. Banks, would say), all those things I worried about, all those things that went round and round in my head, would disappear.

That seems so laughable I might even give it a try. But the things going round and round in my head aren't anything that I just put down here. Well, at least my fifteen minutes are up!

Ms. Cifuentes said she wanted me to do this every day, each time I was sent here to her. My problem is I got a mouth. I wonder sometimes what it would be like if I was made like my friend Jenny Tenorio. Jenny is all long braids and silence in class.

Plus, Ms. C said write about the stuff that's bugging me. So having a big mouth does kind of bug me. It's just that I can only keep things in for so long when there's so much stupid going on around me!

I'm not proud of the fact that my Spanish stinks. There, it does. Jenny's is perfect, and she talks about tortillas and champurrado and enchiladas all with the right pronunciation that would only make me feel awkward trying to say, as awkward as it makes me hearing Jenny say it. Like it's not embarrassing at all to speak Spanish. Like it's not a sign of low rent or house cleaners or janitors or shopping at the swap meet.

I'm not knocking janitors or housekeepers or swap meets. My mom works at La Market, and still has time to make us good food. My dad used to be a janitor, before he became a paralegal, before he gave up. That's what my mom calls it. He gave up on himself, not us, she said. And then she doesn't talk about him.

That's a long way of explaining why I am in Spanish class. Or, more precisely, why I am *not* in Spanish class, but instead here. I am here because I could not stand one more stupid word out of Mr. Torres's mouth. Not one more idiotic thing! He was talking about the Lizard People, and I was thinking, how does an adult believe something so stupid?

He's going on and on and on and then I say, "Do they speak Spanish?"

He shoots me a dirty look, but asks, "What?"

I say it slowly, so he can better understand me: "Do the Lizard People speak Spanish?"

He shrugs as if to say he doesn't know, then, "Why? Why do you want to know?"

I say, "Because this is a Spanish class and it would be great to learn it here."

Another dirty look, then, "Fine. You wanna learn Spanish? Class, pull out a paper and pencil. Thanks to Abigail here, we're gonna do a pop quiz."

Groans from the class and now they all want to kill me.

"I'm sorry," I say. "I guess I was confused. I didn't think enrolling in Spanish 202 was really Lizard People 101."

Referral to Ms. C.

I have been referred twelve times this semester, seven from Mr. Torres. He probably wants to expel me from his class. That might be the sensible thing to do. But I think that would mean I win. He doesn't just tell us about Lizard People, but also about his dirt-poor childhood which I know for a fact all of us kids in this class could totally beat. Who's he trying to impress? Who does he think is going to feel sorry for him?

I don't feel sorry for him, and I don't want to hear any of his sad, sad tales of woe. Ms. Cifuentes, on the other hand, looks at you kinda sad, so you know she's got her own hurt, but she's not gonna lay her grief on you, a kid. She's gonna be a real woman and take care of it, and take care of you. That's right. That's like my mom. When, as she says, Dad gave up, she cried with us. But she never asked us to make it right. To take care of her. Caro, my little sister, tried to make her coffee or ramen, and Ma just said, "No, baby, that's *my* job."

Ma sleeps a lot. That seems right to me. Sleeping is the only form of time travel we got. Something bad happens, go to bed. Somehow it hurts just a little less in the morning.

I guess another thing you could do would be to play *Animal Crossing*. All video games are good for focusing right on what's in front of you, and forgetting about the shit all around. I mean, it's like the house disappears, right?

Another thing is movies. But sometime they're so loud.

Another thing is books. Sometimes a book can make everything disappear. The sleeping mom, the deadbeat dad, the lousy teacher, and the broke-ass school.

These things can make it all disappear, and then it's almost more painful to come back to the barred windows of real life. Even inside our place the street traffic noise runs 24/7. I can smell the bus's exhaust, hear the shriek of brakes. The walls of our apartment smell. I think it's the diesel fumes. Caro and I are good at cleaning, we don't mind (no, I hate it really, but I don't mind. Ma shouldn't have to do everything), but there's a smell inside the walls we can't get rid of. Maybe that's why people go for candles?

Our old home had a yard. I had a bike I could ride to the corner and back, or in the street in front of our house. The bike disappeared with the move. It doesn't matter—it's not like I would ride it anywhere.

It's just me with Ms. C right now. I guess not many kids get into trouble during first period. I mean, if you're coming to school for trouble, just hang back, stay home. Kids get to be antsy, moving around right before lunch. I figure everyone's hungry and bored and that's a sure recipe for bitching at each other.

Just write it out, Ms. Cifuentes said. Don't stop, keep writing. I wonder what *she* would be writing about. Are her eyes sad because of some guy? I hope not. Guys are dopes. Maybe not all guys. My dad was not a dope, he was just at the end of his rope.

Ugh, that's a terrible rhyme.

* * *

Ms. Cifuentes said my time was up, so I just left. That was last week. That was February. Now we're in March and I don't really want to talk about my dad—I don't care what Ms. C says.

I'm here again, it shouldn't surprise anyone that I'm back in the friendly detention area of an empty cafeteria, with, this time, another girl, and the same boys in the back. When do they even go to class? They probably think the same of me, if they ever think of me.

Sherry looked at the composition book Ms. C gave her like it was a dog shit sundae, and then glared at me.

I wasn't gonna help her out on this one. We've been trying to kick each other's ass since fifth grade—you know how someone looks at you and your teeth get on edge? That's me and Sherry. I really thought Ms. C was gonna make us talk it out and work it out together and I was gonna have to gag on the insincerity, but today she barely looked at us, at me, and I admit, my feelings were kinda hurt.

But she's probably got a lot more on her mind than a bunch of stupid kids. Fuck Sherry, she doesn't even rate, but what about me? Ms. C's got more important things on her mind than me?

That makes me stop writing, right there. You get used to certain kinds of disappointment, because you got a little hope in maybe one tiny part of the world . . .

Volleyball season is over. Something about a virus. Annette said they're probably lying about the whole thing. Thought maybe Ms. Jones got sick of paying for lunches and gas and driving us around, only to lose to golden girls.

But Mrs. Jones isn't like that at all. She's got her hair cropped short and kinky, she wears aviator sunglasses even inside the gym, and she doesn't bad mouth the other teams or ever mention just how pathetic we are. We were. She shows us how to spike, how to block, how to anticipate. She's big on anticipating your opponent.

So what do you do when your opponent is the next day?

My mom's been in bed this past week, and she doesn't look good. I wanted to stay at home to take care of her, but she made me get Caro ready for school, and she made me go out. We walked the three dirty blocks to school, a couple of kids behind us, a group of kids in front of us, all walking the same way. I could hear them jeering at the woman in short shorts and a sparkly halter top standing outside of Gus's #1 Tacos. I pointed out the Disney billboards across the street to Caro to distract her. Why do you wanna make fun of some lady who's just hungry? I wondered if her day was ending or just beginning.

When I got to English, Sherry talked smack about what I was wearing; it was worse that it was true. I stood up and flipped my desk over at her and that's when Mrs. Banks sent the two of us here.

Now I'm stuck here glaring at Sherry's stupid face, with her bad skin and thin lips that look like all they talk is garbage.

Friday was the last day of school for what the principal said would be three weeks. I should be happy, I should be leaping up and down, dancing, or at least smiling on the inside, but I am not. We're supposed to, maybe? do our classes online, but I don't know how that's gonna play out. I don't have a laptop, I was hoping to save for one for college. I don't have a phone, and Ma uses hers as little as possible. She's probably got the cheapest data plan in the history of the world.

They were giving out Chromebooks before we left. Jenny got hers, I even saw Sherry shoving hers into her shoulder bag. Yeah, what is she gonna use it for? Sell it?

There was a glitch and I didn't get one. They said they'd call me, I could pick it up sometime next week. Which is now this week, and I haven't heard from them.

It's late Wednesday morning and Caro is happy. She's sitting at the kitchen counter listening to Bad Bunny and coloring.

That's what she really likes to do. She colors everything. There are pictures of me, her, and Ma taped to the refrigerator, the bedroom door, the front room walls. They used to be me, her, Ma, and Dad, but Ma pulled them down. For a while Caro drew only in black, but now she's back to giving all three of us brunettes bright and glossy golden-yellow-orange hair. I tried to let her know that brown hair is us, and it's good! But she just shook her head, smiled, and colored, while the tip of her tongue peeked out the side of her mouth.

I don't feel good. I don't feel sick like Ma, who still hasn't gotten out of her bed so I've been the one in charge, making egg burritos or boiling the beans (yeah, I wasted a pound of beans, burned the first pot, and it still stinks in here, that pot was a bitch to clean and I think I've still got steel wool under my nails), but I don't feel happy like Caro. Like I've got three weeks of school off. I feel worried.

The biggest reason I feel worried is because Friday, our last day, Ms. Cifuentes found me in my English class and called me out of the room. She handed me this notebook. "Use this," she said. "I'm telling you, if you write down what's worrying you, you really will worry about it less."

The way she said it, with her eyes all red and puffy like she'd been crying, though she said it was allergies, made my guts flip inside out. Ms. Cifuentes put her hand on my shoulder, which panicked me even more as she'd never touched me before, and said, "Abigail, we're gonna get through this. Just hang on. One day at a time. And when you feel upset, write about it."

By then everybody knew about this virus, and Italy, and China. But those countries seem so far away. When Carmela told us her family was going back to Oaxaca I was sad and jealous and mad and I just turned away to go pick up Caro.

Right now we are on lockdown, which means nobody's supposed to leave their homes except for essentials and essential workers. Ma's an essential worker, but she can't leave her bed. Her breathing is terrible. She won't let us in the room, so I put her food just outside the door. I made her fideo like she told me, and she didn't eat any of it. She's big and warm, so she's not gonna starve to death, she's got plenty of fat cells to get through first, but still, I'm worried.

On Tuesday she told me to go to the store and buy things. I left Caro to watch TV (that's her second-favorite thing to do— coloring in front of the TV is probably a peak experience for her. I wish that was all it took to make me happy I'm pretty sure even in third grade I wasn't like that).

La Market was crazy! It was terrible! But I didn't realize as I passed all these people, some with blue face masks, some with scarves around their heads like me, that everyone was waiting in line. For La Market! It wasn't until I walked to the front of the line and did a double take. What was I gonna do?

The owner, Brenda, who wore a mask that looked like she made it out of paper clips and paper towels, recognized my wild frizzy hair from behind my glasses and scarf. She walked over to me and said, "Your mother called. We got a box of stuff for her already. I'm gonna drop it off later. I told her you didn't need to come here!"

A coupla hours later, sure enough there was Brenda, with a huge cardboard box at her feet, knocking at our security screen door. "Tell your mother to get better soon," she said. "Tell her it's from everyone at work."

My mom wouldn't let me into her room, so I talked to her through the bedroom door. I told her there was pinto beans, black beans, rice, oatmeal, canned tuna, noodles, two dozen eggs, bacon pieces, packages of chicken thighs, apple sauce, canned tomatoes, Mexican chocolate, canned spaghetti, canned ravioli, canned tamales, and pudding cups. I put things away; there was so much chicken I put it in different packages, like I'd watched Ma do, and froze them. Caro ate half of the pudding cups that night, nothing I said would stop her; she ate the rest of them Sunday for breakfast and looked kinda green the rest of the day. I heated up the canned ravioli for dinner but it was straight-up disgusting, so that's when I tried to cook some beans.

My mom laughed through the door when I told her, and said if I'da been hungry enough the ravioli would've tasted just fine.

My mom's got her phone inside the room with her; it's not like I can text my friends. I got two people in this whole world to talk to, one is eight and one is sick and maybe that's why my guts keep going inside out.

I don't think I can spend my whole day here writing about everything that's worrying me. As much as I appreciate her ideas, I don't think Ms. Cifuentes is right about this. Writing down what I'm worried about, putting it into words, almost makes me feel worse, fills me with a kind of dread, like those stories in English class we read last October by Edgar Allan Poe. All heavy and dark, like there's this mist around me, despite the sun shining out there, despite Caro listening to Taylor Swift. Or maybe like that Stephen King film I watched. It feels like that: like parts of my world are disappearing.

I wonder if she's gonna call Dad.

When it was all of us, we lived in a house with a yard. Until we got evicted, which apparently was when my mom found out there was a problem. Caro was crying and my mom was crying and my stomach was tumbling over and over again—I couldn't cry, I could only glare.

My dad had a pretty decent job. For all I know he still has that job, a paralegal with a pretty snazzy law office downtown. Before we moved here there were pictures of my mom and dad from the holiday party. Imagine a law firm so fancy they pay for a photographer, and then they print them out and frame them, right there for you! Okay, so the frames were paper, but still.

My mom looked beautiful. She'd bought her dress in the garment district, it was green and shimmery and she moved in it like she was dancing. In the photograph she looks so happy.

My dad looks like he looks in every photo I've seen of him with my mom. *Hey, I'm with her? How'd I get so lucky?* He does. I told that to Ma once and she just snorted.

It was probably because I was thinking of Dad, and whether he'd call or not, or whether she'd call him, that I did what I did. I don't feel guilty, but I don't feel good. I wish I hadn't listened.

I heard my mom talking on the phone. Caro was watching TV, I was in the kitchen making us a couple of quesadillas, when I heard her voice. Did she need something? Was she calling me? Was she okay?

"Ma?" I said, walking down the hallway. Her plates were outside. She'd finished eating the can of soup I'd heated up for her.

I tapped on the door, "Ma?"

"Hold on," I heard her say. "What, Abby?"

"Did you need something?"

"I'm fine."

"Okay." I stood there a moment and heard her talking to someone. I stepped into the bathroom. From there you can hear practically everything, because of the way the vents work, or the walls are thin or something.

I could hear her talking. Was it to Dad?

"No, Sandra, you don't understand." Oh, she was talking to Tía. Tía Sandra lives in Rohnert Park, up north past San Francisco, so we don't see her and her boys very often. The last time Dad drove us, it seemed to take a week, but a good week. We stopped everywhere. We saw the Golden Gate Bridge. We saw otters and elephant seals and regular seals and redwoods and Monterey pines. We ate clam chowder out of bread bowls. We stayed with Tía and did more things with them all. Thinking of that, when we were all there together, all of us going to Foster Freeze's for ice cream, made my chest hurt. I didn't want to think about it. So I listened to my ma.

"Would you let me talk?" She'd stopped coughing. "Hell yes I'm worried. Why would she bring over all that food if she didn't think I was gonna die?"

Did she really say that? Did I hear right? Did she really think that?

She continued: "Yeah, I feel like crap. My head hurts like you can't believe and sometimes I feel like I can't breathe." She listened to Tía. "No, how'm I gonna check myself into the hospital and leave my girls? No, I haven't told the girls about him. No, you can't come down here. What if you get sick too? No, you can't—"

I left the bathroom and staggered into the hallway. I went and stood in the kitchen, where I couldn't hear anything at all. Not my ma, not Caro. I looked at the kitchen sink and began running water. I could wash the dishes, that's what I could do.

Later Caro began whining that she was bored. I guess even she has a time limit for crayons and television. I pulled out a book I loved in fifth grade. I sat down and she sat on my lap. By the smell of her it was definitely bath time, probably for me too. I began reading *Esperanza Rising* but after five minutes Caro began to squirm. I get that. No pictures. Next time I'll pick another book. I told her if she took a bath I'd play cards with her after dinner.

With the water running you can't hear anything from the bedroom, but Ma was off the phone anyway. I tapped on the door and opened it. "How you doin'?"

She coughed a long time before she answered me, "I don't want you in here, Mami. Close the door." I did. She called after me: "You just put the food by the door, okay? I'll get it. Don't come in here, I don't want you getting sick."

For dinner I had another quesadilla and Caro ate the leftover canned ravioli. I guess she was hungry enough. We played Fish and I let her win three times, and then I decided it was time for her to go to bed. She argued with me. Of course she argued with me. "If you go to bed when I tell you, you can always have the top bunk."

Deal. She tapped at Ma's door and said, "Mommy? G'night!" I heard Ma's voice answer her.

When Caro was in bed I cleaned the kitchen like I've watched Ma do dozens and dozens of times. I took a bath; the apartment was quiet. I brushed my teeth, I got a clean set of pajamas, then thought, *Great, I'm gonna have to figure out how to get us clean clothes sometime.* I tried watching TV but it was all so stupid. I watched the news, I heard about the virus, and my guts started churning. I came in here and tried to sleep. Then I heard the very worst thing: there were no traffic noises. Like everything outside had stopped, everywhere.

I heard my mom open her door and head down the hallway to use the bathroom, then go back to her room. I waited. I walked to her room, listened, heard her snoring, and opened the door.

Her phone was next to her.

I gently picked up her phone, and walked softly all the way to our sofa. I tapped in Dad's number and held my breath. I could explain, he'd come and help us, things would get better. I was so nervous, I dialed a wrong number. I tapped again.

What? That didn't make sense. Again. This time I made sure of every number and still I couldn't believe it when the recording told me that the number had been disconnected.

I've already tried going to sleep once. Caro was asleep above me, I could hear her breathing. I lay down, hugging the mattress. I could hear my heart pounding and pounding. I tried and tried to go to sleep. Nothing. I got up again. Started to write here.

I feel like that time when I was ten, when I stayed up late. Something was gonna happen, I could feel it. And it did happen.

That night we had an earthquake that woke everyone up except me, because I was already awake.

I'm just lying here, writing, waiting for the earthquake to arrive.

WHERE THE SMOKE MEETS THE SKY

BY NIKOLAS CHARLES

South Figueroa Street

Olin's heart raced as he crouched in the darkness watching the fire. What began as the small flickering flame of a match quickly grew into a furious blaze. A faceless fireman appeared in the doorway, the last one out. Before he could escape, the roof collapsed, crushing him under the weight of a thousand pounds. He let out his last gasp of air in a shrill scream expelling the devil smoke.

Olin awoke to realize the scream he heard was his own. By the time the morning siren sounded at 06:00 hours and the detention services officer announced rise-and-shine over the loudspeakers, his nightmare went silent. The same dream that played on the screen inside his head each night fell dark once more. He shielded his eyes as the fluorescents lit up the dormitory room where other male juvenile offenders snored and passed gas.

A delinquent named Linwood Earle eyeballed him every morning. Other boys warned Olin to keep his distance. He had black-on-black tattoos running up his arms and across his back. He had scruffy growth under his lip and around his chin. He had a permanent scowl and a deadeye gaze. Olin did his best to ignore him. He rubbed the sleep from his eyes. When he recalled the dream, he shrugged it off to his night sweats, one more hardship of life in the hot box called Central Juvenile Hall.

Olin rolled his wiry frame off the low cot and got in line for the latrine. Linwood Earle was still sitting on his bunk giving Olin the stink eye. He wondered how long it would take before the emotionally disturbed youth became combative. As soon as he started sleeping in the group room, this guy zeroed in on him. Honed in like some kind of nuclear missile.

A big Black DSO named Officer Hawkins approached Olin holding a clipboard. He was tall and thick with massive arms and a stern expression. His job was to maintain order and control of the unit and he took his job seriously. He circled Olin comparing the X number on the back of his wrinkled and sweat-stained uniform to his paperwork. "You're Roberts, Olin Raymond," he said. "Your defense attorney, Ms. Klein, is here from the Juvenile Court with some legal documents. She will meet with you in the front office."

Olin walked with his head down and his hands behind his back. He remembered the lady attorney as soon as he saw her. She was damn good looking and smelled nice too.

"I've been handling some aspects of your case," she said. "I brought LA County deputy probation officer Jesus Garcia here today to assist you with your successful transition back into the community. I met with the judge and the prosecutor this morning. The cause has come back as undetermined. Therefore, you're no longer a suspect and the charge against you has been dismissed. You've been granted a release by a court order. Do you have any questions?"

"Am I really getting out?"

"You'll be discharged in the custody of Officer Garcia. He will transport you to your new residence. Fortunately, it's operated by the same staff as your previous group home. You can stay there until a more permanent revision can be instituted."

Olin was glad to be getting out but it wasn't all good news. He walked out to the lobby of the detention center after the three-minute shower they allowed him. His hair was still damp

NIKOLAS CHARLES // 239

and unkempt. He was back in the street clothes he hadn't worn in months. Jeans, a pair of Vans, and a black Public Enemy T-shirt.

Officer Garcia waited for him. He was an older Mexican man, probably fortysomething, Olin thought. He had a gold badge sewn on his shirt and a thick black mustache. Adults are dangerous. Cops even worse. Olin didn't have any reason to trust him anymore than anyone else.

"Okay, amigo. Vamos!" the man said, leading him out of the building.

Olin kept his mouth shut and his eyes on the ground.

Garcia read his body language. "It's all right, my friend. Everything will be better soon. Today is your lucky day." He led the way to a white older-model fifteen-passenger transit van. "You're my only VIP in this, our luxury limousine."

"This is just a van."

"Not just a van. It's a big, ugly van. Climb in."

Olin rode shotgun as Garcia steered over the metal tiger teeth. He waved to the guard and drove onto Eastlake. He passed the food truck selling carne asada to some USC health-care workers. He cursed the road construction. "I drive on surface streets to avoid traffic. Easier for me to supervise my passengers. Some boys fight. Some try to hurt themselves. Best part is you get the nickel tour of South Central just like Huell Howser."

With the downtown Los Angeles skyline in his rearview mirror, Garcia drove south on San Pedro. The day was weary and dismal. The officer reminisced about growing up in the hood, the dark days he witnessed, and how he prayed for better ones. Olin looked out the window. He saw a couch on the curb. He saw homeless encampments near and far. He saw shopping carts filled with trash.

Garcia stopped short and swung the van to the right. One, two, three black-and-whites sped past them. The vehicles came to a quick stop diagonally across the oncoming lanes. The LAFD engines and trucks followed with sirens blaring. "Ay, Dios mío. I hope no one is hurt," Garcia said.

With traffic blocked by the LAPD, Olin had a front-row seat to the incident. He leaned out the open window watching the emergency unfold. A fireman stood in front of a single-family residence within earshot of the probation van. He barked anxiously into a handheld radio.

"Task Force 33 on the scene assuming incident command. Smoke showing at a dwelling on San Pedro and Vernon. Search and rescue in progress." The swarthy man wore an orange helmet and a yellow jacket that was smoke-stained and worn. He looked grizzled, with a deep scar on the side of his face.

"Roger, 33," said a woman's voice on the other end.

Olin could see smoke seeping out of the upstairs window and a sudden flash of hungry flames. A crowd of people appeared in front of the burning house with their necks craned upward. "My baby is still in there!" screamed a woman standing on the lawn. A man held her back.

"Metro, I've got fire throughout with people trapped inside, request ALS rescue unit!" the fireman shouted. A blur of yellow and red ran toward the structure under the blackened sky. Uniformed police officers waved the traffic forward. Garcia merged into the lane. Olin looked back to see a fireman handing a crying baby to its thankful mother. In the gray of the day, the silver soot smudged out what was left of the sun.

The June gloom that hung in the air earlier in the day had turned into precipitation. The light rain mixed with the oil residue on the road created a slick surface. Garcia hit the intermittent wipers and grumbled that Angelenos hate rain, drought or not. He reached behind his seat and propped a clipboard between the console and the dash. It sat on top of an old spiral-bound Thomas Guide. Olin saw his name and the address of the new group home. His heart pounded and his palms got sweaty. He breathed hard and fast.

"I'm not going back there," he said.

"Where, amigo?"

"I'll just run away like I did before."

"My responsibility is to drive you to the address on this paper."

"Let me out," Olin cried. "Bad shit happened to me there." When there was no response from Garcia, Olin panicked and yanked the handle of the door. It swung open and ricocheted against its greasy hinges, knocking him off-balance. He fell out and hung by his seat belt. The van began to hydroplane. It skidded and slid across the wet surface. Garcia struggled to control it.

"Grab my hand!" he yelled.

"I can't reach it."

Garcia pulled the wheel down hard with his left hand and did his cross with his right. The bulky behemoth lurched into the center lane, cutting off the car behind them. The momentum sent Olin flying back inside the cab as it careened into northbound traffic.

"Watch out!" he hollered.

Garcia reacted and the antilock brakes locked. He swerved and smashed into a parked car. The force thrust them forward then dropped them back. They looked at each other, dazed.

"Don't make me go back to those people," Olin said.

Garcia took a deep breath before he spoke. "Could be un gran problema at my work, but I feel you deserve a second chance. I can't take you to a place where there's abuse or neglect. I have an idea."

The van was crunched and crippled but still running. The windshield was cracked. And the body and frame damage made it limp and squeal. The unlucky parked car fared even worse. Garcia scrawled a quick note and stuck it under the wiper. It simply began, *Lo siento.* Beneath it was his name, rank, and main number to County Probation.

Soon after, he turned into a strip mall in the Vermont-Slauson neighborhood, on the corner of Figueroa and Gage, called Angel's Plaza. "We're here," he announced proudly. Olin followed him to some glass doors. "This might be the solution to your problem."

"This is a laundromat."

"Sí. Coin Lavandería, an investment for my family's future." The officer walked inside and pointed at the rows of stainless-steel front-loading washing machines. "New, expensive, very shiny," he said as he smirked at his reflection.

"This is the solution?" Olin asked.

"Maybe not the real solution, amigo. But possibly a bridge from an old place of sadness to a new place of hope. You can work here."

"Doing what?"

"Night janitor. Sweep and mop. Until you find a real home."

"But where will I live?"

Garcia had another idea. He led Olin outside to a heavy iron security door. They walked upstairs to a dank and dingy attic. It was a neglected, cockroach-infested room with a toilet and tub. The space was cluttered with paint cans, tarps, and ladders. It had a window that looked out at the parking lot.

"Live here? Where will I sleep? There's no bed?" Olin frowned at the soiled carpet, the water-stained ceiling, and the dusty window. The air was alternately musty from mildew and sweet from the smell of the bakery below.

"It's only temporary. You're no longer a ward of the court. You have two choices: go back into another group home or make it on your own. Living here means you follow my rules. No cerveza, no Mary Jane, and no happy ladies from Figueroa. Girls like that always want more."

"More what?" Olin asked

"More than you got."

Then he grasped Olin by the shoulders and asked him what he wanted to do with his life. "How will you be a better man?"

Olin wasn't used to being touched but he didn't pull away. He already knew the answer. Garcia waited patiently. "I want to be a fireman," he said as he braced himself for the ridicule. But Garcia didn't laugh. He smiled. "You remind me of another boy I knew. He and his two brothers were in and out of juvenile hall. Always in trouble with the law. But the oldest one found the courage to leave the life of crime behind. He became a fireman." Olin thought that if someone else could do it, so could he.

That night, Olin swept and mopped the Lavandería. Garcia showed him where to find all the supplies. A closet with brooms, mops, and generic cleaning fluids from the 99 Cents Only Store. He emptied the clumps of lint from all the dryers and shined the metal surfaces of the appliances. He turned off the lights and locked the door.

All of the stores in the strip mall had closed. Olin noticed that one vehicle remained in the lot. It was an ugly, colorless pickup truck. He wondered who the owner was. He looked through the windows of each store. He saw signs in different languages. From the Korean dry cleaners and the Vietnamese nail salon to the El Salvadorian panadería, there was no one in sight. He shrugged and went back upstairs. He looked out the sullied window. It still sat there like a dead weight.

Olin examined the set of keys—one was unaccounted for. He walked down to the desolate parking lot and approached the truck. All of the paint had been sanded off. It was bare metal. Olin put the mystery key in the driver's-side door and it opened. He got in the vehicle and clutched the steering wheel at the ten and two positions. He swiveled it back and forth and made car sounds with his mouth. He put the key in the ignition and turned it. It coughed out a black cloud of burnt oil. It turned over and roared. He hit the gas and howled through the window as he peeled out onto the pavement.

The farther he drove the more perilous the neighborhoods became. The South Figueroa Corridor was humming with women selling their wares and men selling dope or mixtapes. He saw a group of rough-looking Black males ambling in the intersection. He got anxious when they glared at him. They heckled and hounded the harlots. They whooped, jeered, and flipped him off when he drove by. The warm night wind caressed his face. It smelled of tortillas and carried with it the sounds of the city. The subwoofers in the two-tone ragtop beside him vibrated in his chest.

There were plenty of girls walking the street. But only one of them caught his eye. From a distance, she looked like a recently pruned palm tree. Tall and slender from her feet to her head. She had an explosion of coiled black hair that grew out in every direction. She had skin like the warm setting sun. And cherry-red lips that blew kisses to the cars passing by. He had never seen a Black girl naked before, or any girl. He turned down the side street to circle back and got a better look this time. The streetlights above her flickered like the bulbs of an old movie theater marquee. She wore high heels and a little black dress—she was busting out all over the place. But what would she see in him? He was just a skinny, pimply-faced white boy in a Black and brown hood. He yanked the wheel and pulled a U-turn, remembering his goal.

He pulled up in front of Fire Station 33. It sat on the corner of Main and East 64th, across the street from a Catholic church. He stopped the pickup on the west side of Main facing south. From that angle he could see the station's redbrick building from the flagpole to the markings on the road that warned: *Keep Clear*. He could see the station's mascot painted on the far wall. Underneath the words *Fire City* was a ferocious bulldog. It had a spiked collar and a resolute expression; it was a symbol of pride and brotherhood. Most importantly, he could see the three large garage doors of copper and bronze. He imagined the valiant and mighty fire engines rolling out of those gates: rugged, brave, and with serious purpose. He envisioned himself wearing the yellow helmet with the red shield. He would carry an ax in one hand and the strength of a hundred men in the other. He would have the respect and admiration of the whole community.

He killed the engine and clicked off the headlights. The street went black. He slid the seat back and waited for the alarms to sound. He took a deep breath and closed his eyes. His body temperature dropped, his heart rate slowed. He felt his whole body go numb. He was floating in midair, a warmth bathed over him. Something between the heat and the light called out to him.

Olin jerked awake to a horrifying face at his window. In his groggy state, he was frightened to see a creepy old man watching him sleep. He had a pointy nose, a high forehead, and sharp teeth. Olin turned to his right to see an equally menacing character. He thought the ugly faces were very strange until their high-pitched voices gave them away. He opened the door and shouted, "Beat it, you punks!" Two kids playing outside late at night. They ran off laughing. The oversized rubber masks wobbled on their small heads. "Little shits."

He pulled away from the station but it was only a matter of minutes before he felt another pair of eyes upon him. These were almost certainly more menacing. The vehicle behind him had the brightest white lights, like bleached snow. It was either coincidentally traveling the same route or trailing him with ill intent. Olin started to get jumpy until he saw the car turn off. Once more, the night was still.

Back in the Lavandería the next night, Olin filled his pockets with quarters from the appliances. He told himself it was for the right reasons. When he locked the glass doors he noticed a strange car parked in the lot—it was some rowdy ruffians smoking pot and drinking beer. They revved the engine and zoomed off. Not paying much attention, he strode up to the bed of the truck. He snatched a rusty gas can out and pumped it full across the street. No more waiting for fire. From now on, the engines would come to him.

He drove down Figueroa past Florence in the Vermont Knolls neighborhood. He parked on 74th Street just past the Parlour Motel. With the can of gas in tow, he walked down the alley. It was dark, narrow, and covered in trash, infested with armies of vermin, maggots, and fleas. The area reeked of human excrement. Large rats brazenly chased each other through piles of rotting food squealing like toddlers in a playground. It had a sickening stench.

Olin jumped when an angry pit bull charged at him barking sharply. It bounced off the chain-link fence that confined him. Olin kept his head down and walked toward a metal dumpster overflowing with garbage in the middle of the alley. He poured the combustible fluid atop the debris and jumped back as it splashed toward him. He found pages of newsprint that had blown against the fence and rolled them tightly, then ignited them with a cheap lighter. He tossed the fiery torch into the dumpster and the contents flared, popped, and roared against the charcoal sky. He watched as it lit up the nearby trees. Flames like red clay and sandstone flashed upward and outward.

Olin dashed to the truck. From his vantage point, slouched in the front seat, he peered down the alleyway. With his window open, he heard the restless neighborhood stir. Station 33 fire engines hastened past him with sirens swirling and shrieking. More fire trucks barreled around the block. Two men in uniform discussed the fire.

Olin focused on the flames. He felt the heat on his face, white-hot and faithful. He smelled the poisonous gases of burning rubber and plastic. The toxic fumes grew stronger and the black smoke thicker. For a fleeting moment, the tremor of the torrid flame quelled his loneliness.

Olin was getting wound up and twitchy, and decided to move

his vehicle down the street. A black-and-white rolled toward him shining its spotlight. Olin froze and looked forward, and the cop rolled on. He checked the rearview and saw the wide-angle view of the chaos. He knew it was all him.

He decided to head back northeast. Before Mario's Tires at 68th he caught another tail. He remembered what the LA County therapist had said about paranoia: "As an abandoned youth, it's expected that you'll have some emotional disturbances." This time it wasn't an illusion. He could spot those headlights any-where. Pure white and piercing.

A group of Black bruisers loitered on Figueroa near Marina's Mini Market. They looked like the same crew who had taunted him before. When one of them waved him over, he rolled down his passenger-side window and pulled the truck in front of them.

"Need some weed? I got the good shit," the dealer said.

Olin said no with a quiver in his voice as the man moved closer. A tall goon with a buzz cut and gauges in his ears stood beside him sucking on a spliff. A big thug in a sweat-soiled wife-beater appeared at the driver's-side window, wide enough to block out the light. The pusherman leaned in with menthol breath and a tobacco-besmirched grin. He had an iced-out chain around his ink-stained neck.

"So, lookin' for what, homie? Blow? Crack? Smack? Crank?"

"I need a firearm. I mean a piece."

"Say what? You wanna buy a gun, New Jack? You fixin' to go on a killin' spree?"

"No. Protection only."

"Dee-fense from the Five-O? I feel ya. How much you spendin'?"

"How much do I need?"

"Depends on what it is, know what I'm sayin'? Could be a revolver like an S&W or Ruger. Or a semiauto like a Glock or Sig.

AKs and shit."

"Just a handgun, I guess."

"Listen, homie, you better not be playin'. Meet me at Florence and Normandie tomorrow night in the alley between the gas station and the hot dog place. Make it midnight and bring a wad."

Olin had second thoughts about meeting with the hoodlum—the guy had neck tattoos and a creepy vibe—but he had to go. He pointed the truck south on Figueroa, turned right on Florence, and continued west, crossing over Normandie. He picked out the drop spot from a distance, a place called Art's Chili Dogs. It was wide and squat with an awning in front. It was closed and dark and butted up against a beige residence with black iron bars across the windows.

Olin turned left between the food stand and the gas station, into the narrow alleyway. The three roughnecks were already there with the trunk popped and their arms folded. Their car was parked in a garage with the back end facing out. "That's him," he heard someone say. They eyed him up and down.

"You're late," the dealer said.

"Sorry."

"Got the bread?"

Olin nodded, tapping his front right pocket. The hoods stole glances at each other, shifting back and forth in low-slung pants and oversized basketball shoes.

"Let's see it."

Olin pulled out a pile of crumpled bills.

"Damn, boy. Count that bitch out for me."

Olin's hands fumbled and shook as he flattened out the bills and counted up to two hundred. The big thug took the money and stuffed it into his pocket. He nodded at the tall goon, who reached into the trunk and passed something to the dealer.

"For that, all you can get is this," the man said, ramming the butt of a small black handgun into Olin's sternum. Olin wheezed and coughed.

The three men disappeared into the garage and yanked the door shut. For a minute, Olin stood there alone in the alley. Now that he had a gun, he was ready for anything.

Olin had to find something to burn. He gathered the mismatched hand towels, stained T-shirts, and ladies' panties that he'd collected from the Lavandería lost and found. He rolled each one tightly and tied it with twine, then loaded them into the bed of the truck along with the can of gas and the cleaning fluids from the janitor's closet. He would soak each one with flammable liquid when he got to the site. It was a good plan, it was solid.

Olin darted out of the parking lot of Angel's Plaza after midnight and drove south on Figueroa. He passed the lizards and the curb crawlers hunting them. There it was on the southwest corner of the intersection, a vacant one-story house labeled with a *Condemned* sticker. It sat on a slab in a small lot of dirt and dead grass. Olin thought he was doing the neighborhood a favor, ridding it of this hazardous eyesore. He turned right and parked on West 65th.

With his supplies in hand, he walked up the darkened walkway. He rattled the handle of the front door—it was locked and sturdy. Olin went around back to find another entrance. A horizontal board nailed across the back door was its only lock. Three kicks was the right combination: the door swung open into an entryway marred by vandals. He stepped over shards of glass and into the front room, treading slowly on the loose floorboards. He bent down to soak the laundry items in the accelerant when a shadow blocked the light from an outside streetlamp.

"What up, playa?" a voice said. In the dim light, Olin saw it was the dealer who'd sold him the gun. Flanked by his two hustlers, they blocked the only exit.

He jumped up to face the intruders. "What are you doing here?"

"Just stopped by to see yer new crib."

"You're the one who's been following me?" Olin asked.

"Wasn't hard with that ugly-ass truck."

"I paid you your money."

"Uh-huh. You know, my kid brutha says you talk in yer sleep."

"I don't even know your brother."

"I think you do, motherfucka," another voice said, stepping out of the shadows. It was Linwood Earle and he looked bigger, stronger, and meaner. He walked from the door to where Olin was standing in three big steps. It was dark but Olin still recognized the hatred in his eyes. That same dead stare he saw every morning in juvie. When Linwood whipped his right arm sideways, Olin leaned and ducked just in time. Linwood regained his footing and grabbed him by the neck.

"I been waitin' for this for a minute," he said sneering, up in Olin's face. He stank of body odor and malt liquor. "I heard you talkin' in yer sleep every night. Cryin', screamin', and sayin' all kinds of shit. That's when I knew you killed our brutha."

Olin flailed and thrashed to get free. His eyes bugged and bulged. Linwood finally released his grip and Olin fell against the wall gasping for air. "What do you want from me?"

Linwood shoved him backward. "You got some fuckin' nerve axin' me that. How 'bout some street justice for my oldest brutha Derrick? He was the closest thing to a real father I ever had. Then he goes and dies in a fire at a home for orphans. Same one you stayed at!"

"That doesn't prove anything," Olin responded.

"But that can of gas does," the dealer said, taking a step toward him. "Maybe the law couldn't prove shit, but *we* can." He slid a Glock semiauto out of his waistband and raised it up to his chest in a two-handed grip.

Olin didn't have anywhere to run. He could taste the fear in the back of his throat. He flinched and stumbled, and clumsily yanked out his own gun. He squeezed the trigger and braced himself for the blast. Nothing happened.

The dealer snickered and said: "That one don't work. Made sure of it after we knew it was you." He aimed again, but before he could fire, Linwood picked up a wooden board and swung it hard and wide, cracking Olin in the back of the head. He dropped like a sack of wet meat.

"Is he dead?" the big thug muttered.

"Let's get the fuck outta here!" the dealer shouted.

Linwood threw his fist in the air and yelled, "Light this place up!"

They slopped gas on the floor around Olin, who was limp and moaning. Linwood lit a match and dropped it in the oily puddle. The dirt and sawdust smoked. The vivid yellow flames swirled and danced like arms reaching for Olin in a tender embrace. The golden-orange and radiant red flashes of blistering heat flared in a deafening blast. Olin's gray world exploded into brilliant colors. Everything was on fire, everything was burning. It was the most beautiful thing he had ever seen.

JAYSON AND THE LIQUOR STORE

BY LARRY FONDATION

Imperial Highway

J ayson robbed the liquor store at gunpoint. He doesn't know why he did it. He didn't then and he doesn't now. He just did it. At least that's what he tells people. Even years later.

The gun wasn't loaded, he says. (If he even had a gun.) But he doesn't tell anyone anything about the gun. (Like what kind of gun.) Least of all Marta.

The cops never came. So he says.

He said he stole a car, and that the car busted an axle in the potholes before he abandoned it outside the Hawkins's joint on Imperial, aiming to come back to the projects that, back then, we all called home. They call them "the developments" now—just to make it sound good and fancy—but we still say projects. Concrete blocks stacked upon concrete blocks forming shoebox units, with thick steel doors to resist bullets and intruders, and bars on the windows. Built as temporary housing for retuning World War II vets—but sixty-plus years later, still standing. Nickerson Gardens, Jordan Downs, Imperial Courts. Nice-sounding names. But inside the apartments are cramped spaces and the same cinder-block construction on the interior, no drywall. You can't nail anything to the walls. No wedding pictures, but it's mostly single mothers. No graduation pix either, but me and my brothers and sisters all dropped out of school. They weren't teaching us jack. So, we don't take photos of nothing. But it'd be nice to have the option.

Jayson had a story. And fifty bucks for his efforts, he claimed.

The fruits of his labor. The store didn't carry much in the way of cash. So he says.

I don't know if Marta was impressed. She didn't act like it. But she's never acted impressed in any way whatsoever. Not for nobody. Beautiful, aloof Marta.

We all wanted her. We all talked but never did shit.

That's what happens most of the time—not doing shit, meaning nothing has happened.

I remember one time we asked—"Jayson, what liquor store?"

"The one on Central Avenue."

Like that narrowed it down.

"What one? R & R?"

That's at Compton and 104th. It's so close. And we would've heard. Word travels. And why the fuck would you steal a car to skip out on a six-minute walk? It didn't add up.

"No, you know, the other one."

Jayson could never prove shit. Of course not. But he just bragged and bragged. He keeps changing his story. Even now. We all know it's just bullshit. But so what? Like the rest of us, he doesn't think he has a real story to tell.

A lot of stuff happened. It just all happened before we were born. Or maybe when we were babies—born in 1992, right when something happened. Boiled over; blew up. Then for us, nothing happened. At least nothing much that we think is worth talking about.

I mean bad things still happen of course—murders, robberies, break-ins—we eye our best friend's girlfriend; we argue, we fight, we want to make something happen. We start shit, we finish shit; sometimes we start shit we cannot finish. But most times we're bored to shit, and nothing happens, nothing at all, and that's the worst. That's when trouble starts. Nobody knows what Jayson did or didn't do—nobody ever will.

But back in 2009 when we were still kids, Jayson made his first play.

It just didn't work.

Nobody got Marta. Not even Marta. She made a few commercials, got her face on the side of the bus, shilling cell phones for Cricket Wireless, some such thing. Then nada.

Jayson is in jail now—of course, not for the liquor store heist. The one that probably never happened. But recently, he got himself into tons of bad shit. He's paying the price.

Right before he got busted, he'd asked me if I wanted to "work with him," meaning he was offering me the opportunity to deal drugs. He said we could be partners, that he could put some money in my pocket.

"Jayson, I got a job. I make a paycheck; I got a payday."

"Come on, man. You bag groceries at Food 4 Less. You don't make shit."

"I'm good, Jayson."

"Really, brother?"

"I'm not your brother, Jayson. And I don't want any part of your fucking bullshit."

"My bullshit? Man, we came up together. Our mothers stayed at the same place, raised us kids in the fucking projects. Now you think you're better than me? Why? Because you got yourself some shit-ass job and you moved out? Your whole fucking family is still here!"

"Fuck you, Jayson. You were born full of shit. Like all that 'I robbed a liquor store' horseshit back in the day."

"Horseshit? I got fifty dollars that night. Just by scaring that little motherfucker. He wouldn't even dare call the cops."

Jayson is a big guy. No mention this time about any fucking gun.

"Still saying the same old shit. You just made that shit up to impress Marta. And she never gave a fuck about your tired ass no matter what the fuck you said."

"I'm telling you, dude, I hit that fucking place! And Marta, man, she never gave a fuck about *any* of us."

"You got that right. But you know what, I'm out of here. I'm tired of your shit, and I don't want nothing to do with you or your goddamn schemes."

For the last time, we went our separate ways. Haven't seen hm since. I think they got him incarcerated out in Chino. But I'm not 100 percent sure. My mother says I should look him up. I tell her I will, but I never do.

So, yeah, I got out. I quit Food 4 Less. I drive a truck now. Delivering for UPS. I'm a member of the Teamsters union. The company pays benefits. I make a decent living.

I moved up by USC. I stay there now. I mostly like it but not always. The people are different. Especially the students. Put it this way: we don't have much in common.

The 901 is a bar on Figueroa. It's like the official bar of USC or some such shit. I don't know why I go there. I mean nobody bothers me. Not physically anyway. Maybe in the back of my mind, I think some rich college chick is going to hit on me, take me home. I look all right. My job keeps me in pretty good shape. LOL, right?

Anyway, one night as I was about to leave—the frat boys' behavior was bugging the shit out of me—who do I see, flirting with some football-player-looking guy? Marta.

I mean back in the day, Marta looked like a young J. Lo, only better. As I got closer, I could see that she's still fucking gorgeous; she just looked tired. I was nervous about approaching her. Not about the guy. Fuck him. But it has been a long time, and we were never really close.

The guy moved on. Started flirting with some really young-looking chick. Like high school young. She probably had a fake ID.

When the guy split, Marta looked around; she saw me and rushed at me. What the fuck? Then she hugged me, she fucking hugged me. I hugged her back.

"Oh my God! It's been forever. How are you?"

We let go of each other. I was even more nervous. I wasn't even sure she remembered my name. So I offered to buy her a drink. She said yes and we talked and we drank for a long time. I asked what she was up to. She was blunt as hell about what happened to her modeling career.

It was her turn to ask me about my life.

"Do you work around here?"

"No, I stay here, I got a place not far from the new stadium. I drive for UPS. I get to see neighborhoods all over town. It ain't bad . . ."

She looked up from her drink and straight at me.

"Are they hiring?"

ABOUT THE CONTRIBUTORS

STEPH CHA is the author of *Your House Will Pay*—winner of the *Los Angeles Times* Book Prize and the California Book Award—and the Juniper Song crime trilogy. She's a critic whose work has appeared in the *Los Angeles Times, USA Today*, the *New York Times*, and the *Los Angeles Review of Books*, where she served as noir editor. Cha is the current series editor of *The Best American Mystery and Suspense* anthology. She lives in Los Angeles.

Maria Kanevskaya

NIKOLAS CHARLES writes about heroes, thugs, and firebugs. Before devoting his time to writing crime fiction, he was a music journalist and photographer. His work has been published in *Rolling Stone, Playboy, People, Life,* and *US Weekly*. He was embedded in the Los Angeles Fire Department at Station 33 in South Central. He's currently contributing to *Time* magazine and writing noir stories. Follow him on Instagram: @nikolascharlesauthor.

TANANARIVE DUE is an American Book Award–winning author who teaches Black horror and Afrofuturism at UCLA. She has published several books including the novels *My Soul to Keep* and *The Good House,* and the collection *Ghost Summer: Stories.* She was an executive producer on Shudder's *Horror Noire: A History of Black Horror.* She and husband Steven Barnes cowrote an episode of *The Twilight Zone* for Jordan Peele and two segments in Shudder's *Horror Noire* anthology film.

Melissa Hibbert

LARRY FONDATION is the author of six books of fiction, primarily set in the Los Angeles inner city, where he works as a community organizer. Three of his books are illustrated by London-based artist Kate Ruth. He has received a Christopher Isherwood Fiction Fellowship. In French translation, he was nominated for Le Prix SNCF du Polar. His work in progress is called *Single Room Occupancy*, set on the fringe of Skid Row.

Tolu Solanke

GAR ANTHONY HAYWOOD is the Shamus and Anthony award–winning author of twelve crime novels, including the Aaron Gunner private eye series and the Joe and Dottie Loudermilk mysteries. His short fiction has been included in *The Best American Mystery Stories* anthologies and *Booklist* has called him "a writer who has always belonged in the upper echelon of American crime fiction." Haywood's spiritual thriller, *In Things Unseen,* was published by Slant Books in 2020.

Donna Haywood

Mayumi Hirahara

NAOMI HIRAHARA is the Edgar Award–winning author of traditional mystery series and noir short stories. Her first historical mystery, *Clark and Division*, follows the release of a Japanese American family from a World War II detention center. The seventh and final installment of her Mas Arai series, *Hiroshima Boy*, was published in Japan on August 6, 2021. Currently living in her birthplace, Pasadena, California, she was an editor of the *Rafu Shimpo* newspaper.

Theodora Stewart

EMORY HOLMES II is a Los Angeles–based journalist and short story writer. His reporting has appeared in the *Los Angeles Times*, the *Los Angeles Daily News*, the *San Francisco Chronicle*, the *Los Angeles Sentinel*, and other publications. His short stories have appeared in *The Cocaine Chronicles*, *The Best American Mystery Stories 2006*, *Los Angeles Noir*, and *44 Caliber Funk*.

Alexis Terrazas

ROBERTO LOVATO, a journalist and teacher, is the award-winning author of *Unforgetting*, a memoir picked by the *New York Times* as an Editors' Choice. He is also the recipient of a reporting grant from the Pulitzer Center. His essays and reports from around the world have appeared in numerous publications including *Guernica*, the *Boston Globe*, *Foreign Policy*, the *Guardian*, the *Los Angeles Times*, *Der Spiegel,* and other national and international publications.

Peggy Blow

PENNY MICKELBURY is the author of twelve mystery novels in three different series, two novels of historical fiction, and a collection of short stories. She has also contributed short stories to several anthologies. Her first career was as a journalist, and in 2020 she was inducted into the National Association of Black Journalists Hall of Fame. The Atlanta native lives in Los Angeles.

Gilda Haas

GARY PHILLIPS has published novels, comics, and short stories, and edited numerous anthologies. *Violent Spring*, first published in 1994, was named one of the essential crime novels of Los Angeles. *Culprits*, a linked anthology he coedited, has been optioned as a British miniseries, and he was a staff writer on FX's *Snowfall* about crack and the CIA in 1980s South Central, where he grew up.

Armelle Bodiguel

ERIC STONE is the author of the Ray Sharp series of detective thrillers set in Asia and based on stories he covered during many years of working as a journalist. He also wrote *Wrong Side of the Wall*, a biography of Ralph "Blackie" Schwamb, the greatest prison baseball player of all time, for which he took a very deep dive into the history and culture of Central Avenue in South Central Los Angeles during the 1940s.

Michael Walker

JERVEY TERVALON was born in New Orleans, raised in Los Angeles, and got his MFA in creative writing from UC, Irvine. He is the author of six books including *Understand This*, for which he won the Quality Paperback Book Club's New Voices Award. Currently he is the executive director of Literature for Life, an educational advocacy organization, and creative director of the Pasadena LitFest. His latest novel is *Monster's Chef.*

Craig Westerson

JERI WESTERSON, an LA native, writes the acclaimed Crispin Guest medieval noir series, two urban fantasy series, and a gaslamp fantasy-steampunk series. Her medieval mysteries have garnered thirteen award nominations, from the Agatha to the Shamus. Westerson has served as president of the Southern California chapter of the Mystery Writers of America, and president and VP of Sisters in Crime Orange County and Sisters in Crime/Los Angeles.

Skye Moorhead

DÉSIRÉE ZAMORANO, a native of Los Angeles, is the author of the highly acclaimed literary novel *The Amado Women*. An award-winning and Pushcart Prize–nominated short story writer, her work is often an exploration of issues of invisibility, injustice, and inequity. A selection of her writing can be found in publications from Akashic Books, Catapult, and Pen + Brush, and in *Cultural Weekly* and the *Kenyon Review*. She is a frequent contributor to the *Los Angeles Review of Books*.

Also available from the Akashic Noir Series

LOS ANGELES NOIR
edited by Denise Hamilton
318 pages, trade paperback original, $16.95

BRAND-NEW STORIES BY: Michael Connelly, Janet Fitch, Susan
Straight, Héctor Tobar, Patt Morrison, Emory Holmes II, Robert
Ferrigno, Gary Phillips, Christopher Rice, Naomi Hirahara, Jim
Pascoe, Neal Pollack, Scott Phillips, Diana Wagman, Lienna Silver,
Brian Ascalon Roley, and Denise Hamilton.

A *Los Angeles Times* best seller, SCIBA best seller, and
SCIBA Award winner; includes Edgar Award–winning
story "The Golden Gopher" by Susan Straight

"Noir lives, and will go on living, as this fine anthology proves."
—*Los Angeles Times*

LOS ANGELES NOIR 2: THE CLASSICS
edited by Denise Hamilton
336 pages, trade paperback original, $15.95

CLASSIC STORIES BY: Raymond Chandler, Paul Cain, James Ellroy,
Leigh Brackett, James M. Cain, Chester Himes, Ross MacDonald,
Walter Mosley, Naomi Hirahara, Margaret Millar, Joseph Hansen,
William Campbell Gault, Jervey Tervalon, Kate Braverman, and
Yxta Maya Murray.

"If you love either mysteries or tales about our corner of the world,
pick up *Los Angeles Noir 2* . . . Hey, the concept of 'noir'—dark,
steamy mystery stories—was invented here."
—*Los Angeles Daily News*

ORANGE COUNTY NOIR
edited by Gary Phillips
312 pages, trade paperback original, $15.95

BRAND-NEW STORIES BY: Susan Straight, Robert S. Levinson, Rob
Roberge, Nathan Walpow, Barbara DeMarco-Barrett, Dan Duling,
Mary Castillo, Lawrence Maddox, Dick Lochte, Robert Ward,
Gary Phillips, Gordon McAlpine, Martin J. Smith, and Patricia
McFall, with a forword by T. Jefferson Parker.

"The fourteen stories selected by Gary Phillips take readers on a
hair-raising ride through a landscape of quirky brutality and mysterious beauty . . . Orange County crime fiction fans will treasure this
book." —*OC Metro*